This was a madhouse, a loony bin. Walter pouted his toothless mouth and felt a surge of rage. They were all mad here, not certified or else they'd be in a proper asylum. This was a sort of private nursing home full of nutters . . . He had to get away from here, escape, this very minute.

A step at a time, one foot in front of the other, taking a wavering course towards the door because it was the only logical route. Always the fear that his tortured, ageing brain might slip and catapult him back into a state of mindlessness, vegetate him.

Also by Guy N. Smith in Sphere Books

FIEND

MANIA

Guy N. Smith

SPHERE BOOKS LIMITED

SPHERE BOOKS LTD

Published by the Penguin Group
27 Wrights Lane, London W8 5TZ, England
Viking Penguin Inc., 40 West 23rd Street, New York, New York 10010, USA
Penguin Books Australia Ltd, Ringwood, Victoria, Australia
Penguin Books Canada Ltd, 2801 John Street, Markham, Ontario, Canada 13R LB4
Penguin Books (NZ) Ltd, 182–190 Wairau Road, Auckland 10, New Zealand

Penguin Books Ltd, Registered Offices: Harmondsworth, Middlesex, England

First published by Sphere Books Ltd 1989
Copyright © 1988 by Guy N. Smith

1 2 3 4 5 6 7 8 9 10

Printed and bound in Great Britain by
Richard Clay Ltd, Bungay, Suffolk

For Mike and Di Wathen

You are about to embark upon a journey into the darkest recesses of the human mind, an exploration of the unknown. Travel at your peril for your safety, your sanity cannot be guaranteed. For some there may be no return.

PROLOGUE

Walter Gull had lain soaking in his own bedwet for the past twenty-four hours. It might have been longer, he had no means of measuring time in this gloomy cubicle of a room with its closed frayed curtains and peeling dirty wallpaper. Grey daylight like an autumnal mist that never dispersed, a square shadowy world which encased his ailing, skeletal body beneath the grimed sheets, a twilight of silence broken only by his rasping cough and the gurgle of phlegm in his wizened, scrawny throat.

He shifted uncomfortably, cursing the pain from his bedsores, lifting his bald head off the stained pillow and staring about him with hollowed eyes. Seeing and comprehending, sometimes understanding during those intermittent fits of lucidity. Then it slipped from him and he gave up the struggle, writhed with discomfort and knew only one thing; that he was a prisoner in this place.

He tried to claw the clinging pyjama material from his bony bottom, saturated material which gave off a sharp, nauseating odour, and started the coughing again. He'd messed himself, he might even be bleeding but the bastards didn't give a damn. Lie in it, old man, and maybe you'll die soon. Then you won't be a nuisance to anybody any more. Would you like us to put you down?

They had removed the hand bell from the bedside table so that he couldn't call them. The beaker of water was gone, too, knocked on the floor when he last tried to reach it with a shaking hand. He croaked another curse with a parched tongue, lay back and closed his eyes. Sleep was out of the question, he slept little these days. It was more of a conscious doze, listening for footsteps coming down the passage beyond the door, willing them to enter, afraid in case they did. Because they would only torture him again. For Christ's sake, why don't you kill me and get it over with? You want me dead, don't you?

He mouthed inarticulate cries of terror every time the door opened. It was worse when Mrs Clements came on her own, the sadistic old bag. George, her husband, was a bastard, too, but he was a kind of steadying influence on her, stopped her from going too far.

'That'll do,' he would shout, and grasp the wrist of her hand which held the hypodermic needle; once he had caused her to snap the needle off and then he had had to hold Walter down whilst she got the broken bit out with a pair of tweezers, digging deep in the buttock to find it. Thumping the patient as though it was his fault.

They tortured his bum every day as though it gave them some perverse pleasure. Then they rolled him back to lie in whatever he had done as a kind of punishment for still being alive.

Whenever they gave Walter a blanket bath and changed the sheets he knew that the doctor was going to visit. Dr Gidman was kind in a rough sort of way. He examined the patient but never inflicted any pain, not deliberately anyway.

'And how are you today, Mr Gull?' The greeting was always the same, the features made military by the heavy moustache, an M.O. who was still dealing with rookies trying to get sick leave. 'You don't look so bad to me.'

The Clementses hovered in the background, threatening ghouls who were afraid that the speech might suddenly become coherent, accusing, cackling words of truth.

'His hallucinations are becoming more frequent, doctor. Sometimes he gets violent. We had to sedate him twice yesterday.'

'Hm!' It was impossible to tell whether Dr Gidman believed them or not, he gave nothing away. He checked the pulse rate, placed a thermometer under the armpit and removed the instrument a couple of minutes later. Without comment, he made some notes on his jotter and put it back in his pocket.

'They're trying to kill me!' Walter Gull shouted, but the words came out different, a high-pitched shriek of frustrated senile dementia. Brenda Clements stepped forward, a small woman with a shrill voice, and pushed him back down on to the pillow.

'See what I mean, Dr Gidman?'

'Hm.' Either the doctor saw or he did not see, it was impossible to tell. 'I'll give him another prescription, something a little stronger, more relaxing.' He scribbled on another pad, tore off a sheet and held it up between finger and thumb. *Take it, one of you, come on!* A silent reprimand, the woman snatching it, relieved that it was all over for another day or two.

'Thank you, doctor. George can pick it up from the dispensary this afternoon when he goes into town.' Something to say, an instinctive cover-up. 'We'll just have to see how he goes on. He's been very trying lately.'

'Which is what you're being paid for!' Gidman's tone was suddenly sharp, habitually reprimanding an army nurse who had spoken out of place. *Don't try to tell me my job, just do yours.* Sweeping up his bag, he turned towards the door as though he, also, was eager to be away from this place.

The door closed. Walter listened to the receding footsteps, let himself drift again and tried to ignore the stinging bedsores which would surely infect those torture wounds on his bottom before long.

Hours passed, night merging into the greyness of day and then darkening again. Lifted upright by the insensitive Mrs Clements so that he could slop porridge or soup, spill it and be slapped for it. Hazy disjointed thoughts, remembering decades past easier than he recalled recent months. Lying there and waiting for the blood to flow to his brain again, pumping lucidity, however brief.

Once every so often the mist seemed to lift from his mind, uncaging the anger within him. It seemed to give him physical strength, too, enough to sit upright and stare at the closed door, the barred window behind the curtain. A release of adrenalin which if he wasn't careful fogged his mind again and left him groping in uncertainty. He had not learned how to control it; it controlled him.

Understanding, realization flooded back, a surge that hit him with the force of an icy wave. Of course, it was Margaret that was doing this to him. Well, indirectly it was his daughter's fault that he was here in the Donnington Nursing Home, Ronald his son-in-law's really, a plot to get him out of the way, mentally unfit to change his will and hope you die soon, Dad. No hard feelings but it has to be this way, the Clementses will take care of it for us and maybe there's a backhander in it for them too . . . But more likely not. They're just getting a good rake-off for watching a mentally sick patient die.

Senile dementia they called it. At bloody sixty-eight! It was the drugs that were doing it, all that stuff they pumped into his arse to keep him under. Make him ill and hang on as long as possible, a lingering investment. And don't you worry about your dad, Mrs Hambrook, we'll look after him. There's no hope, though, just make him as comfortable as possible.

This was a madhouse, a loony bin. Walter pouted his toothless mouth and felt a surge of rage. They were all mad here, not certified or else they'd be in a proper asylum. This was a sort of private nursing home full of nutters. Maybe half of them had made wills in favour of the Clementses, there was no way of knowing. Walter would bloody well change his, make sure that Margaret and Ron didn't get a penny. He'd . . .

It wasn't easy, everything was loaded against him and before long his brain would fog again and that would be that. Back to square one, peeing himself and more needles in his bottom. He had to get away from here, escape, this very minute.

He was stronger than he thought, or rather, not as weak as he imagined himself to be. He sat upright and threw the stinking bedsheet off him. A feeling of slight dizziness, but it passed. He swung his legs to the floor, held on to the table for support. Stood up. Everywhere threatened to go black, the room tilted crazily, steadied. There – he could even walk. A step at a time, one foot in front of the other, taking a wavering

4

course towards the door because it was the only logical route. Always the fear that his tortured, ageing brain might slip and catapult him back into a state of mindlessness, vegetate him. It didn't and he reached the door. It wasn't locked. There was no point because they had not envisaged this. He was too damned clever for the dirty bastards!

Out into the corridor, standing there in the gloom trying to get his bearings. Right or left? A seemingly endless corridor either side of him, the flooring a furling roll of linoleum. He listened; nothing. He moved off to the left, supporting himself against the wall, shuffling his bare feet along the smooth surface. He came to the staircase.

The descent was an awesome prospect. A wave of vertigo swept over him, had him clutching desperately at the stair rail. A giddy drop down to the flagged hallway beneath, the quarried squares of deep red heaving up like a restless sea of blood. Walter dropped down to a crouch, began to ease his body down the uncarpeted steps, oblivious of the soreness of his chafed buttocks as he did so.

Voices drifted up to him, meaningless chatter that came from behind a closed door in the hallway. The dining room; it was mealtime for patients, those that weren't confined to their beds. He could not work out whether it was breakfast, lunch or the evening meal, for time was a commodity that had become of little interest to him. Alone in his room he gauged it by greyness and darkness, day and night; there was nothing in between. A prisoner in solitary confinement, forced to lie in his own filth. He began to hurry. No way was he going to be dragged back up there.

Nearly downstairs, just another two or three steps to negotiate. He slid, landed in an awkward heap, had to use every ounce of his frail strength to drag himself up. They were laughing loudly in the dining room, shrieks of uncontrollable laughter, accompanied by a symphony of clanging cutlery. Sometimes they went wild, got over-excited, and then George Clements burst in and raged at them to quieten them down. Once he had hit Fred Ainslow, cut the old man's lip.

5

Fear now, in case the proprietor of the Donnington Nursing Home suddenly appeared from out of his private quarters and discovered Walter Gull trying to escape. Flinching at the thought, angry. They didn't have any right to treat patients that way, they should be reported. To whom? Dr Gidman? The Reverend Hurrell, the vicar who paid infrequent visits 'for the good of your souls', as he often explained his supercilious grinning presence in the place? A lot of good that would do, the Clementses always had the answers. Nobody believed folks in a head farm.

The mirth was reaching a pitch, everybody in there was surely banging on the table with their forks (they weren't allowed knives). It was probably Vera Brown causing the commotion. The simple young girl couldn't leave herself alone and it mattered not to her if she did what her body demanded in full view of the rest of the inmates. She seemed oblivious of their presence when she got in one of those moods. Well, good luck to her and her audience. Walter shuffled for the door, gasped his relief aloud when he found it wasn't locked. Goodbye Donnington, and I hope I never see you again.

Outside it was full daylight and raining a steady, heavy drizzle, a depressing late autumn afternoon. Across the fields in front of Walter, maybe a quarter of a mile away, he heard the swish of passing traffic on a wet road. Hedges and trees devoid of their foliage seemed stark and forbidding, the only greenery the unpruned laurel bushes lining a weedy gravelled driveway which snaked ahead of him and disappeared in a wide bend and was lost to sight. The route to freedom, the way of escape.

He walked forward, swayed as his limbs rebelled at this sudden activity. He staggered, almost fell, a pathetic figure in saturated pyjama bottoms that were clinging tightly to his thin legs and already beginning to chill him. His striped jacket flapped in the wind, tore another button free.

He tried to work out some plan, a destination. It wasn't easy when you had only decided upon a bid for freedom a matter of minutes ago. But the moment they discovered he was missing they would be after him; George Clements, an infuriated workhousemaster from the last century intent on personal revenge upon an escapee; florid faced, overweight and breathing heavily, cursing, huge fists clenched so that the knuckles whitened, raised to strike. But so far Walter Gull's impromptu flight had gone unnoticed.

He followed the drive, looking back just once, seeing the forbidding red-brick house with slatted eyes that frowned beneath glowering gables, its open door a spiteful mouth that hissed after him, 'You won't get far, they'll catch you.'

They couldn't do this to him legally. Not even Ron and Margaret. He hadn't been certified. They had just booked him in here and hoped he'd die soon so that they could get their grasping fingers on what they wanted. He needed to see a solicitor, make a will that ensured that they didn't get a penny; that'd spite 'em and after that it didn't much matter. Leave it all to a cat's home. He had never owned a cat but he liked them all the same.

But to get to a lawyer he needed transport, a lift from a passing motorist on the road yonder. Surely somebody would stop and pick up a poor old man? But, please, don't take me back *there*.

Out of the grounds and on to a narrow country lane with steep grassy banks and high hedges on either side, but room enough for two cars to pass. But there weren't any cars, wouldn't be until he reached the main road. Keep going. Oh, God, his legs felt like they were going to buckle under him any second and throw him to the ground. The loose chippings were cutting into the soles of his bare feet, making him limp. Just keep going or they'll catch you.

He had to get to the road and . . . He stopped, bemused, closed his eyes, tottered. Get to the road and . . . what? It was as though a bank of mist had rolled in on him, fogged his thinking. He struggled with his brain but nothing came. Only that he had somehow got away from that terrible place where they kept him locked in a room and tortured him by sticking pins in his bum. He'd escaped but where was he . . . where

7

was he going? Standing there in the deserted lane not knowing, sobbing his frustration, afraid of what would happen to him when they caught him.

Just keep going. An injured foot thrust forward, bleeding from the gravel which adhered to it. He fought to keep his balance, hearing traffic somewhere in the distance and sensing that he could find help there. Shivering, coughing and throwing up mucus, gasping for breath. An overwhelming desire just to lie down, to give in, but somewhere in that muddled brain a dim spark drove him on, kept him upright and moving. Don't let them find me, don't let them take me back. I want to die, but I don't know how.

There was no pursuit, just the dusk and the brightness of vehicles' headlights not so far away now, the roar of speeding engines louder, the rushing of tyres on wet tarmac like roaring rapids. A 'Give Way' sign but it meant nothing to the old man, the lane veering to the left and then white markings where the major road began. Cars and lorries like racing monsters eager to be back in their lair before deep darkness fell, the drivers only intent upon where they were going.

Walter Gull knew that he had to stop one of them. Just one. Take me with you, *please*. Anywhere will do, just take me away from that place where they keep me prisoner and torture me.

But nobody was interested. Perhaps they did not see the near-naked bent form shying from the bright lights on the edge of the verge, shouting at them with a voice which was now no more than a hoarse unintelligible whisper. The twisted stubbled features pleading, yelling; gesticulating as the wind threatened to whip the remnants of that upper garment from the almost fleshless body. If they saw him they ignored him; it was none of their business; it was too dangerous to stop on a busy clearway on a wet night when everybody was driving too close to the vehicle in front. You risked a multiple pile up, a line of twisted metal. The life of one old man, if it came to that, did not warrant the risk. So keep going, you haven't seen him and if you did see something then it was a trick of the lights on the wet road. And, in any case, it was not wise to pick up hitchhikers after dark; you could easily get a knife in your ribs

Walter Gull cringed from the flying spray; they weren't going to stop, not a single one of them, unless he *made* them. It was an instinctive reaction from one who was unaware of the dangers of traffic: the lurch forward, stumbling on to the smooth surface, arms upraised. Stop, I command you!

It was a large van, possibly a furniture removal van, braking too late, slewing instantly. The driver hauled the steering wheel over to his right, felt the impact as he clipped an over-taking car, was dimly aware that the other careered crazily into the path of the oncoming traffic, but he had eyes only for that spectral figure in front of him, a Canute who thought an upraised hand was sufficient.

The driver screamed his terror, prayed that maybe it was some kind of mirage and in a second he would be back to reality and it wouldn't have happened. Then there was nothing, just something bumping up beneath the floor of the cab, a brittle tree branch cast into the road by a gale, snapping beneath wheels and whacking the undercarriage. Insignificant. You wouldn't have given it a second thought if you hadn't seen that ghastly figure in your path.

Braking, feeling another impact as a car went into the tail-board, seeing the beginnings of the carnage in his wing mirror and knowing that it was terrible reality. And all for one old man who might just have collapsed and died safely on the verge and gone unnoticed.

PART ONE

THE UNBORN

CHAPTER ONE

'I *can't*!' Suzannah Mitchell held the small square of paper aloft and waved it angrily, her long scarlet thumbnail piercing a hole in it. 'Rosie, I just can't do it. It isn't fair to ask me.'

'But you *have* to, Mum.' There was anguish, desperation on the fourteen-year-old girl's finely cut features, her dark eyes already beginning to flood with tears. She clenched a fist, stamped a foot and was on the verge of one of her tantrums. 'Mrs Blower will kill me if I don't attend every rehearsal!'

'Blow Mrs Blower.' Suzannah thought about trying to make a joke of the whole thing, ridicule the much-feared drama teacher, but knew that it wouldn't work. Not with Rosie, anyway. Her daughter took everything so seriously, gave her all to whatever she did. Because she was talented, second best was a failure. 'Look, Rosie –' She lowered her voice, tried to be rational. 'It is now November the twenty-fourth. A month ago Mrs Blower gave you the list of rehearsal dates and I've put myself out to get you to every one. Now she's panicking because she can't organize a . . . simple pantomime, and to try to save herself she's decided to hold three extra rehearsals. It just isn't on. It's a twenty-mile drive each way, which adds up to one hundred and twenty miles for *her* benefit. Not to mention the cost of the petrol, the wear and tear on the car . . . and on me! If your father was here . . .'

Oh, God, now I've gone and put my foot right in it. Rose blames me for the break up even if Charles did go off with another woman. And, anyway, I've put all the arguments forward before. Too great a strain on a young girl who has piles of homework and is only a year off 'O' levels, Grade Four piano exams next month and . . . Forget it, the child will have her way in the end.

'Daddy would have taken me.' Sullen, defiant, trying to

fight back the tears. 'I know he would. And if I don't go to the extra rehearsals I'll lose my part. Don't you understand that, Mum?'

'Yes, I understand it.' Suzannah sank down into a chair by the kitchen table, longed for a cigarette but Rose would only complain about that too. 'Passive smoking' was the term she always used: 'Do you want to give me lung cancer too, Mum?'

'I understand it only too well. Though God knows how I'm going to afford it. All right, I'll take you, even at half an hour's notice, even though it's been snowing this past two hours and I had a job to get the car up the drive when I met you off the school bus.' Even though . . . pack it in, you won't help matters. Emotional blackmail doesn't work with Rosie and you ought to know that by now.

'Thanks, Mum.'

There was an uneasy silence, mother conceding the issue, daughter perhaps feeling a little guilty. A confrontation lost and won. Suzannah glanced towards the window, saw the large snowflakes swirling, smattering silently and starting to form a white curtain on the outside of the pane, stark against the darkness. What a night to have to go out! She had been looking forward to a quiet evening, a doze in front of the telly.

'Finish your tea, darling, and then go and get ready. There's no hurry. We don't need to leave till five-thirty even if the roads are going to be tricky.' Perhaps when we get down to the bottom of the estate we'll find that they're so bad by then that even Rose will accept that we have to turn back. Some chance!

Suzannah Mitchell was thirty-five, tall and slim with long dark hair that fell below her shoulders. The divorce had left its mark on her, a fleck or two of grey in her hair and the odd line etched in her otherwise unblemished features. Men still cast sideways glances at her in the street, occasionally a passing motorist wolf-whistled. She had had offers since Charles left, but she had to sort herself out first. Maybe one day . . . but in the meantime her life revolved around Rose. Which was why she was going to drive all the way to Ryton tonight. At least it was a main road for most of the way.

All the same she was angry with Rosalind Blower. It was typical of the woman. The teacher thought that ballet, dancing and drama were more important than schooling, said as much to your face. The last thing Suzannah wanted was for her daughter to suffer the heartbreak of a career on the stage. But for now she would let her go ahead with the production of *Where the Rainbow Ends*. It would give her confidence. Maybe Mrs Blower was going to play one of the dragons! A wry smile creased Suzannah's mouth at the thought. The old bat!

Then the sadness rolled back. She and Charles had everything going for them. The perfect marriage for fifteen years and then, without warning, crash, bang, wallop and she was on her own. A girl of twenty-two, nothing special but her husband had made his choice. She'd take him back tomorrow if she had the chance but she had finally resigned herself to the fact that Charles wouldn't be coming back. Sunday afternoons were the worst when he called round to take Rose out. Often Suzannah had to shut herself away upstairs when she heard his car draw up outside. Why, oh why, did you do this to me, my love? There was no answer to that, none that she could accept, anyway.

'I'm ready, Mum.' Rose stood in the hall clutching a plastic holdall bag. Her resemblance to Charles was hurtful sometimes, but at least he couldn't take Rose away from her. The heartache had all been worth it just for Rose.

'Right then.' Suzannah took her old duffle coat down from the back of the door. 'Let's give it a try, but I warn you; one slight skid and we're coming straight back.'

'It'll be all right.' It would have to be really bad for Rose to accept a surrender.

It was snowing harder than ever now, the wind had freshened and the flakes were slanting down venomously, piling up against the doorstep; there was maybe three inches already. Rose slid into the back seat of the Escort, slammed the door and a pile of snow slid off the roof. Suzannah began scraping the windscreen clear, using an old rubber children's beach spade which she kept for that purpose. Christ, what a weak fool I am! Far better to have had a shouting match and stayed in the warm but it was too late now. It was Charles's fault. Rose had too much of him in her. Never give in and to hell with the consequences.

A van went by on the estate road doing about ten miles an hour, exhaust fumes clouding in its wake, getting slight wheel-spin on the incline but managing to hold its course.

Suzannah backed slowly out on to the road, revved. The wheels slipped then got a grip. A glance in the mirror showed her Rose's anxious face peering out through the window. She was worrying about Mrs Blower and the rehearsal again, not about the hazards of driving tonight.

Even the main road was deserted, the few faint tyre tracks already filling in. The wipers began to form a wedge, their arc restricted by the build up of snow. Before long she would have to pull into the side and knock the snow off; already she was peering through an aperture which was growing increasingly smaller. She dared not exceed twenty-five miles an hour and it was a job to tell where the road ended and the verge began.

A few miles further on she pulled into the side.

'What's up, Mum?' Anxiety; we aren't turning back, are we?

'I'll have to clear the windscreen.' Suzannah opened the door, had to hold it against the wind. 'My God, there's a gale and a half! There's as much snow blowing off the fields as there is coming down out of the sky. It's already starting to drift.' Weird patterns were forming where the snow had blown through a gap in a thick hedge, concave and convex shapes, beautiful but terrifying.

'We won't have to turn back, will we?'

'I don't know.'

'Oh Mum, you said . . .'

'I said one skid and we head right for home.'

'But we haven't skidded yet.'

'Not yet.' But do we really have to?

The tarmac was buried beneath a treacherous covering of powdery white snow, deeper in some places than others. Rose noticed a sign out of the corner of her eye, the lettering plastered by the drifting but she knew it by heart: Ryton, twelve miles. Christ, we're not even halfway yet!

A couple of oncoming cars passed, vanished behind. Surely Mrs Blower would call off the rehearsal tonight! If only there was a phone box where they could stop and phone; maybe Rose would be satisfied if the old dragon herself said it was cancelled. But there weren't any call boxes, all part of a cost-cutting scheme; you can die of hypothermia on a snowy night but we're not going to install non-profit-making telephones just so you can phone for help.

The engine wasn't picking up; there was a kind of blind spot where it threatened to cut out. Suzannah accelerated, changed down to second but there seemed to be a lack of power beneath the bonnet. She tensed; perhaps there was a bit of dirt in the carburettor and it would clear itself in a minute. It had happened to her once before and a short while afterwards it was all right. It didn't clear.

'What's the matter, Mum?'

How the hell should I know? 'The engine doesn't seem to be picking up. I thought perhaps it was dirt in the petrol. It might be. Or it could be one of the leads has come off. I think I'd better pull into the side and check.' She sensed the child's tenseness, not because of their predicament but because of what Mrs Blower might say if they were late or didn't get there, which was now a very real possibility.

Again Suzannah stopped the car. She got out and lifted the bonnet, a metal shield to protect her from the driving snow-storm. At least the torch worked! She peered into the engine and checked the leads. They were all tightly in place so it had to be the snow. The engine wasn't ticking over very smoothly, so maybe she should slam the bonnet down and rev it up before it . . . Too late. With a final stutter the engine cut out, died and abandoned her in a world of silence where the only sound was the soft pattering of snow flakes.

'Damn!' Suzannah said. 'And damn again!'

This time Rose did not ask what the trouble was, but just

sat there white-faced on the back seat. Suzannah climbed in, tried the ignition again. The starter-motor whirred, whined but refused to fire. Again and again, now becoming slow and sluggish.

'Oh, Mum!' Rose was close to tears. That was the last thing they needed.

Suzannah switched off the headlights, but left the sidelights on. A feeling of panic which she fought down. Maybe in a minute or two the engine would fire and if it did they were going to swing round in a U-turn and keep going until they reached home. Whatever Rose said.

'We'll be late, Mum.'

'I don't think we'll be getting there at all. In fact we'll be damned lucky to get back home tonight.' She recalled those television pictures last winter of motorists stranded in Derbyshire; one man had died of the cold. It wasn't a pleasant prospect.

'I'm going to try it once more.' She spoke out loud because she needed to, and she was almost afraid to grip the ignition key and turn it. She held her breath, aware of how her right temple was pounding. Please fire this time. Oh please!

The motor whirred lazily, groaned and died with an alarming finality. Suzannah was sweating in spite of the cold. She peered through that fast-diminishing gap in the snow on the windscreen, looking for a pair of oncoming headlights. In which case she would dash into the middle of the road and wave the approaching driver down. Please give us a lift, get us away from here.

But there was only empty blackness ahead and behind them, no twin pinpricks of light to be seen. Nothing. Which wasn't altogether surprising on a night like tonight; this main road wasn't an industrial route nor a commuter one. A link between rural towns, and when you finished work you went home and if it blizzarded like it was doing now you stayed there. It was quite possible that there wouldn't be another vehicle along until after daybreak and that might be the council snowplough. And for Christ's sake, child, don't ask what we're going to do now because I just don't know.

CHAPTER TWO

Owain Pugh was already regretting not having booked in for the night at the Kerry Hotel. But at three o'clock that afternoon, when he had left Kerry, it was only just starting to snow. The skies were leaden but there should have been plenty of time to have cleared the twenty miles of moorland road before there was anything in the nature of a serious fall. Particularly in the four-wheel-drive Subaru.

Sure enough, he was away from the desolate moors before dark but these rural main roads were presenting a very real problem. He engaged the low-ratio gear, dropped his speed to twenty and stared fixedly ahead at the neverending white road.

Owain was just thirty. Slight of build, his jet black hair falling in a fringe over his forehead, he had escaped the marriage trap more by good fortune than anything else. At twenty-five he had been a nine-to-five insurance broker's clerk, and had been engaged to a girl he had courted on and off for three years. They had planned to marry, or rather Sylvia had, but when word had reached her via local gossips that he had been seeing another girl she had broken the engagement off. Owain foolishly presumed that the way was clear for him to bring his relationship with Karen out into the open but the tittle-tattlers saw to it that she got to know about his previous engagement and two-timing, so in the space of one week he found himself on his own. Two months later he gave up his job and threw off the shackles of routine boredom.

With the prospect of an immediate marriage gone, he had only himself to think of and security was no longer a priority; he would sink or swim by his own efforts, earning his living by his hobby, something which had brought in a part-time income for the past few years. With no wife to support he reckoned he ought to be able to get by, eke out a living of some kind, and what he lost financially he would gain in freedom.

Owain had begun book-collecting in earnest when he was in his early twenties. He added to the nucleus of a childhood collection, complete runs of all-time favourite comics and boys' papers, progressing to detective and science fiction, fantasy and horror. He had only realized their worth when a fellow collector had offered him seventy-five pence each for his *Eagles* (he had refused, naturally!), publications which had originally cost four old pence. So he began scouring jumble sales, Oxfam and second-hand shops for similar material. This had resulted in the erection of Dexion shelving in the living room of his bachelor flat until his hobby took over. He decided to prune his collection somewhat and spent two whole weekends typing up a catalogue of items surplus to requirements, then advertised it. The response was overwhelming, with two dozen replies with stamped-addressed envelopes for lists on the first day. It was encouraging, but in all probability nobody would buy; just a host of collectors who were curious. He had surely been greedy, overpriced the publications.

A week later Owain had virtually cleared his list and banked a couple of hundred pounds, proportionally a lot more than he was earning at the office. So he went book and comic hunting again and his catalogues became monthly. Dare he risk it as a full-time business? In fact Sylvia and Karen had done him a favour, wiped the slate clean for him to embark upon a totally new way of life, working from his flat. He didn't want a shop, he didn't need one because his customers were scattered the length and breadth of Britain.

Two years later he was earning a comfortable £10,000 a year, drove a Subaru estate and apart from the 'paperwork', cataloguing, invoicing and mailing, he spent some enjoyable trips visiting bookshops and second-hand shops throughout the country. An idyllic way of life – except when you were caught out in a blizzard as he was today. Still, he wasn't far from home now.

The snow was several inches deep on the main road, and in some places he had to plough his way through small drifts where field gateways had channelled the snow across the highway. It was the depth of the snow which was beginning to worry him. A Land Rover with its high clearance would have had no problems, a firm four-wheel-drive grip wasn't the sole answer to hazardous conditions like these.

Another drift up ahead; he accelerated, hit it at thirty m.p.h. in a cloud of fine white spray and bumped over it. Christ, soon you wouldn't be able to tell where the road was.

He swerved suddenly to avoid a huge white mound, recognized it as an abandoned car, slid, but the tyres miraculously found a grip. And then he ploughed into the big drift.

He felt the seatbelt jerk, check him, almost cried out. Sudden darkness as the headlights were buried, a grinding noise and then the engine stalled. He stared dazedly at the ignition warning light, a sinister pinpoint in the blackness, a glittering jewel of evil. This is the end of the road, pal.

He almost panicked. He grabbed for the gear lever with a shaking hand, grated it into reverse and trod hard on the throttle. Tyres spinning, the Subaru moved sideways a little, jammed. He revved again, smelled a faint tang of burning rubber and disengaged the gears. Stuck solid, bloody great!

Owain fumbled for his torch in the glove box, found it and switched it on. He tried to open the door but there was a wall of snow pressing against it. He could not open it more than a couple of inches, just enough for cold, wet chunks of snow to fall in off the roof. He shut it again, and felt the beginnings of panic once more.

Take it easy, you've got to think this one out. Try the passenger door. He scrambled across the seat, found the catch. Momentary relief as the door opened, no more than a foot but enough for him to squeeze through, knee deep in soft snow and having to hold on to the side of the car. I should have had enough sense to bring a pair of wellies and a spade, he thought. But I don't have either so I'll have to do without. At least I'm being philosophical.

The torchlight confirmed his worst fears; the drift was a big one, several feet deep and a good three or four yards wide. The Subaru had gone right into it, its nose buried, the underside a ramp of compressed snow due to the weight of the vehicle. Until the wheels and the chassis were dug out the car wasn't going anywhere. And it was snowing harder than ever, plastering his sheepskin coat.

He had a choice; get back in the car, and keep the engine running and hope that a snowplough arrived before long, or start walking. People died trapped in their cars overnight. There had been warnings on television about carrying blankets and food in case of such an emergency and Owain Pugh had neither. Likewise he wasn't equipped for walking. He was wearing a pair of light shoes which were already soaked through. He could get lost, collapse in a state of exhaustion and not be found until the thaw. Two ways to die: in the car or out here in Arctic conditions. He shivered but his mind was already made up and he began moving away, sinking up to his thighs in the drift, extricating himself. Which direction? The elements determined his course, forcing him to walk with the wind and driving snow at his back. It was the only way he could breathe.

Out of the drift and on to a flat surface. In places you even glimpsed patches of black where the wind had blown the road clear. Another drift, but not nearly so bad as the first one, no more than knee-high. He wondered how far it was to the nearest habitation or shelter of any kind, even a farmer's hay barn where he could snuggle amidst the bales for warmth. Anything would have been acceptable.

But there was nothing, not so much as a deserted roadside fruit-seller's stall constructed from corrugated tin sheeting. Just white uneven walls that were ragged hedges, and more drifts where there were gaps in the growth. His feet were numb. Somehow he managed to light a cigarette, shielding his lighter with his coat. The tobacco glowed fiercely in the gale, showered sparks and tasted bitter. He threw it away.

An unending white desert, it went on and on into the blackness of a winter night. The world was gone, the new ice age was here. Hadn't there been a programme recently on television which forecast its imminence? Civilization gone, buried or fled south to a milder climate, just himself left behind because he had been foolish enough to set out without a spade and wellington boots. All gone. He was going to die. Maybe he should surrender, lie down and get it over with. He had read somewhere that dying in such conditions could be quite pleasant, warmth and drowsiness, oblivion. It was a tempting thought.

And then he saw the small side road on his left. At least he thought it was a lane because there was a wide gap and there were snow-covered hedges on either side. He stumbled towards it. If it was a lane then surely he stood a better chance of finding some form of human habitation down it, perhaps an isolated farmhouse where he could seek shelter.

The wind wasn't so vicious here, the hedges gave some protection. The snow was deep and getting deeper but it hadn't drifted. He swung his torch from side to side; just keep between these hedges and you're bound to end up somewhere. It could be a lot worse. Suppose he had been caught out on that stretch of moorland up above Kerry village? Try to think positively.

He had lost all conception of time, did not even consult his wristwatch. The blizzard howled over the top of the lane, he walked on, bowed, still hoping.

Another gap in the hedge. It could be a farm gateway minus its gate or somebody's drive. He hesitated and then made out the oblong shape of a signboard. Torch in one hand, he began scraping the snow from it with the other. Large blue lettering: in all probability it would be something stupid like 'No Tipping'. All the same he had to find out; it was a matter of life or death.

He experienced the urge for tobacco again, resisted it. Stupid. Maybe he was going light-headed. Before long he would spy the welcoming lights of a cottage but when he approached they would vanish and there would be nothing there. Just a snow mirage, either his eyes or his brain going funny.

He stood back, shone the beam of his torch on the board and read the words several times over. DONNINGTON COUNTRY HOUSE HOTEL.

That was what it said, and he rapped on the flimsy woodwork with his knuckles just to make sure it wasn't some cruel trick perpetrated by his imagination. It was solid enough and he read it once more just to be sure. This was a driveway then, and somewhere at the end of it there was a hotel, one with a bar that sold drinks and a dining room that served meals. Food and drink. And bedrooms with beds, maybe even electric blankets. And baths and showers.

Owain Pugh began to laugh hysterically as he moved forward, tried to run and slipped headlong in the snow. And he was still laughing, only getting himself under control when he rounded a bend between twin lines of bowed laurel bushes and saw the lighted squares of downstairs windows. And he realized then that he wasn't going to die after all.

CHAPTER THREE

'Fred's been smoking again,' Brenda Clements shouted as the kitchen door banged open and her husband entered and deposited a tray of dirty soup bowls on the table. 'I know he has, I smelled it on his breath earlier. Where's he getting his fags from?'

George Clements sighed, glanced heavenwards and hoped his wife didn't see him. She was in one of her moods, there was no doubt about that; she was always in a mood but worse around the time of the full moon. He had kept a record in his diary, proved that point.

'I expect he's caught a bus to town and bought them from a shop.'

'Then we'll have to stop him catching buses. That's your job.'

'Mother —' He had always called her 'mother' right from the day little Elspeth was born, their only daughter who had died of meningitis at seven — 'this isn't a nursing home anymore. We don't have any *control* over those who live here. Or had you forgotten?'

Brenda Clements turned from the chip pan and regarded him steadily; her eyes glazed over for a second or two then cleared, filled with resentment.

'It's the same place, the same people. You can't change people no matter what you do.'

'Except that they're not *patients* any more, they're residential guests. They *pay* us to live here.'

'We're responsible for them because they're not responsible for themselves. They're under our care.'

'Try telling that to the health authority and they'll close this place down, board it up. God, they tried to do that after old Walter esca . . . wandered off and got himself run over.

You can thank Mansell for finding a loophole for us to carry on but, mark my words, they're watching us. They're only looking for an excuse. Which is why you ought to clean this kitchen up. The health inspectors could walk in any day and that'd be curtains for us. They're out to get us one way or the other.'

'They can mind their own damned business.' Mrs Clements returned her attention to the chips. 'This is *my* hotel and I'll run it *my* way. None of the guests are complaining and that speaks for itself. But I'm not having Fred Ainslow fagging it on the sly. If he lives here he doesn't smoke. Or drink. And there were a couple of empty beer cans in the dustbin last Wednesday and no prizes for guessing who put them there. You can speak to him right after dinner, George.'

'Leave it to me.' George began loading plates of pie and chips on to another tray, glancing at his wife as he did so. Jesus Almighty, if an inspector walked in now and saw her working in the kitchen in her wellies the hotel would be bolted up tomorrow. Not that anybody was likely to turn up on a night like tonight; anyway, nobody could get in because the snow had blocked the lanes. Gave you a sort of relaxed feeling for once in a while. Yes, the full moon certainly did *something* to Brenda. Look at that long stringy grey hair that hadn't been washed since last week, that dress she'd made herself and was up one side and down the other, showing a few inches of leg above the wellington boot on her right foot. A proper bloody shower.

'They're making a lot of noise in there.' She jerked her head in the direction of the dining room without looking round. 'Is it that Vera Brown again?'

'Yes.' There was no point in denying it, Brenda only had to open the door and see for herself.

'I've told her before that it's unhealthy but if she must do it then go and do it in her own room. It's Barbara Withernshaw's fault, she brought her here in the first place. I should have refused to accept the girl. She's a bad influence on the others and before we know it some of the men will be getting ideas.'

This time she turned round and fixed her husband with a threatening stare. And don't let it be *you*, George Clements.

George shifted uncomfortably, dropped his gaze and lifted up the tray. 'Vera's harmless enough.'

'She's a dirty little whore. Didn't Barbara find her sleeping rough in a subway somewhere? Just like she did Fred.'

'Mrs Withernshaw pays their keep here so what have you got to complain about?'

'What have *I* got to complain about? Just that I'm not having this hotel turned into a house of ill-repute, that's what. You know the rules, George, as well as they do. At Donnington you don't smoke, drink or . . .'

Which includes me, George thought, and his thick lips tightened. I haven't fucked for the last ten years and, anyway, who'd want to fuck an old biddy in wellies who stinks as bad as Fred Ainslow? Vera Brown's got the best idea, keep it to herself and those who want to watch, can.

He was glad to get out of the kitchen, a clumsy balancing act through the door and back into the dining room, almost afraid to look across to the table in the corner where Vera Brown always sat on her own. An inaudible sigh of relief; she was all right now, sitting there with her crumpled old-fashioned flowery dress pulled back down, resting her arms on the table, a beaker of water knocked over, its contents soaking the grubby tablecloth. Eyes closed, exhausted as though she had just completed a cross-country run out there in the snow. She'd sure taken it out of herself this time but it would have to stop. Maybe Barbara could do something about it, but the old bat seemed to condone it. Do-as-you-will seemed to be her code.

Vera's eyes flickered open, took time to focus behind her steel-rimmed spectacles, a vacant expression on her moon face, her mouth hung open. Long fair hair, straight and straggling like her figure, George Clements thought. A twenty-year-old Plain Jane and a halfwit to boot. Like the bloody rest of 'em.

'Oooh, *chips*!' Vera came alive suddenly, rocked the table precariously as she jumped up, went over on her ankle and fell. A shriek, but she bounded up again. '*Chips!*'

'*Vera!*'

The commanding deep tone stopped the girl in her tracks and seemed to jerk her back, a lifesize puppet on a string. Turning slowly, she looked at the well-built grey-haired woman who sat two tables away. Respect that bordered on awe, mutely apologizing for her behaviour, she sat down again, embarrassed.

'Calm yourself, Vera.' Barbara Withernshaw spoke kindly but firmly, even smiled. Once, long ago, she might have been attractive, it was hard to be sure. Features that had thickened and coarsened over half a century, a waistline that had spread so that even the voluminous dress was unable to hide it, layers of badly applied cosmetics buried the lines in her face. Cultured certainly, imposing if you let yourself be imposed. 'Vera, I've been trying to get you on a proper diet for ages. I know it's not your fault, Mrs Clements should know better. This is the third time we've had chips this week and it's only Wednesday. And that pie, it's a mass-produced one out of the freezer, the pastry made with white flour and loaded with harmful additives. Not to mention the filling. I shudder to think what that is. Second-rate meat, in all probability, the poor beast injected with Lord-knows-what and so damned scared in the slaughterhouse that it's pumped its body full of adrenalin. An instant coronary on a plate, if you're lucky. That's the quick and easy way out. None of us would be in here today if society wasn't intent on slowly poisoning us. No, Vera, you are *not* having pie and chips.'

'Oh, *please*, Auntie Barb.' Vera Brown's lower lip trembled and her glasses started to mist up. 'Please, just this once and . . .'

'Most definitely, no.' The older woman turned her gaze on George Clements and she rapped on the table with a fleshy knuckle, caused a wave in her own tumbler of water which threatened to slop over. 'You can take Vera's back to the kitchen. And Fred's. And mine. They are *my* responsibility. You can do what you like with that mush, only please don't send it off for pigswill like you do the rest of the waste. I'm

passionately fond of pigs and I don't want them harmed deliberately. As for the rest of these ... guests, well, they're old
enough to make up their own minds. I've tried to educate
them but it's no use. Go on, man, back you go with three
plates of that rubbish!'

'But ...' The plates slid on the tilted tray and only a fast
reaction by George Clements stopped them from avalanching
on to the floor. Jesus on a moped, it was the full moon all
right! 'But, but ... Mrs Clements will be most ... offended.'

'Frankly I don't give a fuck whether Mrs Clements is offended or not.' Barbara waved a forest of jewellery-laden
podgy fingers disdainfully. 'Go on, man, back you go through
that door.'

Clements took a couple of backward steps and halted. There
was going to be another almighty rumpus for sure.

'Go on, Barb, be a sport, let us 'ave a few chips for a treat,'
the hunched white-haired man wearing a knee-length frayed
navy blue overcoat seated at the next table grunted. An un-
shaven chin failed to hide a mass of blackheads which he
stroked almost lovingly. 'It won't 'urt and ...'

'Don't *you* start interfering, Fred!' She stabbed a forefinger
with undisguised anger. 'I am doing this for your benefit as
well as Vera's. And don't you forget, if it wasn't for me you
would still be sleeping rough in a disused shack on a railway
embankment at Lampeter.'

'And better off.' Ainslow spoke beneath his breath, hoping
that the other didn't hear. 'At least I'd 'ave a fag and a jar
when I wanted.'

'Well, *I'm* going to eat pie and chips,' a bearded man in his
mid-thirties said aggressively. His pale blue eyes bulged out of
their sockets as though they might burst like bubbles at any
second. Tall and slim, he wore a casual sweater, the elbows
out, and a pair of dark brown trousers which at some stage in
their life had belonged to a reasonably well-cut suit even if
they were too large for their present owner. 'We should be
grateful for the food which the good Lord provides. He would
not send contaminated nourishment. You're mad, woman, but

I pray that you will be restored to sanity when Jesus comes again. He will . . .'

'And a lot of good he's done you, Jack Christopher. Three times up before the beak for indecent exposure and you think you're Jesus Christ waiting to be reborn.'

'There is nothing to be ashamed of in the human body, made in the Lord's own image.' Twin red spots appeared on Christopher's cheeks. 'You seem to condone what *she* does.' He pointed venomously at Vera Brown.

'She will . . . grow out of it, like perhaps you might one day,' Barbara Withernshaw said, not to be deterred. 'But you are not my responsibility, thank God.'

'Perhaps you could . . . well, leave it untouched and I will discreetly remove it with the other plates later.' George Clements took a step forward, glanced nervously back towards the kitchen door.

'No!' It was a shriek from Barbara Withernshaw this time. 'I will not be party to deceit. That woman must learn that we will not have dangerous and unpalatable food forced upon us. I must remind you that we are paying guests here. This is no longer an unqualified private nursing home.'

A moment's silence, a confrontation that had suddenly become stalemate, as though the actors in a crazed drama had forgotten their lines and were waiting for a cue. And then the kitchen door burst open and a wild-eyed, grey-haired woman in an uneven dress that swirled around her wellington boots stood there, arms akimbo.

'What's going on?' Brenda Clements screeched. She moved an arm and brandished a bottle partly filled with a pale yellow liquid. *'Will somebody tell me what's going on?'*

George Clements stepped to one side and put the tray down on an empty table. Once, not all that long ago, he had been able to placate his wife on occasions such as this, but no more. Nowadays he tried to keep out of the fray. But she was barring the door, there was no escape back to the kitchen and he did not fancy running the gauntlet across her to the door leading out into the hall.

'Yes, I'll tell you.' Barbara Withernshaw spoke evenly, her tone almost devoid of expression, as though this was a kind of recitation which she might have learned by heart and quoted often. 'On many occasions I have tried to educate you on the necessity of foods low in animal fats and free from harmful artificial additives. Yet we have had chips for the third time this week; bacon and sausage with them on Monday, in spite of the fact that we had bacon and sausage for breakfast on that day, corned beef on Tuesday that might well have given us all salmonella poisoning, and tonight some indescribable yukky pie, contents unknown. Neither I nor my two charges are going to eat them, and I have advised the others against doing so. That is what the matter is, Brenda. Now, go and prepare something nourishing and palatable like a good girl and show us what you really can do if you try.'

Another silence, longer this time, all eyes focused on Mrs Clements. The occupants of the dining room saw how her expression became vacant, puzzled. And then angry again. The bottle in her hand was levelled like a pistol, trained unwaveringly on Fred Ainslow.

'*He's* been smoking.' Her words were the hiss of a deadly snake about to strike vengefully. 'And drinking. So what do you say to that, Mrs Withernshaw, who's always trying to put the world to rights?'

'I'm sure he hasn't, have you, Fred?'

'Naw, I'm TT, you knows that and I wouldn't touch a fag neither.'

'He's lying!' It was a scream from Brenda Clements this time, the boot on the leg beneath the raised half of her dress stamping on the lino in rage.

'Hey, come off it.' Ainslow shuffled uncomfortably, looking down at his feet.

'That's a fucking insult and I must ask you to withdraw the accusation and apologize to Fred,' Barbara said haughtily.

'And I'll ask you not to fucking swear in my dining room!'

'I'll swear when the occasion demands.'

Brenda Clements's features screwed up, a rubber face mask

being crunched into a ball, mouthing obscenities which her throat refused to utter aloud. Her arm went back, the bottle was held aloft.

''Ere we go, again –' Fred Ainslow, moving with surprising agility, slid to his knees behind the table, pulled the cloth and showered cutlery and his glass of water on to the floor, the toughened glass bouncing and rolling unbroken. *'Duck!'*

The others moved fast, following his advice as though it was some pre-planned evasive action, and crouched down behind their respective tables.

Brenda Clements managed another screech as her arm shot forward and the bottle left her fingers, a spinning, scintillating missile that sped for the far wall and hit it with force, shattering and spraying its contents in all directions. Fragments of glass tinkled on the floor and liquid poured down the grimy wallpaper in a dozen different rivulets.

The occupants of the room stampeded for the hall doorway in an ungainly flight, napkins or handkerchiefs clasped to their faces, cursing and pushing one another. Jack Christopher pulled the door open and was first through. Fred fell, was helped up by Barbara and Vera Brown.

'And don't you bloody well come back!' Brenda Clements yelled after them and turned to her husband who was making his own exit through the kitchen door. 'George, where d'you think you're going? You come back here this . . .'

She began to cough, clawed at her eyes and staggered after him, crying aloud as the ammonia fumes reached her, a vile, pungent, stinging stench that threatened to suffocate her.

But it was her own husband who took her into his arms afterwards, let her sob until the fit of anger was out of her system. It was always the same and he cursed those people for doing this to her; they should know by now that it always ended this way.

After a time he left her and went through to the dining room to clean up. And that was when he heard the front door knocker hammering, booming through the big house, demanding to be answered. He had numerous fears as he went to answer it; it might be the police, or a food inspector come to check the kitchen, or even the health authorities come to charge the Clementses with running an unlicensed nursing home again.

But he had not anticipated the callers being an attractive young woman and a child, saturated with snow and on the point of exhaustion.

CHAPTER FOUR

Suzannah was grateful for the warmth of the old stove in the kitchen, the plate of mushy pie and luke-warm chips, the chance to dry her clothes and Rose's as well, draping their coats and sweaters over the back of a chair, their footwear laid out on the floor close to the fire. Safety and warmth when she had begun to despair, but she felt decidedly uneasy, almost afraid. This middle-aged couple was strange to say the least. The woman had obviously been crying and now she appeared to be sulking, sitting in an upright chair in the furthest corner of the room staring white-faced at the blank wall. Her husband was helpful, certainly, but you had the sneaking feeling that with hindsight he would not have answered the door.

'You won't be staying, will you?' He spoke from the sink where he was washing up, sleeves rolled up to his elbows. He did not turn around. Forthright, certainly, there was no mistaking the meaning of his words. Eat up and be on your way.

'I'd *like* to go home,' Suzannah replied. Oh God, I wish I'd never left it! 'But I'll have to phone for help. The A A, perhaps, I'm a member. You've no idea how bad it is out there. The drifts are several feet deep. We're lucky we didn't get lost. We only found you by sheer chance.'

George Clements dried a cup, his forehead furrowed. He glanced over at his wife but she appeared to be totally oblivious of the fact that they had callers. Maybe she wouldn't speak for days, for she didn't come out of those fits of rage easily. He pursed his lips and laid the cup down on the draining board. The last thing they wanted was outsiders in here, gossips who would go and spread wild stories.

'I'll try the phone,' he muttered. 'Maybe a breakdown lorry could get through and take you and your car away.'

'Thank you.' Suzannah watched him shuffle across the

34

kitchen and go through to the hallway, closing the door behind him. She wrinkled her nose. There was an overpowering smell of ammonia and it was starting to make her eyes water.

'Mum, what's that smell?' It was the first time Rose had spoken.

'I think it's ammonia.' She glanced at the woman again but there was no reaction. Mrs Clements was lost in a strange world of her own. She looked upset. Maybe Suzannah and Rose had arrived in the middle of a full-scale marital row. It was all very embarrassing. 'I expect they've been washing the floors.' God, they must use the stuff neat.

Rose's hand found Suzannah's, held it and squeezed it; Suzannah detected a slight trembling, a nervousness in her daughter. Poor kid, it had been a terrible experience battling through the snow and now they were stuck in this strange house and might even be staying the night. Mr Clements clearly did not want them to but they might have to if nobody could come and rescue them. She listened, tried to pick up sounds of a telephone conversation out in the hall but there was nothing. Silence except for the ticking of the cheap clock on the mantelshelf. Her stomach tightened. If it wasn't for the snow she would have taken Rose and walked back to the main road, tried to hitch a lift. That woman in the corner was giving her the creeps; there was something wrong with her, like she had had a stroke. Not so much as a flicker of an eyelid, just staring continually at the wall. Suzannah shivered. It was all Mrs Blower's fault, blast the old bat!

Footsteps, slow shuffling ones, the doorknob turning. Mr Clements was coming back. Suzannah turned and rose to her feet. His expression told her nothing, neither a frown nor a smile offering anything in the way of news. He closed the door quietly in case, perhaps, he disturbed his wife.

'Well?' For Christ's sake how did you get on?

'Phone's off. He shuffled back wards to the sink.

'Oh!' Her heart sank. Rose tightened her grip. 'I suppose the snow must have brought the lines down then.'

'Not necessarily.' He picked up another cup, studied the

inside of it, and wiped it. 'They're mostly underground cables here but that's worse. It's these bloody farmers that are to blame, ploughing through them or cutting them when they put land-drains in. And the selfish bastards don't even bother to report what they've done. They just leave it. I've complained to the telephone people, managed to get a rebate on the rental. Just a couple of quid, better than nothing, but it's the principle of the thing.'

'What are we going to do then?' I won't let you turn us out into the blizzard.

He did not reply immediately. He finished wiping the cup, and set it down.

'I don't rightly know. I'd better consult Mother.'

George Clements turned to face his wife, flinched visibly and when he spoke his voice faltered.

'Mother, these folks are stranded, what are we going to do with them?'

Suzannah felt a sudden pang of terror. The woman never acknowledged that she had even heard and continued to stare straight ahead of her. Her mouth opened a little and her tongue darted in and out, reminding Suzannah of a reptile fly-catching in a cage at the zoo. But no word was spoken.

'Mother's leaving the decision up to me.' He leaned up against the cupboard units and sunk his head as though deep in thought.

'We'll have to stay the night.' Suzannah Mitchell tried to speak calmly for Rose's sake. These people were crazy and if this was an hotel then were there any other guests? There had to be judging by the washing-up in the drying rack. Then where were they? 'I'll pay you, don't worry about that.'

'You'll have to.' He spoke abruptly, aggressively, meeting her gaze for the first time. 'We don't take non-paying guests, Mother wouldn't allow that. It's fifteen pounds a night, bed and breakfast and evening meal. You've had your evening meal so there'll just be breakfast in the morning, and we like guests to vacate their rooms by ten. There are a couple of spare rooms on the second floor.'

'One room please,' Suzannah replied sharply. *Christ, I'm not leaving my little girl to sleep on her own in a madhouse like this. She'll have screaming nightmares.* 'And if it isn't a double room we'll manage.'

'I'll have to charge you for two rooms then.'

'All right.' She checked her annoyance. *The greedy bastard, he knew she had no choice.* 'And we'll be away in the morning as soon as we can, I'll promise you that.'

'I'll go and get your room ready.' He folded the tea towel and draped it over a length of string stretched between two cup hooks. Mother still showed no interest; there was definitely something wrong with the woman.

'Have you . . . any other guests staying?' A question Suzannah had to ask, one that took courage. She didn't really want to know.

'Yes.' Once more avoiding her eyes, he made for the door.

'I take it they're having an early night then?' That old clock on the mantelshelf claimed it was 9.40. It was probably wrong but couldn't be too far out.

'They are.' His guarded reply sent a little icy shiver up her spine. 'I won't be long. Stay here, please. Mother is an introvert and she isn't feeling too well tonight so I'm afraid you'll have to excuse her.'

'Of course.'

Suddenly a loud banging destroyed the awkward silence, a frenzied hammering that echoed and reverberated in the hall beyond the door. Suzannah stiffened, felt Rose jump. George Clements stopped in mid-stride and froze, but his wife appeared not to have heard. *Thump-thump-thump.* Something heavy pounding on solid wood. Suzannah tried to identify it. It was so familiar but it eluded her for a second. And then she remembered; the heavy iron knocker on the front door. *Somebody was banging on it.*

'I think there's . . . somebody at the door,' she said, since Mr Clements was apparently making no move to go and answer it. This was crazy, you couldn't pretend that you hadn't heard it.

'Yes' – A hoarse whisper, a slight paling of those ruddy, unhealthy features. 'It's the door. At this time of night. Who can it be?' He turned, demanding an answer, which made her feel foolish. How the hell should I know? Go and damned well find out.

'I'd better go and see,' he said.

The hall door was closed gently and she listened to his receding footsteps, almost furtive. Afraid!

'I don't like this place, Mummy.' It was always 'Mummy' when Rose was frightened.

'Sh, dear.' Mother might hear you and we've got to stay whether we like it or not. 'You're tired. A good night's sleep and you'll feel better in the morning. I doubt that you'll be going to school'.

'I expect Mrs Blower's angry because I wasn't there for rehearsal.' The girl was close to tears. 'I might lose my part.'

'I doubt very much if anybody got there tonight,' she said, trying to comfort her. She strained her ears and thought she picked up a snatch of distant muffled conversation. Then the front door slammed shut: either the visitor had been admitted or else he had been left outside in the blizzard. They would soon know.

Footsteps coming this way; Suzannah found herself tautening, holding Rose to her, eyes fixed on the door. Oh, God, what next?

It opened. George Clements came in first followed by a younger man in stockinged feet that left a trail of melting snow in their wake, a bedraggled figure with a snow-covered sheepskin coat over his arm.

'Hi!' Pale and exhausted but managing to smile, the visitor made for the stove, spread his hands to warm them and dumped his coat on the floor. 'My name's Owain Pugh and my car's stuck in a snowdrift on the main road.'

'Snap.' Suzannah experienced relief, a knight in shining armour in their hour of need. Or, at least, a companion who was *sane*. 'I'm Suzannah Mitchell and this is my daughter, Rose. We're staying the night.'

'Me, too, it seems.'

'We're fully booked,' Clement was eyeing his wife cautiously but again there was no response.

'Then I'll sleep on the floor in front of the stove,' Owain snapped. 'No way am I going back out there.'

'Mother, there's another one wants to stay.' Clements spoke fearfully, and the others could not fail to notice how he braced himself: Mother, I'm afraid my football's gone through the window. Waiting for a reprimand, perhaps a punishment. Neither. 'You can stay, we have one small room left on the second floor. Bed, breakfast and evening meal. Fifteen pounds.'

'That's fair enough. I'd appreciate something to eat as soon as possible. I see you're a hotel, Mr Clements. Is there a bar for residents?'

George Clements stiffened, his face turned even paler and he cast yet another frightened glance towards his wife. He turned back. His lips moved but he seemed to have difficulty getting the words out and when he did they were barely audible.

'You'll not drink under this roof, sir. Not a drop of alcohol shall pass your lips whilst you are a guest here. Otherwise I'll have to ask you to leave immediately, snow or no snow. Do you understand me?'

'All right,' Owain replied, shrugging his shoulders, 'but I'd appreciate a cup of coffee. Or tea.' His hand had strayed to his pocket, and emerged with a crumpled pack of cigarettes.

'*Stop!*' It was a strangled shout of anguish from Clements, and a flabby hand thrust forward as though to snatch the cigarettes from Owain's hand. 'Not in this establishment, sir. Mother allows neither drinking nor smoking.' The hand remained outstretched as though asking for the cigarettes to be handed over, a confiscation by a schoolmaster who had caught a pupil smoking.

'All right, all right –' Owain dropped the packet back into his pocket. 'I'll abide by your dogmatic rules but I'd be glad if you wouldn't shout. I'm not here by choice, I'm here by circumstance and I bloody well wish I wasn't. But as my car's stuck in a drift and your phone is out of order I'm willing to pay for board and food. Now, may I please have something to eat and some kind of non-alcoholic drink? Is that too much to ask in return for my money?'

George Clements seemed to recoil, and there was a slight pause whilst he recovered his composure.

'Of course, sir. I will get you something to eat as soon as possible. But if you'll excuse me I must help Mother to bed. She's not well, you know.'

They watched as he crossed the room, and slipped an arm around the transfixed woman and helped her to her feet. Slowly he assisted her to walk towards the door. Her skirt, lifted by his hold, displayed legs that were marked where she had scratched them, disappearing on down into those ridiculous rubber boots. Any other place, any other time, it would have been comical but tonight in the Donnington Country House Hotel it was decidedly sinister.

Somehow they got through the door, closed it behind them, and the newcomers listened to those dragging steps going along the corridor and then a door opening and closing.

'Is this some kind of a nuthouse?' Owain asked in amazement, sniffing as he detected and recognized the smell of ammonia.

'I'm beginning to think so.' Suzannah smiled, relieved that this man had come out of the blizzard to join them. 'By the way, it's warmed-up mushy pie and cold chips for supper.'

'Frankly, I don't care what it is.' He noticed the steaming kettle on the stove and went in search of a clean cup and a jar of instant coffee. 'I'll complain in the morning. Still, this is the height of luxury compared with what's happening out there. If this wind and snow doesn't let up the drifts will be ten feet deep by morning.'

'I'm not staying after breakfast,' she said, wondering how long it would be before their room was ready. 'I can't wait to get away. There are supposed to be others staying here, and I dread to think what *they're* like.'

'Don't worry.' He seemed so confident, so masculine, that she fleetingly wished that they were sharing a room tonight. But that was silly, she had only known him a matter of minutes. 'We'll be away after breakfast tomorrow. Think yourself lucky, we could be lost out there in the blizzard.'

She shivered, and it was not only at the thought of a night spent out in those arctic-like conditions.

CHAPTER FIVE

Harry Clements's eccentricities had become obsessions as adolescence merged into manhood. A doctor had once diagnosed his compulsion with having everything in neat piles or straight lines as 'symmetrical neurosis', an illness which had turned him into a recluse and set him apart from his fellow men, made him the subject of their ridicule although he was totally impervious to the remarks of those around him.

George Clements's younger brother was forty-nine. He had a gaunt frame that weighed no more than eight stone, stooped shoulders and aquiline features, and his hair, that had scarcely a hint of grey in it, was brushed back because it could be kept neat that way. He had a worn suit – the trousers put in a press every night – and for outdoor wear a knee-length macintosh. He always wore a cap, donned meticulously with the aid of anything that gave a reflection if there was not a mirror handy. He frequently used shop windows for this purpose, much to the amusement of passers-by.

Harry had taken early retirement from his job with a security company and moved south to live with George and Brenda. In the 'nursing home days' Harry had occupied a room on the first floor, but his collecting hobby had ensured a move to a larger basement room when the ceiling of the room below his had shown signs of bowing under the colossal weight of his boxed collection of books.

The basement suited him better. He felt more apart from the rest of the household. A long narrow room with no window, it had become a corridor of neatly stacked cartons with an inventory of the contents written on each. On entering by the door, one turned sharply to the left, then right again, and ten feet further on reached a well which comprised a bed and a small table. The latter was piled with vintage magazines, nu-

merically sorted in order working upwards; the remainder of the
run of this particular title was to be found under the bed.
Harry cleaned his own room, dusted the boxes weekly, on
Tuesday mornings, and latterly had taken to preparing his
own food in the kitchen and carrying it downstairs to eat on a
tray whilst sitting on the bed.

He was nocturnal, a habit that stemmed from his working
life when he manned the telephone of the security firm from
eight p.m. to eight a.m. He was accustomed to being awake
during the night hours and then sleeping until mid-afternoon,
which meant that at Donnington he missed both breakfast and
lunch. He came to a compromise with Brenda via George:
from now onwards he would buy all his own food – he was a
small eater – and prepare it in the kitchen after everybody else
had retired for the night. No, Brenda was emphatic: he
couldn't have a reduction in his keep, but if he wanted to live
that way then that was up to him.

His nourishment consisted of two night-time feeds, one
around eleven p.m. and the second just after six a.m., when he
ate in the residents' lounge and watched breakfast television.
The central heating was not switched on at that hour, so he
wore his macintosh and an additional pullover in the winter.

That Withernshaw woman had already poked her nose into
his diet. She had obviously been foraging in the kitchen and
examined his neatly stacked pile of groceries on the working
surface, Harry's own square foot of reserved space. A small
loaf, purchased every other day, white sliced; a jar of the
cheapest commercially made raspberry jam. A cheaper brand
of crackers than the proprietary ones Brenda used when the
guests had biscuits and cheese instead of a sweet. Honey,
cheddar cheese, fancy cakes with the necessary preservatives
in them to prevent them going stale so that they would last the
week, and teabags for brewing an extra strong cuppa in the
cup itself.

'No wonder you're ill –' Harry reckoned she had deliberately
waited up that night until he emerged from his 'den' just to
have a go at him. 'You're short of vitamins and protein, you

43

don't have any fresh vegetables or fruit. And I saw that can of corned beef there last week. Now listen, I'm going to write you out a diet sheet, one that will be easy to follow and with a minimum of preparation, and I guarantee that within a fortnight you'll . . .'

Harry had turned and gone back down below. Damn the bitch, when he returned an hour later she had left a list of what he should eat and drawn up a daily menu for him. He had screwed it up and thrown it in the stove and carried on as before.

Those night hours were busy ones for Harry Clements. Parcels of books arrived regularly for him from dealers; he was a compulsive catalogue buyer. These books had to be examined page by page, returned if there was a flaw not stated in the description, any pencilling in the flyleaves removed with a rubber, dog-eared pages pressed and straightened, and then entered up in his inventory book as well as on the outside of the box in which it was stored. And during the rest of the time, if there was any to spare, he read. He was knowledgeable, gloated over bargains and hated spending money except on books, which were an investment. Time itself was an investment, he once told his brother, inflation was a benefit if you used it properly.

On the whole he kept himself remote from the other residents and had as little to do with his landlord as possible; it was too bad of George charging him just a fiver a week less than everybody else was paying. Damn it, he didn't cost them anything except a little bit of electricity. He didn't even eat their food these days and his laundry was infinitesimal in with everybody else's.

And both George and Brenda were queer, there was no doubt about that. His brother had once hinted that she had had to 'go inside' for a while some years ago. Harry was surprised they had let her out. He remembered one night, a fortnight or so ago, when he had gone up to the kitchen for his first feed of the night, he had heard raised voices and had stopped outside the closed door listening. Brenda was shouting insanely, 'I'm going to poison the lot of them, it's dead easy, I'll just sprinkle some of that rat poison on their porridge. Or mix it with the sugar and they can poison themselves. No, that won't do, Barbara Withernshaw doesn't take sugar and she won't let Vera or Fred have any, so they'd escape. Don't you see, George? I'm doing them a favour, sparing them the agony of this life, sending them early to a better one.'

'They'd put you away. I won't let you.'

'They're conspiring to murder me, I overheard them. Fred said he was going to kill me and Barbara said she'd give him a hand. *They're going to murder me if I don't kill them first, don't you understand?*'

'They were speaking figuratively.'

'They're going to kill me. Just like those doctors took it upon themselves to kill our Elspeth.' There was crazed hysteria in Brenda Clements's voice now.

'She died of meningitis.'

'They let her die, they could have saved her. She spoke to me afterwards and told me.'

'She is going to be reborn.' George spoke evenly and somehow his words penetrated his wife's madness.

'*What! When?*' She stared, leaned forward. 'How do you know, George?'

'I know a lot of things, just have faith in me. But Elspeth will be returned to us before very long, that I promise you. Have faith in me and wait, and I will prove it to you. *Elspeth will be born again in this very house, a babe that has to grow again.*'

It had been very frightening and Harry had crept away, gone back to his room and had remained there. Brenda was crazy enough to do what she threatened and maybe from now onwards he ought to keep his victuals in his room rather than leave them in the kitchen where they could be tampered with. She was crazy enough to do it, she should be put away.

Now Harry was cautious, keeping more to himself than ever. Which was why he was both surprised and concerned that evening when his door was opened and George entered.

'It's snowing,' George said. 'Hard. The roads are drifted and the telephone is off.'

'That won't bother me. I thought it was cold, though.'

'I'm worried about Mother.'

Harry tensed. Oh Lord, had she gone and done something desperate, either to herself or some of the residents?

'She's had another of her fits,' George went on, 'a bad one, worse than usual, threw ammonia again. I can't get through to her at all. I've put her up in her room and locked her in.'

'She'll be safe then.'

'Until she starts having screaming fits as she surely will. And we've got strangers in the house tonight. It would all happen at once. A full moon, a blizzard, Mother and strangers.'

'Who?'

'A woman and a kid, and a chap who turned up later. Got their cars stuck in the drifts. But it's Alison I'm worried about even more than Mother.'

'She's still ill then?'

'She hasn't been out of her room for a week now. Mother had a look at her yesterday, diagnosed stomach pains, might have been an appendicitis. But *I* know what's the matter with her, Harry. *She's pregnant, she's going to have a baby any day, any hour!*'

Harry sat down suddenly on the bed. His legs had gone weak and the shock seemed to have affected his breathing.

'I . . . don't believe it.'

'It's true. I've been talking to her. She went into labour and then it went away again. But she'll have the baby soon.'

'Can't we get help?'

'We don't want anybody interfering in this, Harry. She'll be all right. But I'd like you to go and keep watch on her. I've got my hands full with Mother.'

Harry went cold, the light seemed to dim a little. Only too clearly he recalled that conversation he had overhead between George and Brenda in the kitchen. *'Elspeth will be born again in this very house!'*

'I . . . I wouldn't know what to do.' Stalling, there had to be

46

a logical explanation. A sudden thought: could George be the father of Alison's child? That would explain it, a way of trying to placate Brenda when she found out. 'But it's *our* child, Mother. Elspeth reborn.' But suppose the baby was a boy? There was something about this business that had the back of Harry's neck prickling.

'I'd like you to go and sit with her anyway.' George's attitude changed, a favour-seeking grateful brother. 'And if she goes into labour come and get me. I'll be with Mother. You won't have to do anything other than that, I promise you.'

'Oh, all right.' Harry cursed himself for agreeing and watched as his brother turned and left the room. That prickling had crept right up from his neck into his recently brushed scalp and his mouth was very dry. A confirmed bachelor's nightmare, being present at a birth. But he would run for George long before the baby came.

CHAPTER SIX

Alison Darke-Smith had been institutionalized from a very early age. In her own way she had accepted it, grown up with it. She could barely remember what her parents looked like. They didn't bother with her now and in many ways she was grateful for that.

When she was six years old a private tutor had come daily to teach her at her parents' huge black and white timbered house on the rolling downs. She still remembered Miss Mason, a well-built, stern woman with thick rimmed glasses who, on occasions, had slapped her because she was unable to make any progress with her reading. So at the age of eight Alison was sent away to a girls' boarding school, but that only lasted a term; the other girls teased her, bullied her, and no matter how hard she tried she could not become 'one of them'. She began to realize then that she wasn't quite as other children were; her speech was different, she had trouble making herself understood and understanding others. Once she tried to run away but she didn't get far, and that was when she was re-turned home.

Her parents' attitude towards her had changed. Where once there had been a glimmer of love now there was nothing but disapproving looks and silent exchanges between her mother and father. Money was no obstacle. Numerous specialists' appointments, forbidding waiting rooms with piles of magazines which meant nothing to her, examinations, head-shakings, pursed lips, conversations with her parents in low tones.

Another school but not like the last one. Here they didn't get cross if you didn't understand and they gave you paper to draw on, things to play with, long walks on fine days under strict supervision. They didn't scold you when you wet the bed because most of the girls wet their beds from time to time.

Life was conducted at a casual pace, there was no pressure, and Alison grew into 'a bonny big girl' as Miss Sollis, who ran the establishment, repeatedly reminded her.

Alison was not wholly unattractive. She had rich chestnut hair that was cut short, her broad features were a mass of freckles and she was large of build rather than fat. The dentist removed the brace from her upper teeth: it had worked as well as he had hoped, the protruding upper set only slightly prominent by the time she was sixteen; they would not improve any further.

Home again for a brief spell and then she was sent to the Donnington Nursing Home. She didn't care much for Mr and Mrs Clements, but so long as you behaved yourself they left you alone. The boredom was the worst part, which was why she was glad when Mrs Withernshaw brought Vera Brown here. At least they could go for walks together and Vera was doing her best to teach her how to play croquet on the lawn at the back. For a brief spell Alison was happy, and then she was sent back home because the 'hospital' was 'closing for alterations'.

Those few months were a nightmare. Her parents had gone abroad and left her in charge of Miss Jeavons, a private nurse who was very strict and used to lock her in her room so that she could go off for the day. But eventually Alison found herself back at her former institution, only now it was different and they were calling it a hotel. Several of the former patients had returned and in some ways life was much the same as before, except that now the Clementses didn't bother with her and there was no supervision. She could do as she liked provided she was in the dining room for meals, a kind of thrice daily roll call.

Now she lay in the semi-darkness of her room staring at the reflected patterns on the wall cast by the snow outside. It was still snowing. She could hear the soft, eerie patter of the flakes on the windowpane as the wind drove the blizzard relentlessly, as though intent on burying the landscape, hiding it from human view beneath a barren white desert.

She was exhausted. Those contractions had taken it out of her and she had writhed and screamed but there was nobody to hear her, to comfort her. As had happened throughout her life, she had been shut away to 'get on with it'. She was going to have a baby. Mr Clements had broken that news to her yesterday and she was quite philosophical about it; most women had babies, didn't they? Why should she be any different? Her parents had always tried to make out that she was different so now perhaps they would realize that she wasn't. They wouldn't care, though; they wouldn't even come to see her.

Alison had had few visitors to her small room during her second spell at Donnington. Mrs Withernshaw seemed too taken up with Vera Brown to bother with Alison lately and she lacked young company. She hated George Clements and wished that she had been able to lock her door to keep him out. Sometimes Harry Clements would wander in here during the middle of the night, and if she was still awake he would stay talking to her for hours. She could not comprehend the bulk of what he said. He mumbled to himself a lot of the time, spoke in low tones as though he was afraid of being discovered here.

And Jack Christopher frightened her. At least he had last night when he had intruded upon her privacy, uninvited.

The pain had subsided and she lay there sweating, eyes closed, and when she opened them again Jack Christopher was standing by the side of her bed. She recognized him by his silhouette, the way the eyes seemed to stare and glow out of the shadowy bearded features, boring into her. She started.

'You are in pain, my child. I heard your cries.'

She nodded, didn't reply. It was no good telling him to go away because he never did. He would go when he was ready.

'Let me see if I can help.' A deft movement and he flung the sheets back, exposing her body, her lower stomach an unsightly mountain of white flesh where she lay naked on the damp sheets. Instinctively she grabbed for the bedclothes but they were beyond her reach. 'You're in child, girl.' A statement, his voice emotionless, neither scolding nor sympathizing.

'Yes, I'm going to have a baby. I don't know when but it can't be long.'

His soft slim fingers stroked her abdomen. She pressed her thighs tightly together in case his hand strayed lower down but it made no move to. Just an examination, the way Dr Gidman had done that time when they thought she might have had appendicitis, but hadn't. The fingers were withdrawn. Jack Christopher stepped back, those piercing eyes now searching out her own.

'With whom have you lain, girl?' An accusation, but his voice shook slightly as though he was afraid of what her answer might be.

'I . . . I don't understand.' She swallowed, thought she knew what he meant but had to be sure.

'With whom have you copulated? Who is the father of your child to be?' The head was thrust forward, the stooped shoulders lowered. Alison imagined those features screwed up in anticipation of her reply. Silence, except for her own laboured breathing.

'I . . . haven't been with anybody. I swear it!'

A sharp intake of breath, a hiss as it was expelled. The face came close to her own and the fingers which grasped her wrist were trembling. 'What! Tell me again.'

'I . . .' She had difficulty getting the words out, her lips moved but only inarticulate whispers came. 'I . . .'

'Tell me. *Quickly!*'

'I . . . haven't been with anybody, I swear it on the Holy Bible. No man has touched me.' A gabble of words, almost a confession. He wouldn't believe her but he had asked for the truth and she could do no more than tell him. 'I don't know how it came about. My parents will be furious, they will call me a liar, have the baby taken away . . .'

'*No, they shall not touch it. Nobody will!*' He tightened his grip on her wrist. 'You're not lying, are you?'

'I swear it.'

51

Jack Christopher pulled back, loosened his grip on her, walked over to the window and stood staring out at the moonlit sky as though searching for something. Immobile, just watching until at length he turned and came back to her.

'It has happened,' he said, and there was a fever of excitement in his voice. 'And I believe you, girl. It *had* to happen sometime, but I feared that it would not be in my own time. But now the moment is nigh and I must prepare myself.'

'What is the matter?' Alison felt very frightened, the prospect of childbirth frightening enough in itself without the fear of something else. 'Please tell me.'

He hesitated by the door, turned back towards her, deliberating as though undecided whether or not to impart to her what he believed.

'I suppose it is only right that you should know.' His whisper was scarcely audible. 'If you have not had intercourse then . . . *But are you a virgin?*' An afterthought of a question, fired with a suddenness that shook her, temporarily robbed her of her speech again. 'I must know: *are you a virgin?*'

'Yes.' She had no doubt. She was a simple maiden who, on occasions, had done to herself what Vera Brown was always doing, but she hoped he didn't ask about that. 'I'm a virgin.'

'Then it *is* true!' He smacked a fist into the palm of his hand. 'There can be no other explanation. *You* are the chosen virgin, sent here to this place so that I can watch over you and ensure that nothing goes wrong.'

'Please tell me what it's all about.'

'*The Second Coming*, my child,' he said in a hissing euphoric voice. 'We knew that He would come again, it was only a question of *when*. The Son of God is returned unto us and this time we must protect Him from those who would harm Him, destroy the Holy Babe, crucify Him again. Do you understand now?'

She nodded, experiencing a feeling of faintness, a slight difficulty in breathing as though her childhood asthma was about to return. The pain was in her chest and back this time and not in her womb. It couldn't be true, not *her*, Alison

Darke-Smith whom everybody tried to shut away from human eyes, the ogre child of a wealthy family. No, there had to be some other explanation. Some freak of nature. But the Second Coming was a freak of nature, a miracle. They had done something to her, made her like this . . . a cruel trick of the Clementses, perhaps. Or Jack Christopher. Or even Harry Clements.

'It can't be,' she moaned, 'not *me*.'

'Stop blaspheming!' His voice was raised now, angry. 'Do not speak of the Holy Babe with contempt. You have been chosen by God to bear His Son and *I* have been chosen to look after both of you. Now –' He lowered his voice again suddenly – 'speak to nobody about what I have told you. I shall be close to you throughout, watching over you. They shall not harm you, nor the Child, I promise you that. All we can do now is watch and wait, and after the birth the Babe must be removed to a place of safety because if they guess, they will kill Him. And believe me –' His lips were right up against her ear now, as if he feared there might be an eavesdropper close by. *'There is evil in this very house, an evil so terrible I scarcely dare contemplate it, and for that reason we must remove ourselves and the Child from here as soon as He is born!'*

And then Jack Christopher was gone, closing the door softly behind him and leaving Alison alone with her terror, the darkness and her labour, and the knowledge that he was right. For she, too, sensed an evil in this place, an invisible presence that skulked in the shadows and watched her day and night. Waiting for something to happen. And now she was more afraid than ever.

Jack had not returned since last night and she found that disconcerting. Not that she liked him, but in the light of this latest knowledge his presence would have been better than solitude and the feeling that unknown, hidden eyes were focused on her from out of the dark.

She had lain listening to the eerie softness of the snow piling up against the house, its reflection lighting up the walls of her room and then, later, the soft ethereal glow of the full

53

moon. The pains came and went. She had not had them for hours now, and she told herself again that it was some cruel trick, perhaps played by her own body, and she was not pregnant after all.

There had been a lot of activity going on elsewhere in the house. Shouting from down in the dining room; doubtless Mrs Clements had had one of her turns again, and everybody had vacated the room and come to bed early. Silence for a while, then there had been a banging on the front door and more voices; she thought she heard a child's but she could have been mistaken. Then a second knocking on the door and, after a time, somebody else came up the stairs. They were using the rooms next-but-one to hers, the 'spare' rooms, which meant that there were strangers in the house tonight. She tensed. The evil was very strong, a cold, cloying dampness that was in no way due to the snow and the fact that the antiquated central heating had gone off.

They had not brought her any food since tea-time, some bread and jam and a slice of stale cake. But she wasn't hungry, she didn't want anything to eat. Oh God, if I'm going to have this baby let me get it over and done with. And then she heard footsteps coming down the landing corridor. She tensed and became afraid because they were not the fast, stealthy footfalls of Jack Christopher but rather a slow shuffling, their owner muttering to himself under his breath.

Once more Alison wished that there had been a lock on the door. Somehow she would have got to it and turned the key. But there wasn't and anyway it was too late now. The handle creaked as it was pushed down. She pressed herself back against the headboard of the bed and stared with frightened eyes as the door began to edge open.

George Clements had managed to get his wife back to their ground floor bedroom, had her lying back on the unmade bed, still staring vacantly at the wall. She was still there when he returned from talking to his brother, had not even moved her head, her expression still the same. He wondered if he could talk to her, he had to. About the baby which would surely be born at any hour. Elspeth, *their* long-dead loved one returned to them from the womb of a rich man's halfwit daughter. George smiled grimly and remembered that awful night, sometime back in the early spring. He tensed, his forehead damp with cold perspiration. Oh God, better to have let Elspeth rest in peace than . . . *this*.

The residents had been late going to bed that night, with the exception of Alison Darke-Smith who had turned in early, soon after nine. Oh, little did he guess *why* right then. They had sat around in the lounge with the television on, watching some late movie, impervious to the fact that the heating had long gone off. It had been so very cold, too.

He was agitated. He wanted them all in their rooms so that he could turn off the lights and lock up. Late-night telly viewing cost electricity. Mother had already turned in.

He opened the door of the lounge and left it open, a direct hint. Christ, they weren't even paying attention to the film! Barbara Withernshaw was yakking away, delivering one of her lectures to which nobody was listening about her own views on schizophrenia and how it was caused by harmful additives in food and could be cured by their withdrawal. Fred Ainslow was asleep in the chair next to her, head back and mouth wide open, snoring loudly. Vera Brown was . . . doing what she always did to herself when she got bored, a leg draped over the side of the old armchair and her right hand up her skirt, an expression of euphoria on her pinched face. Jack Christopher was immersed in a tattered Bible, reading avidly; George half wondered if he might have a dirty book hidden in its pages. How could a guy who had on three occasions shown his whatsit to middle-aged spinsters, and sent them screaming all the way to the nearest police station, adopt this holier-than-thou image? The crazy thing was the bugger thought he was the chosen saviour of mankind. There was no sign of Harry. He was probably reading or arranging his vast library in lines of neat little piles, the spines of the books all facing the same way.

Come one, you lot, I want to go to bloody bed!

It was after one when the last of them went upstairs. They even left the television running with that awful screeching whine and George had rushed in to turn it off. Off with the lights, then, he had fiddled for a few minutes with the front door lock – it needed a new one and he'd have to replace it soon. After that he had checked the kitchen; what a bleeding mess! He almost didn't go upstairs but if he didn't then somebody was sure to leave a landing light on all night. He sighed and began mounting the stairs, now in his stockinged feet. He didn't go shoeless solely for the benefit of the guests – his prime reason being that if anybody was up to anything he'd surprise them.

He wasn't going to bother going down to see Harry tonight, he was too tired. His brother would be mooching about the house as usual, but at least he didn't disturb anybody, or, rather, there had been no complaints.

Wearily he began the climb up to the second floor landing. Damn it, he could do without this and it looked like the light was off anyway. Would that he had retraced his steps then, but in the long run would it have made any difference? He didn't know.

He had no need to walk the full length of the corridor. He could have turned back and gone downstairs. But he didn't, he crept on in the darkness. Christ, it was bloody cold, it . . . Alison Darke-Smith's door was ajar and a wan shaft of moonlight coming from the window slanted out into the corridor. George Clements decided he would just take a discreet peep, see that she was all right. She was a troublesome lass at times, and a comely one, too. He grinned to himself in the half-darkness; you got to thinking like that when you had somebody like Mother to put up with day in, day out.

There was somebody in the room with Alison, and . . . *oh, my Jesus!*

A scene that was enough to snap a brain that already wavered on the narrow, shaky bridge that separated sanity from madness, an obscenity that transcended eroticism. George thought it was a man, at least a *male* . . . a creature that knelt between the spread legs of the girl on the bed, powering hips and buttocks with unbelievable strength and ferocity, strangled grunts of lust emanating from the throat. The bed creaked, threatened to collapse under the weight and strain, and some cheap ornaments on the dressing table clinked and vibrated. Alison, if it was her for it was impossible to see beyond this monstrosity, submitted in silence. She might even have been dead. George Clements stood transfixed. The cold was intense, like a wind that wafted direct from the Arctic and penetrated the old, ill-fitting window. And the *stench* . . . he recoiled, tried not to breathe in the foul air, a smell reminiscent of an uncleansed stable that seared the lungs. On and on, a blasphemous mating that ended and began again, this . . . *thing* barely checking its rhythm, such was its lust for a mentally impaired virgin.

George could not remember creeping away, only that he found himself back downstairs in the bedroom and thanked God that Mother was already asleep for he could not bring himself to relate that happening up on the second floor. He lay on the bed fully clothed, afraid to put out the light in case whatever it was that had visited Alison Darke-Smith in her room came down here. But it didn't, not that night anyway.

The next morning he went up to check on Alison. Her door was closed. He stood outside listening, afraid to enter in case . . . There was no sound to be heard from within and in due course he eased the door open just a fraction and peered fearfully inside.

Weak early morning sunshine bathed the room in a pale golden glow. Thank God the girl was all right, lying there sleeping peacefully with the bedclothes pulled back over her, her breasts rising and falling rhythmically. She looked peaceful enough and there was no sign of anguish on her sleeping features. Perhaps he had imagined it all, he tried hard to convince himself that he had. But no, it had been so real and . . . he sniffed the air, caught a lingering whiff of that putrefying stench and fled back downstairs. Whatever, whoever, it had been had taken the virgin and gone. Pray God it did not return.

It did; three nights later but in a different way. George was dreaming, he was sure of that, but the dream was so vivid it might have been reality. He was aware first of the coldness, a drastic drop in the room temperature that had him clawing and pulling at the bedclothes, believing in his half-slumber that Mother had become restless again and in her tossing and turning had dragged the blankets all over to her side. A fumbling, tugging, trying to get a grip and then aware of the awful smell which permeated the bedroom.

He struggled up into a sitting position. It was not totally dark, for the deep gloom was relieved by the starlight coming through the frayed curtains. Light enough to enable him to make out a figure standing at the foot of the bed.

'Who . . . who's that?' He was suddenly very afraid.

'I want to talk to you.' It was a man, tall and lean, his features hidden in shadow, dressed in some kind of loose dark material, a cloak that rendered him almost invisible against the background. 'I want to speak to you about Elspeth.'

A shock like that caused by a mild electric current passing through his body had George trying to jerk away, but his back was up against the headboard of the old-fashioned utility bed and there was nowhere to go.

'Elspeth?'

'Your daughter. She died, you remember?'

George Clements nodded, swallowed. He couldn't get his words out, his vocal chords were constricted with sheer terror.

'You'd like her back, wouldn't you? Just as she once was, a newborn baby to start life all over again.' The nocturnal visitor was smiling. George couldn't see his face but he knew by the leering grin in his tone.

But, please, I don't want to look upon your face.

'Yes,' he grunted, 'but that's not . . .'

'Oh, yes it is. Everything is possible with *me*. In fact, I have already made it so that she will be reborn into this very house. The same child you once had, ready to begin life all over again. You see . . .' He paused for a second . . . 'I've been looking after her for you. She was taken because we had need of her. We still do, but in a *different* way.'

George glanced down at his wife. She was sleeping peacefully, turned on her side. Thank God!

'You don't thank God, you thank *me!*' The words were like a whiplash. George cowered. He had not spoken the name of God aloud . . .

'I do thank you,' he mumbled.

'Good, then you shall have your child back . . . Things will be a *little* different, but you need not worry. So long as you remember that I am your master and you must obey me implicitly.'

'I'll do anything you ask.' Even in the midst of stark terror George would have pledged his soul for the return of their baby. It was Elspeth's death that had made Mother like she was; maybe now everything would be all right again, Mother her old self, his own mind no longer tortured by grief.

'Good.' The stranger glided rather than stepped back into the deepest shadows. 'We know where we stand then. The time is almost nigh for me to return to this world from which I was banished, longer ago than you can possibly be expected to recall. I have my followers but I need more than a smattering of converts. I need a place in which to be worshipped, a temple, and what better than this place, inhabited by outcasts from the world outside? You see what I mean?'

George did not, but he nodded his head in agreement just the same.

'Good. Now, as I am returning your beloved babe to you there will be a price to pay. Put it this way, I need *disciples* if I am to overthrow those who worship the one they call God. When religion has been eradicated from the face of the earth, prosperity and happiness will return, I promise you that. But sacrifices will be necessary, the blood of those who are against me must be spilled, and even in this place there are those who worship God. They must die, as must all those who follow the mythical God. You must convert those you can, the rest must be removed. Do I make myself clear?'

'Yes.' It was all very confusing but George wasn't going to argue.

'I took from you a young girl and in return I am giving you a babe. Listen carefully: when the babe is born, another young girl will come into this household and she you will send to me. A life for a life. There is no other way.'

George was trying to work it all out. Cold and shaking, being forced to breathe that awful putrefaction down into his lungs, he guessed but was afraid to accept what he saw and heard. He sat there in the bed and stared at nothing, an empty blackness and the chill of an early Spring night. Whoever it was had gone . . . if he had ever been. Clinging to the hope that it was just a dream, that he had imagined that fearful copulation in Alison's room. Tricks of the mind, and that would be the end of it.

Until Alison Darke-Smith was suddenly pregnant. And now George Clements had to tell his wife. At least part of it.

He turned back to face her, a pathetic woman who should be certified and locked away, looked after for the rest of her life. Himself, too.

'Mother –' It wouldn't be any good, he wouldn't get through to her – 'they are going to give us Elspeth back.'

Perhaps an eyelid flickered. The expression softened into a deep sadness, but Brenda Clements did not move.

'Elspeth, Mother –' Going over to her, thrusting his face close to hers, shouting at her like he used to do in his boyhood in those caves which threw your words back at you, where you made echoes until you became bored. 'Elspeth . . . Elspeth . . . Els . . . peth . . . E-L-S-P-E-T-H.'

He almost felt it penetrate her, a bullet sinking into the armour-plated hide of a rampaging elephant, the pain taking time to spread, the wound opening up but the beast still unaware of its injury. Brenda Clements's features tightened, her sunken eyes filmed over then cleared, stared at him and *saw*. The jolted brain was reeling, needed time to steady. Then she stirred, took a deep breath and her lips moved.

'Elspeth is gone.' The words were hollow, the voice trembled. 'She's dead, snatched from us in childhood.'

'But she will be returned to us. I was promised that and now it has come true. Alison is about to give birth to *our* child – any hour, any minute. And when she does . . .' Mother would never understand, there was no point in telling her the rest. *And when she does we have to pay the price, give him back that child that came in here tonight out of the blizzard.*

'It's impossible. Unless . . .' Brenda's eyes hardened, a hand was raised and a finger pointed at him accusingly.

'No, no, Mother, I swear to . . . I swear by that which is now sacred to me that I have not touched Alison. It is he who took Elspeth from us who has sown the seed by which she will live again. Let me explain . . .'

It wasn't easy explaining. She stared at him in amazement and there was no way of telling if she understood. But she didn't try to shout him down because she would do anything just to have her baby back again after all these years. Perhaps she did not believe him and was forcing herself to, clinging to vain hope and enjoying raising it to its highest pinnacle, putting off the hour when it would be dashed to irretrievable fragments and the heartache would start all over again.

'Suppose . . . suppose the baby isn't . . . a girl?' she whispered hoarsely, and there was a haunting fear reflected in her sunken eyes. 'It could be a boy!'

It was as though an invisible blow struck George Clements, staggered him. Shock and pain, reeling, then somehow forcing himself out of it. His lips steadied and he glared fiercely at his wife.

'It won't be a boy, it'll be a girl. Because *he* said so. He took her, now he's giving her back to us.'

She nodded unconvincedly.

'But we have to do what we must do.' It took courage. His fingers started to shake so he clenched them. 'After all, it's worth anything to have her back. That young girl, she has to go. Leave that to me. After all, we didn't ask them to come here. I tried to get them to go but they insisted on stopping. And if they'd gone –' He smiled for the first time as though a weight had suddenly been lifted to ease his troubled conscience. 'If they had gone back into the blizzard they would have died. Likewise, if they hadn't found us they would have perished. So it comes to the same thing in the end, doesn't it?'

'I suppose so.' She pulled the quilt from under her and wrapped it around her. That was how she would remain for the rest of the night. 'I *felt* it tonight, George, I knew something was about to happen. It was like all the demons from hell had got inside me, were torturing me. I wanted to kill those fools in the dining room. So you see, he'd got to me too only I didn't know it. It has to be right what he says. I'll help you, anything so long as we have her back again.'

But George wasn't listening. His thoughts were on the Mitchell girl upstairs and he was wondering how he was going to sacrifice her to the Lord of Darkness in return for their dear Elspeth being returned from the grave. It wasn't easy, but he'd find a way.

CHAPTER SEVEN

Suzannah had dreamed that they were back out there in the snow. They had not been able to find a place of refuge, instead they had stumbled on and become lost, finally lying down, huddled together, in the snow. It was wrong what they say about feeling snug and warm when the end was near. You were frozen. Rose was pawing at her, sobbing.

'Mummy, Mummy, wake up. I'm cold and I'm frightened.'

Embracing her daughter, holding her to her. Try to get some sleep, my darling, at least we're together. Oh, God, we're going to die!

'Mummy, Mummy, wake up!'

Fists pummelled Suzannah's shoulders, stirring her. I don't want to wake up, I just want to go to sleep and die. But the child was insistent and she would have to stir, try to comfort her with lies that soon everything would be all right and that somebody would find them . . . Shocked realization, a wave of near-euphoria, overpowering relief. They weren't out in the blizzard, they were safe in some dowdy old hotel even if the bed was cramped and damp and the room icy cold.

'Mummy, wake up, *please*.'

Rose was whispering frantically, as though for some reason she was afraid to speak aloud, clinging to Suzannah. And it was very, very cold.

'It's all right, darling, we're safe. We're . . .'

'There's somebody outside the door.'

'I expect it's one of the residents going to bed late, or Mr Clements . . .' Suzannah heard then, heard the stealthy, shuffling footsteps, tne low voice muttering incoherently, muffled words that could not possibly have any meaning. Insane ramblings. Her flesh goosepimpled and she found herself clutching Rose to her.

'It woke me up,' Rose whispered, even lower than before, 'and then I heard somebody shouting as though they were in pain.'

Suzannah fumbled for the light pull then changed her mind. Perhaps it was better not to draw attention to themselves. And there wasn't a lock on the door — she had made that disconcerting discovery earlier when they had retired for the night. Just what did you tell a frightened child in such a situation? This place was like a lunatic asylum except that it could not possibly be. Or could it?

'It'll probably go quiet in a minute,' was the best she could think of saying.

Whoever was out on the landing had stopped, right outside the door to this very bedroom. They could hear laboured breathing, as though whoever it was was exhausted. Or lost. Rose's teeth were chattering; Suzannah could feel her shivering.

'Steady, love, I'll look after you.'

And then the footfalls started up again, a slow dragging, slithering like some legless beast in search of its prey. It was even colder now and in the bright moonlight the snow on the windowpane sparkled in patterns that defied the talent of any human artist. It must have stopped snowing, Suzannah concluded, which meant that they would be able to get away from here first thing in the morning. They might not even stop for breakfast.

The shuffling sounds grew fainter. At least whoever — or whatever — it was had passed on and wasn't coming in here. She expelled her relief in a cloud of vapoured breath. And then, suddenly, a female voice cried out, just once . . . a single scream and there was no mistaking the terror. The screech seemed to hang in the air, dispersed, and the silence rolled softly back.

'Oh, Mummy, I'm so frightened.'

'Well, it's gone quiet again now.' Don't say 'It's all right', because it most certainly isn't. Whoever screamed might be dead, a corpse lying only yards away up the passage. Suzannah wondered if it might be possible to jam a chair under the door handle, but the futility of it was not worth alarming the child still further.

Rose cuddled up to her, pressing herself hard against her mother, and between them they managed to generate some warmth. Both of them lay listening, aware of the pounding of their own hearts, the trembling of their bodies. But there were no further sounds from beyond their unlocked door and much later they slipped into a fitful doze.

Outside the moon reached its zenith and began to dip in the velvet, star-studded sky.

Harry Clements pushed the door softly shut behind him and leaned up against it.

'I hope I'm not intruding,' he said. 'They tell me you're going to have a baby.' He spoke nervously, since such matters were not part of his normal conversation. He was embarrassed and, he was shocked to discover, a little jealous. Not of the birth but because of the *cause* of it. Alison had given herself to a man, and that eavesdropped conversation between George and Brenda came back to him like a record with a damaged groove in which the pick-up needle had stuck. 'Elspeth will be born again in this very house.' And then George had come down to Harry's room only a matter of hours ago and told him that Alison was pregnant and asked him to keep an eye on her. It could only mean one thing. The dirty bugger, and fancy her letting him do it! It hurt, and made him angry as well as jealous.

'I think it might be going away.' Her voice sounded strained, exhausted.

'Don't be silly, babies don't go away. You've either got one or you haven't.'

She clutched the sheets tightly to her. I'm not going to let you look at me, you dirty old man. Everybody wants to look at me. 'I'm a virgin,' she said proudly and laughed, a schoolgirlish giggle.

'You can't be, not if you're going to have a baby.'

65

'I am. You ask Jack Christopher.' Go on, clear off and talk to him and leave me alone.

'What's *he* got to do with it?' Harry Clements advanced a couple of steps, bowed and frail, openly angry now.

'He told me.' She pushed herself even further down the bed until only her eyes and her auburn hair were visible in the moonlight. 'He says it's the Second Coming. I've got Jesus Christ inside me.'

The other stared in disbelief and experienced a rare urge to laugh, to disturb his humourless character with a peal of helpless mirth. She was mad, of course, although he had always thought she wasn't as crazy as some of the others here. Somebody had been having her, all right. If not his brother then Christopher, or maybe both of them. They'd fed her a pack of lies; George claimed that she was going to give birth to the daughter they'd lost years ago, whilst Jack was trying to abdicate responsibility and wipe the slate clean by claiming it was a virgin birth. So *that* was why they hadn't called the doctor or a midwife. They were trying to hush it up. But it would all have to come out in the end. Bloody cowards! George was scared to come near her and Christopher had just buggered off and left her to it. The poor kid!

'I'll see you're all right.' He was shaking visibly. 'I'll get Mrs Withernshaw to have a look at you. She's delivered babies in the past and if we can't get anybody else now that we're snowed in I'm sure she'll . . .'

'No!' A shriek. 'I don't want anybody. Just leave me alone.'

'You can't . . .'

And that was when Alison Darke-Smith screamed, a piercing yell, her body heaving up with the bedclothes then thumping back down again. She lay there white and still, an ungainly, huddled form under the blankets.

Harry Clements peered cautiously at her, wondered if that was how babies came, a sudden screech and they shot out of their mother's womb. Maybe he ought to take a look and see but it was going to need a lot of courage to lift those blankets and look beneath them. So he stayed where he was, watching

66

and listening for the cries of a newly born infant. And when there were none he wondered if it might have been stillborn.

After a time he began to discuss the possibilities with himself in whispered incomprehensible tones.

Morning arrived in stages, the faint moonlight merging into a murky greyness that struggled to find a way in through the worn curtains and snow-plastered windows that had frozen in the early hours. A world of ice and snow, a barren windswept landscape of beautiful drifted patterns. Nothing stirred, even the wildlife seemed to have deserted and left this white waste-land.

Rose wakened and pushed up even closer against her mother. It would be light soon and it wouldn't be so bad then. Oh, hurry up and shine, sun, and then we can get up and leave.

It was some time before Suzannah awoke, came to with a start and forced a smile.

'All right, darling?'

'Yes. Can we get dressed?'

'Not yet, it's barely light and I doubt whether the others will be up yet. We'd best stay here for a bit.' It was warmer now, that dreadful cold of the night hours had lessened. But they were alive and unharmed and that was a lot to be grateful for, Suzannah told herself and hugged Rose.

They dozed for a while, talked in hushed whispers. There was nothing but silence and you were frightened to break it; frightened, in a way, of what you might disturb.

It was eight o'clock by Rose's watch when they slid out of bed and hastily pulled their clothes on over their crumpled underwear. Suzannah ran the tap in the wash basin but there was only cold water.

'We'd better go downstairs,' she said. She didn't relish the prospect but neither did she wish them to remain here in this cold, inhospitable bedroom. 'Perhaps Mr Clements will allow us to sit by the stove until breakfast is ready.'

As they emerged on to the landing they heard the adjacent

door opening. Owain Pugh stepped out, looking reasonably spruce in a woollen pullover and corduroy trousers.

'Hi, there.' He smiled. 'Slept well, both of you?' He could tell by the child's expression that they hadn't. Pale and drawn, her fearful eyes roved from side to side as though she expected to find some awful monster lurking in the shadows. 'What's up?'

'We were disturbed,' Suzannah said, walking on towards the stairs, eager to be away from whatever had made those slithering and muttering sounds in case it was still around. 'Somebody was mooching about. We heard a girl scream. At least, I *think* it was a girl.'

'They're an odd lot here.' He grinned reassuringly. 'But harmless. Apparently it was a private nursing home once but the health authorities closed it down. So it reopened as a residential country hotel and all the former inmates came back to live here. At least, that's what I gather, reading between the lines of what the old boy Clements told me.'

'Oh!' Suzannah felt cold fingers clutching at her heart.

'Nothing to worry about.' Owain glanced at Rose and wished he hadn't spoken. 'Eccentrics rather than nutters, if you see what I mean. Anyway, I'm starving so let's get some food inside us and then see what we can do about getting back on the road. It's stopped snowing so maybe the snowploughs will be busy soon. They'll clear the main roads and providing we can walk back down the lane we should be all right.'

Suzannah felt a surge of hope and, again, a feeling for this man which she tried to dispel. Don't get thinking that way, she told herself. He's probably got an anxious wife waiting for him back home. But she couldn't stop herself saying, 'I expect your wife will be worried about you, it was awful not being able to phone last night.'

'Wife?' He laughed as he pushed open the dining room door. 'I don't have one of those. I should be so lucky!'

Suzannah felt a tautening in the pit of her stomach, a slight racing of her pulses and this time she did not try to check it.

The dining room was empty, the tables not even laid. It

reminded her of a deserted transport café, the floor swept in readiness for the next day and if you wanted any food you went up to the counter, ordered it, and helped yourself to eating irons out of the tray. And there was still a faint smell of ammonia, enough to make you catch your breath until you became used to it.

'Let's see what's happening in the kitchen.' They followed Owain in the direction of the adjoining door. 'I can smell bacon frying so breakfast shouldn't be long.'

He pushed the door back on its hinges and all three of them stared in astonishment at the scene which greeted them. They had expected to see Mr Clements, dressed as he had been on the previous evening, bent over the frying pan on the stove. Instead it was a grimy, white-haired old man, clad in dirty overalls, who turned to greet them, grinned with a toothless mouth and stroked a three-day stubble of beard.

'Breakfast in five minutes.' Fred Ainslow laughed coarsely. 'A right fry-up this'll be. Cornflakes in that cupboard there if you want it.' A fit of coughing shook him and with his other hand he flicked cigarette ash on to the floor. 'Rough and ready, Fred-style, but, by Christ, it'll be good. Learned me cooking in the army, did for three 'undred once and you should've seen 'em get it down 'em!'

'He's drunk!' Owain could not hide his disgust. 'Been on a blinder all night unless I miss my guess.'

Rose coughed, exaggerated it. 'I *hate* cigarette smoke. It ought to be banned.' She turned her head away.

'It *is* banned. In kitchens and places where food is prepared,' Suzannah snapped. 'I've a good mind to report this man. And just look at the state of this kitchen! I'm surprised there aren't cockroaches crawling all over it.'

'Where's Mr Clements?' Owain's tone was abrupt.

'In 'is room, I expect.' Ainslow turned a rasher of bacon in the frying pan and it gave off a cloud of smoke. 'The old gal ain't well, not that 'er's ever too good. Good riddance to 'er I say, chuckin' ammonia bombs at the guests.'

Owain Pugh stepped forward. 'You can put that cigarette

out, and you can also get away from that stove. We have all paid good money to stay here and if *I've* got to cook the breakfast then I damned well will. So far, since I arrived, I've had an indescribably awful pie with a morass of cold chips, a damp bed and a room with no heating. Come on, I'm going to get us some breakfast if there's nobody else around to cook it.'

''Ere, leave off!' Fred Ainslow tried to grab the frying pan handle back from the other and received a push that almost toppled him over. 'You can't do this. And that's assault, I'll 'ave you know.'

'Assault or not I'm getting the breakfast. Now, Suzannah, Rose, what would you like? There appears to be bacon, eggs, some tins of tomatoes, and probably some sausages in the fridge if one of you would like to take a look. And . . .'

'What on earth's going on in here?' The door opened and Barbara Withernshaw bustled into the kitchen, clad in a green and black checked housecoat with a pair of silver moon-boots protruding from beneath it. 'What are these people doing, Fred?'

'We are doing our best to prepare a reasonably wholesome and hygienic breakfast,' Suzannah said. 'This man has not only been drinking, he's smoking over the stove, dropping cigarette ash everywhere, and just look at the state of his hands! He hasn't washed them for days!' Out of the corner of her eye she saw a younger, bearded man appear behind Barbara, his bulging eyes stared at each of them in turn and a thick shock of hair flopped over as the head was shaken, as if this latest visitor to the Donnington kitchen was forcibly bringing him out of a trance. Her spine tingled. God, why didn't they just leave right now and forget breakfast?

'You don't understand Fred, that's your trouble,' the woman said, her tone condescending, as though she was addressing a group of infants at a primary school. 'You don't know him like *I* do. My dears, if it wasn't for me he would still be dossing down in an old shack, he might even be *dead* by now. I know he drinks and smokes, but one has to be a little tolerant. Really, Fred, you ought to have washed your hands. Still, there's less harm in a bit of good old-fashioned dirt than there is in all the additives they put in food today. Why don't we forget the bacon and sausages? If you look in that cupboard down there behind where Fred's standing, there's some muesli and shredded bran, bought in by Brenda Clements on *my* instructions. Our bodies need fibre, it is essential and . . .'

'We are having bacon, sausage, egg and tomato, thank you.' Owain scooped some rashers of bacon out of the pan on to an aluminium plate. 'You can have just what you like, provided you get it yourself.'

'Ow's the babby coming on?' Fred Ainslow asked Barbara, nipping the end off his cigarette and grinding it out on the floor with the sole of his dilapidated shoe. ''As he come yet or not?'

'Not yet. I'm going back to sit with Alison after breakfast.'

'*You're not!*' The shriek came from Jack Christopher as he bundled his way into the kitchen and thrust his anguished bearded features into her face. 'You will keep away from that girl, d'you hear?'

'I shall not,' she retorted, 'and certainly not on *your* say-so, Jack. Whatever's the matter with you?'

'Bloody well leave her alone!' Christopher shook a clenched fist, and a dribble of spittle oozed from between his lips and lodged in his unkempt beard. 'I'll kill you if you so much as go near her!'

'Is everybody mad?' Owain pushed the frying pan to safety and rounded on the others. He saw how Rose clung to her mother, how Suzannah had gone pale.

''Course we're bloody mad,' Ainslow cackled harshly. 'Why d'you think we're bloody 'ere, mate? This used to be a looney-bin and it still is, except now it's got a posh name. The Donnington Country 'Ouse 'Otel. Same thing, though.'

'Shut up, the lot of you.' Owain turned on Christopher and the other dropped his aggressive pose and stepped back. 'We are going to cook our own breakfast and damn you all. If you want to fight and squabble, go ahead, but please keep out of our way.'

71

Jack Christopher turned on his heel, stalked out into the hall and they heard him stamping upstairs. Barbara Withernshaw made as if to follow, but changed her mind.

'I'll have muesli,' she said haughtily, 'as will Fred. And so will Vera, though God alone knows what time we'll see *her*! She gets up later and later these mornings.'

'Probably tossin' 'erself off,' Fred Ainslow guffawed.

'Cut that filthy talk out!' Barbara's cheeks were red, her eyes narrowed angrily. 'I'm not putting up with all this. And if you lot want to give yourself early coronaries or bowel disorders with that rubbishy food, then don't say I didn't warn you.'

Owain, Suzannah and Rose carried their plates to the furthest table in the dining room and went through the motions of eating. And when they spoke it was in whispers.

'Let's get moving right away.' Suzannah wiped her fingers on a tissue and passed it to her daughter. Obviously serviettes were unheard of here.

'I think perhaps I ought to take a walk down to the main road first, just make sure that it is being snowploughed,' Owain replied. 'I mean, it's a bit of a waste of time if it isn't and you never know how early these councils start work.'

'We're both coming with you. God, we're not stopping *here*.' She scraped her chair back and stood up. 'I don't want to spend another minute in this madhouse.'

'Please yourself.' He led the way to the door. 'But the snow in the lane is sure to be deep.'

It was. In places it had drifted to several feet, and on more than one occasion they had to clamber up the slippery bank to avoid the big drifts. Once Rose went in up to her waist and Owain had to help her out. She was white-faced, frightened; her stay at that hotel had not done her any good. And that goes for all of us, he thought grimly.

Surely they must reach the road soon. The narrow lane twisted, the high banks and snow-laden hedges screening the surrounding countryside from them. It was slow going, and he had not realized it was quite as far as this. Once they paused for a rest and as he became aware of the total stillness, the unbroken silence, he began to feel uneasy. The road ahead *was* a main road even if it wasn't a commuter route; there should at least be the distant growling whine of a snowplough forging a path through the soft, white depths, or a JCB digging out the bigger drifts. But there was nothing. Just the wind blowing, not as strongly as on the previous evening but still sending up clouds of misty whiteness off the fields, adding to the drifts. There had been a sharp frost sometime before dawn but now the sky had clouded over again, an unending sinister greyness. Odd snowflakes were whipped along by the wind, and it was difficult to tell whether they came off the hedges or whether it was starting to snow again.

'Well, there's the road. I think it is, it has to be because there's a signpost pointing this way and the hedges and banks end just there.' Owain tried to speak with confidence but his optimism was already waning. Ahead of them there was nothing but snow and more snow. High drifts that wound back on themselves, mountains of virgin snow like a desert of white sand dunes.

'And where's the snowplough got to?' Suzannah experienced an urge to burst into tears, but she had to fight the inclination because of Rose. And damn that bloody Mrs Blower once again.

All three of them stood listening. Then, in the far distance, they heard what might have been a chainsaw, its whine rising to a crescendo, dying, picking up again. Or a scrambling bike. Or . . . there were just too many options; you dared not build your hopes on the possibility of it being the long-awaited giant machine with its huge blade pushing the snow off the tarmac. They waited, trying to estimate how far away it was; certainly a mile, maybe two.

'Is it . . .?' Suzannah was worried about Rose. It was bitterly cold and they weren't clad for long periods of exposure to these conditions.

'Could be.' Christ, what was there to say? The bloody thing might be travelling in the opposite direction, back towards Kerry.

'Perhaps if we walked in that direction we might meet up with it.'

'No.' And I'm not allowing you two to attempt it, either. 'Look at those drifts, they're twice, three times the depth of the ones back there in the lane. We'd never make it. You would get buried alive in that lot with nobody around to pull you out.'

A long silence. And to add to their hopelessness it was beginning to snow again, the flakes slanting down with a grim persistence. Owain looked at his watch. 10.35. They had about six hours of daylight in front of them, six hours to stand here in the freezing cold and risk pneumonia. Or . . .

'We could always go back to the hotel and come back later. This road is sure to be snowploughed sometime.'

Today? Tomorrow? The day after?

Suzannah did not reply, she merely held Rose's hand even tighter. At least that inhospitable nuthouse was shelter, there was food . . . of a sort. They did not really have a choice, she was just trying to stall. Hoping for a miracle, a helicopter perhaps . . . Don't be daft, nothing will come before the snowplough and that could be hours yet.

'Mummy, what are we going to do?' It was 'Mummy' again and that was a bad sign. That place wasn't healthy for a young girl. There was something more than just the superficial madness; anywhere else it could have been a real-life comedy show. You sensed . . . an *evil*. Suzannah had felt it last night and it wasn't any different this morning.

'I think we ought to go back. Just for now, darling. We can come out again in a couple of hours. The snowplough will surely have got through by then.'

'I don't want to go back, I hate that place.'

'So do I, but if we stay here we'll freeze to death. Come on, we'll go back and have a warm by that old stove.'

'We won't be . . . be staying there the night again, will we, Mummy?' Rose's lips trembled as she spoke.

'No, I wouldn't think so, darling.' Suzannah turned her head away so that her daughter could not see her face. I've got

74

a terrible feeling I'm lying to you, Rose. I just hope I'm wrong.

With Owain in the lead they turned back, treading in their own outward footprints which made the going easier, enabling them to skirt the few deeper drifts into which they had blundered earlier. And as they walked, Suzannah recalled that heated conversation in the kitchen earlier and wondered about the girl called Alison who was apparently on the verge of giving birth. Poor girl, in a place like *that*. She might even have had the baby by now.

CHAPTER EIGHT

'Gone! What d'you mean, *gone*?'

George Clements's jowls seemed to expand as though they were being inflated to their limit and a purplish hue spread across his cheeks. Eyes narrowed beneath the bushy brows, he gave the appearance of a fierce bird of prey suddenly deprived of its victim, hands raised as though he was about to strike Fred Ainslow.

The old man seemed unaware of the threat, the remnants of a Woodbine about to burn his lips depositing its last length of ash down the front of his grubby shirt. He dropped a couple of sausages into the frying pan, splashing fat which sizzled on the stove.

'Just what I said, gaffer, and bloody good riddance to 'em. Bleedin' snobs! If my breakfast ain't good enough for 'em then they can bloody well do without. There's plenty that'll eat my fry-ups and not complain. When I was in the army . . .'

'Just listen to me, damn you!' George grabbed him by the front of his shirt and a sausage plopped on to the floor. '*Where* have they gone, man?'

'How the bleedin' 'ell should I know? I didn't ask 'em, none o' my business. Out the front door, where d'you think? Up the fuckin' chimney?'

Clements released his hold and closed his eyes for a second in an effort to get himself under control. It was now past midday and Ainslow was doing yet another of his greasy fry-ups for lunch. There was no sign of anybody else. They were probably all in their rooms. The man and the woman were gone; that was fine, he didn't want them snooping around here but he needed that young girl. He could not afford to let her go, it was unthinkable. His whole pact with the Master hinged on it.

'When did they go?' His tone changed, for he would not get anywhere by ranting and raving. Mother did enough of that.

'After breakfast. They got their own, took it through there, ate it, and then got their coats and went.'

'But what *time*?'

''Alf nine, ten. Can't rightly say, I'm not a clock-watcher. Clock-watchers 'ave suicidal tendencies – you ask Barb about that.'

George Clements turned, moved surprisingly swiftly through the door into the hall and saw the front-door was still open. They were in such a hurry to leave they hadn't troubled to close it behind them. He didn't bother about a coat or wellington boots, there wasn't time.

Their footprints showed clearly down the driveway, avoiding the deep patches of snow. Follow them and bring the girl back at all costs – he would need her within a matter of hours. Alison was close, she had had contractions again. There was no time to be lost.

A sudden thought struck him, halted him knee deep in the cold wet snow. Even if he caught them up – and they had maybe an hour and a half's start on him – how was he going to get them back? He had to use cunning, something to lure them back to the Donnington Hotel. You're wanted on the phone, Mrs Mitchell. Liar, the phone isn't working. It is now, they've repaired it, just an exchange fault. No, it wouldn't do, they'd find out the phone wasn't working and leave again straight away. An idea made him forget the discomfort of the snow that saturated his trousers: the girl's giving birth, we need help, we can't get a doctor or a midwife. Help her, please, Mrs Mitchell you've had a baby, you must know all about childbirth. *Please!* That would do, and surely Alison Darke-Smith would be going fully into labour by the time they got back. Elspeth's life depended upon it.

George was breathless. He forced himself through the snow, once falling full-length. He dragged himself up again. Perhaps the other three had not reached the road yet; stop, come back, I need you! It was snowing hard again now.

And then he saw them. Pugh was in the lead, Rose perched on his back piggyback style, Suzannah struggling to bring up the rear. Their feet were dragging, they looked all in. George shielded his eyes, afraid in case it was all in his mind, a mirage of some sort. The snow was coming fast and he could not be absolutely sure it was them. But it *had* to be: a man, a woman and a young girl, it couldn't be anybody else out there. He stood at a loss for words, his cunning lies temporarily deserting him. Suffice that they had returned; it *was* them!

'Well, if it isn't Mr Clements!' said Owain Pugh.

'You . . . you're . . . all right?' Clements resembled a comical children's snowman, snow adhering to his clothing where he had fallen, his unkempt hair a white mass. A red mask for a face, dark eyes like coals pushed deep into the head, a slit for a mouth.

'Apart from being wet and cold, tired and fed up, yes. There's no sign of the plough and the road is drifted worse than it was last night. We're going to try again later.'

'I doubt it'll come today.' Words that were tinged with hope rather than despair. 'You're welcome to stay at the hotel as long as you like. I'm sorry if I was rude last night but the wife's not well, you see. She gets very trying at times. I was worried you'd get lost in the snow but thank goodness you're okay. Lunch won't be long.'

'Cooked by that dirty old tramp, I suppose?' Owain's lips curled in a contemptuous sneer. 'No, thank you very much.'

'Oh, don't worry, I'm going to see to it myself. There's some nice plaice in the freezer if you'd like it. Or lamb or pork chops. We have quite an extensive menu, it was just that you arrived after dinner last night.'

Which was disgusting, commercially mass-produced pie and frozen chips gone cold and soggy. Owain refrained from voicing his thoughts. 'I suppose we'll have to eat it, whatever it is.'

'There won't be any charge. I feel I shouldn't have charged you for last night since there wasn't any proper food available and I hadn't had a chance to get the rooms done and the beds aired. But I'll see all that's attended to. We'd better get back, it's going to snow hard for the rest of the day and we'll catch our deaths standing out here.'

Owain felt his stomach tightening, an in-built warning system. His scalp began to prickle. There was something damned fishy about all this. Clements hadn't come out into the snowstorm to look for them just to make up for the previous night's inhospitality.

It took them twenty minutes to reach the hotel, the big house seemingly more gloomy than ever, looming up out of the driving snow like a squat monster, its mouth wide and hungry waiting to devour them. And even as they stepped through the door Suzannah was aware of the evil once again like cold, clammy invisible fingers reaching out of the shadows to stroke her flesh. She tried telling herself that it was her imagination and that before long they would be leaving again. But it didn't ring true. She had an awful feeling lurking at the back of her mind that the three of them were going to spend a second night in this dreadful place with its unexplained noc-turnal terrors.

The front door banged shut behind them, echoing in the hall and up the stairs with a frightening grim finality. And Rose started to sob.

It was with a sense of trepidation that Barbara Withernshaw approached the door of Alison Darke-Smith's room. She hesi-tated, her hand stretched out to turn the handle. A lingering fear that had grown stronger all the way up the stairs, a tiny voice somewhere inside her urging her to turn back. She ignored it. She wasn't afraid of Jack Christopher in spite of all his threats of violence. Flashers were seldom violent, she knew that from experience, *personal experience*. They got their kicks from showing their erections to helpless women but all the time they were scared to hell, a kind of erotic fear. They nearly always fled. She had never come across an exhibitionist who had been a rapist, not even in those days when she had turned her own house into a home for misfits, hoboes and anybody with a social problem. Her attempts to help these

79

people had led to financial disaster; she had been the victim of fraud, theft and had even been raped twice, but not by a flasher. Afterwards she had come here, a rest cure for six months, and when she felt better she had carried on helping folks. Fred and Vera, and poor old Walter Gull who had run off and stepped under a truck. She was here to help. First and foremost that meant seeing poor Alison through this unfortunate birth; afterwards there would be plenty of time to work on Jack Christopher, get to the root of his problem. She pushed the door open and looked inside.

Jack wasn't here and that was a relief. He would have been an added nuisance, even though she definitely wasn't afraid of him. Alison lay there with the bedclothes on the floor. Why wasn't she cold? She was a revolting sight really, Barbara thought, lying with her legs wide open like that; anybody in this madhouse was likely to come in at any time. No wonder she had got herself pregnant; at least Vera Brown only played with herself and any man who tried to get anything from her was likely to get his eyes raked out with her long fingernails. Two girls totally obsessed with their sexual feelings but in different ways; you had to know something about psychology to understand them and it was a damned good job that Barbara was a bit of a psychologist. Still, this was no time for being smug.

'Is anything happening yet, my dear?' Barbara moved into the room, closing the door softly.

Alison's eyes flickered open, took time to adjust. She had been dozing obviously, and she was confused. Frightened, too, and that was Jack's fault. Barbara thought about sneaking along to his room and, if he was inside, locking him in. There were bolts on the outside of the doors here for that very purpose, dating back to the nursing home days. Later, perhaps.

Obviously nothing was happening, Barbara concluded. Labour pains came and went, some babies came quicker than others; when it was ready it would come yelling into the world. Until then they must wait.

Alison's expression changed, her glazed pale blue eyes clearing, staring. And in them the older woman read fear, a fear that transcended the natural terror of a first birth.

'You have absolutely nothing to worry about.' Barbara took the other's hand in her own and unclenched it; it was rigid, sticky with sweat. 'You'll just pop it out when the time comes and it'll all be over bar the squawking.'

The girl's expression was anguished, mentally writhing, trying to look away. She attempted to pull her hand free but Barbara held on to it tightly. Damn it, Alison was in a bad way and the last thing she wanted to happen was for her to become hysterical. Sometimes sympathy had an adverse affect; there were times when it was kinder to be sharp, even brutal.

'Now, look here,' she said briskly, 'you've got to face up to the fact that you're going to have a baby, whether you like it or not.'

'I want it taken away.'

'You should have thought about that seven or eight months ago. It's too late now.'

'Then I'll kill it!'

'No, you won't, that's murder and they would lock you away in a place far worse than this for a very long time. I shall see to it that no harm befalls the child and then, later, if you really don't want it we'll have to get it adopted. But you'll change your mind when you hold it and feed it. You'll breast-feed it, the proper way. None of this ridiculous titty-bottle stuff. God gave you tits for that purpose, not just for some feller to feel at inside your blouse. And another thing, the father has a responsibility towards this baby and I don't see why he should get away with it now he's had his fun.'

'There isn't a father.'

'Of course there is! I don't want to hear such nonsense, and unless I miss my guess it's somebody in this hotel. It has to be, you never go out anywhere. Come on, my girl, who's been fucking you?'

'Nobody has, I swear it. I swear it on the Bible.'

Barbara Withernshaw sighed loudly. 'That won't do,

Alison. Come on, you can tell *me*. Is it old George Clements? Or Harry? Or is it that religious maniac, Jack Christopher?'

It had to be one of them. Not Fred. It couldn't be Fred Ainslow. Soon after Barbara had taken him away from that tumbledown shed, he'd blundered into her room one night, pissed out of his mind naturally, and unzipped his trousers. 'Come on, Babs,' he'd said. 'It's 'igh time you and me got round to a bit of love.'

Dear God, it had been pitiful. There was no way he was ever going to get a hard-on, so she'd thrown back the bedclothes, lifted her nightdress and said, 'All right, Fred, if that's how you feel about me, carry on.' He'd tried and she'd almost passed out in the beer fumes. In the end he'd fallen asleep on top of her so she'd rolled him off on to the floor and left him there until morning. He'd approached her again a few nights later but she'd told him, 'Fred, you and I do *not* have a relationship, so please stop being a silly bloody old man who's had his day. Take a leaf out of Vera's book if you're really desperate.'

He had never troubled her since. No, it wouldn't be Fred, she wouldn't even add him to her list of suspects.

'It isn't anybody. I'm a virgin.'

Barbara checked her sharp retort, and decided to humour her. 'All right, you're a virgin then. So it's a virgin birth, is it? Jesus Christ's return, eh?'

'That's right.'

Lord above, you felt your own sanity was in danger sometimes.

'I'll look for the star tonight after it's dark,' she said.

'Jack is looking, he says the signs are there.'

'All is explained.' Barbara raised her eyes to the ceiling. 'Ask no more. Silly Jack has been filling your head with fantasies to suit himself. So he's the father, undoubtedly.'

'No, he's never ... I wouldn't let him anyway. But ...' Her lower lip began to quiver and those fear-filled eyes began to glisten with tears. 'Uncle George says ... oh, I'm so frightened, Auntie Babs.'

'What's George been saying, my dear?'

'That . . . that I'm going to have Elspeth, the child he and his wife lost years ago. That she's going to be born in me and that . . . that they're going to take her away from me!'

George had finally flipped, Barbara thought, but at least he might have had the decency to keep it to himself.

'You're sure George hasn't been in your bed?'

'*No!*' A shrill cry of indignation. 'I wouldn't let him touch me. Nor Harry. Harry's been told to keep an eye on me and go and tell George when I start having the baby. But Harry sleeps in the daytime so unless I have it at night he won't know, will he?'

The crazy coots! Barbara let go of Alison's hand and walked over to the window. The snow was falling again, looking like it had set in for the day. Which meant there was no chance of getting a doctor or a midwife if anything went wrong. That in itself was bad enough, but with one loony claiming Christ was about to be born again and another anticipating the re-birth of his long-dead child, there was trouble brewing. Boy or girl, whichever the baby was, there was going to be big trouble.

Barbara glanced at the door, and found herself wishing that there was a lock on the inside.

Harry Clements had set his alarm clock, the wind-up one which the office staff had presented him with on his twenty-first anniversary with the firm and which, although not wholly reliable, usually went off provided it didn't stop. This morning it rang shrilly at ten minutes past eleven, rang for a full minute.

He stirred restlessly, reached out an arm to turn it off, knocked the upturned carton on which it was placed, and sent it rolling across the floor, still jangling. It carried on ringing, started to wind down to a pathetic whirr, then stopped.

He shivered – it was damnably cold this morning – pulled the bedclothes right up to the bridge of his nose and stared up at the ceiling. He thought it was Thursday, but he could not be sure without consulting the calendar and his eyesight wasn't good enough to read it from here. Yes, it was surely Thursday and the alarm had obviously been set for a specific purpose. Because he had something to do which the night hours did not allow time enough for . . . It all came back to him. Oh yes, open and check that parcel from Black Hill Books which had arrived over a fortnight ago and the bloke was bleating for his cheque. But the books had to be checked first, every page scrutinized for dirt stains, scribbles, the odd tear. Nothing but 'fine' condition was acceptable to Harry Clements and anything which did not come up to his high standards would be returned with a curt note, written in his spidery scrawl, and the amount deducted from the invoice. It would take time, five or six hours at least. And the sooner he made a start the better.

In spite of the cold, he dressed with his usual fastidiousness, and hastened up to the kitchen. He tried to ignore the mess as he made his usual cup of tea with a teabag in the cup and ate a couple of slices of toast with margarine scraped on. He sat in the corner by the stove, and noted from the disarray and filth – worse than usual – that Fred had done the breakfast chores this morning. This kitchen really ought to be tidied up, the cups put back in neat rows on the shelves, the plates stacked in the cupboards. There wasn't a grain of organization outside his own room, he concluded. But that was *their* worry.

Back downstairs. Goodness, his door was open and the light was on. Now *he* certainly hadn't left it that way. He habitually switched off the light and then closed the door behind him. Always. A spark of uneasiness somewhere inside him was fanned to a flame: somebody was in his room who shouldn't be there.

A kind of guessing game, stalling because he was afraid. It wasn't George because his brother would have known where to find him; it surely wouldn't be Brenda, she wasn't well enough anyway. It might be that cheeky old man, Fred Ainslow. Or Barbara Withernshaw come to remonstrate with him over his unhealthy diet if she was in a bad mood and had a bee in her bonnet.

It was Jack Christopher! The bearded young man was pacing up and down, hands clasped behind his back, staring angrily from one pile of boxes to another. He whirled round as Harry entered, stabbing an accusing finger in the air.

'I want a word with you!'

Harry Clements swallowed. The other had obviously worked himself up into a rage, was going berserk inside. He might explode outwardly and resort to violence.

'You've been seeing Alison. Don't deny it, don't lie because *I* know.'

'I have been keeping a watchful eye on her and I shall continue to do so. In fact, I have been instructed to do so. Now, will you kindly leave my room.'

'Did that old whore Barbara Withershaw send you up to her or have you taken it upon yourself?'

'Mrs Withernshaw and I are not on speaking terms at the moment,' Harry replied haughtily. 'It isn't any of your business but I'll tell you; my brother has asked me to keep a strict eye upon Miss Darke-Smith.'

'He has, has he!' Christopher leaned forward, eyes blazing so that Harry stepped back a pace. 'Then before I leave this room there's something I want to know, and may the Good Lord have mercy upon you if you lie to me . . .' A pause, an intake of breath, as though the forthcoming question required deliberate courage. 'Have you, or your brother . . . at any time . . . had sexual intercourse with her? Come on, answer me man!'

Harry could almost feel the other's intensification coming at him, an invisible force loaded with electricity burning into him. An issue that was more important than anything in Jack Christopher's life.

'Most certainly not.' Harry swallowed, the words slipped out before he could stop them: 'I am celibate. And I am sure that my brother has not committed an act of adultery with the girl. I would swear on the Bible to that effect.'

'Thank you.' Christopher straightened up, eyes closed, sweat running down his deathly white features in rivulets in spite of the coldness of the room. 'I believe you, I believed her but I had to be absolutely sure. For a brief time my faith wavered but it is strong again now.' He moved forward, pushed past Harry and headed slowly for the open door, speaking to nobody in particular in a kind of sing-song whisper as he went. 'For unto Alison shall a boy Child be born, and on the eighth day I shall circumcize him. I shall baptize Him and protect Him in infancy, and He shall be holy and go forth and spread the Word of God.'

Harry Clements experienced a feeling of faintness and lowered himself down on to the box of unopened books. And again he heard his brother's words behind that door, saying with the same conviction: 'Elspeth will be born again in this very house.'

Harry shivered. The cold was intense, and the light seemed to have dimmed to a wan candle-power, casting strange shadows over the walls of boxes. *His visitor had gone but he was not alone. He could sense a presence, a cold living evil all about him.*

Sheer blind fear forced him back on to his unwilling feet, and he made, in a headlong shamble, for the door, knocking over boxes in his flight, seeing daylight at the top of the basement steps and wondering if he was going to make it. Pain stabbed at his chest like sledgehammer blows intent on felling him, and something reached out of the darkness and touched him with a cold, dead hand.

He attempted to scream but it was no more than a strangled whisper, a wheeze of pain and fear. Those corpse-like fingers were holding him, trying to pull him back. A roaring filled his ears, a thousand screeching demoniac voices. He grabbed the rail, tried to haul himself up the steps, knew at the height of his panic-stricken terror that he was not going to make it.

And knowing, even as the blackness closed in on him and started to suck him down into its icy whirlpool, that up above a terrible child was going to be born. Whether it was male or female, it was one that had no right to exist in this world.

CHAPTER NINE

It was agonizingly clear to Suzannah that Rose was not well. At first, upon their return to the Donnington Country House Hotel, she had put it down to cold and exhaustion, not to mention the terror of last night that had had them both huddling together under the bedclothes. Damp bedclothes. All that was bound to take its toll.

Now Rose toyed with her food. Normally a healthy eater, she chewed on small mouthfuls and was perhaps too embarrassed to push her plate away. She was flushed, too, an unhealthy feverish tinge, and unless Suzannah missed her guess her daughter was starting to shiver too. Oh my God, the last thing we want now is for Rose to go down with a fever, stuck here in this awful place with its unknown terrors and all these crazy people. And we can't even get to a doctor.

'Are you sure you're all right, darling?' Suzannah asked. Owain was looking at the child, too, and even a bachelor with no experience of juvenile ailments guessed that the young girl was sick.

'I'll be okay, Mum.' The standard reply to such a question, like last February when she was going down with 'flu and had insisted she was well enough to go to Mrs Blower's ballet class on the Saturday morning; Rose had fainted halfway through and Suzannah had had to drive out and bring her back.

'No, you're not well, love,' she said, firmly, unable to hide her anxiety. 'Leave that food if you want to.' Suzannah looked at Owain. 'Do you think the plough might have got through by now?' Oh, please say it might have. The anxiety on Rose's fevered face was heartbreaking.

'I'll go and see shortly.' He glanced at his watch; it was almost two o'clock. Two and a half hours of daylight left. They were cutting it fine. He didn't relish the prospect of another trip through the deep snow down to the main road. If it hadn't been for the child he would probably have opted for staying another night. 'You never know, they might have got through.' Noncommittal, he wasn't going to raise their hopes and then dash them.

'We ought to come with you.' Suzannah knew that they couldn't, not with Rose sickening for something, and in any case if the main road was clear they'd have to go anyway. There was no point in subjecting Rose to a useless journey.

'Don't talk daft.' He smiled. 'You know the old saying "he who travels fastest travels alone". I'll be back as soon as I can.' He stood up, turned and walked across the room, without looking back. That poor kid; he had to get her out of here before nightfall, if possible. If not . . . she was beginning to look very ill.

Outside the snow had eased off into a fine mizzle you might have mistaken for rain until you looked at your clothing and saw the minute flakes that had settled. Warmer but damp, it ate into you. He shivered, and set out along the track they had trodden out and back earlier which was still just visible under the fresh covering of snow.

For himself, he would have preferred to stay on till tomorrow and sod the Clementses. He told himself he was doing it for Rose; sure he was, but not *just* for the young girl. His mind conjured up a picture of Suzannah, tall and slim, her long dark hair seemingly unruffled by the weather and that arduous trek this morning. She wore a wedding ring but she had not mentioned her husband, and neither had there been a reference to a father by Rose; and no anxiety at not being able to get a message through somewhere to say they were safe. Which all spoke of a single parent, perhaps a divorcee. She might even be a widow. Wishful thinking, stick to reality. In any case a woman with her looks was sure to have a boyfriend. There was no place in that set up for Owain Pugh . . . Still, there was no harm in fantasizing. It helped to take his mind off this decidedly inconvenient and unpleasant situation. Of all the places he might have chosen to seek shelter from the storm, he had picked a nuthouse. But there was nowhere else out here.

His ears picked up a sound, a harsh grinding noise which vibrated the atmosphere and broke into his daydreaming. Suddenly hopeful, he paused in his step to listen, to make sure. It was a snowplough, all right, heavy machinery working slowly, incessantly, fighting the elements. Might versus might.

He resisted the urge to run. That plough was a good way off, perhaps half a mile down the road and making slow progress. If he took his time, it would be that much nearer when he eventually reached the road. His pulses quickened and that was partly due to the fact that his thoughts had returned to Suzannah Mitchell. If he got her and her daughter out of here before nightfall then the chances were he would never see her again . . . Stop being a selfish bastard, he told himself.

Twenty minutes later he reached the end of the lane. The fine snow had merged with a mist, one that would probably thicken with the coming of night, forming a depressing murkiness which reduced visibility to about 150 yards. Darkness would come early tonight, perhaps by four o'clock. The landscape looked unchanged; he could still hear the snowplough somewhere, that steady whine, not hurrying because it was an unending task; tomorrow would be exactly the same, and the day after that; just pushing up a wall of snow on to the verges, leaving the road a hard-packed, treacherous surface.

Somewhere in the depths of the opaque dampness he spotted a flashing yellow light, a sail on the horizon to a shipwrecked mariner. He surged forward, heedless of the snow which was deep but not drifted here, wading almost up to his thighs. A quarter of a mile, no more. The plough would surely be here within the next half-hour. But he had to go and see for himself, make sure.

Now he could see its outline, an angry yellow monster with a cab above the sweeping bade, the silhouette of a lone figure seated at the controls. Back, forward again, the ten-foot blade sweeping diagonally, piling the snow up, spilling chunks that rolled and powdered.

'Hey, just a minute!' Of course the operator could not hear him. He was wearing protective ear-muffs, a robot immersed in his own thoughts to alleviate the boredom. Perhaps he, too, was thinking of a woman somewhere.

Owain stood on the edge of the unploughed road, arms raised, gesticulating. The machine backed off, lowered its blade and then the engine died, letting the stillness back in. The driver was taking off his ear-muffs, opening the door, leaning out. Smiling. Any break in the monotony was welcome.

'Hiya, mate. Okay?' A young fellow, blond-haired, wearing orange council-issue trousers and a duffle coat.

'I'd be better if I could get back to civilization,' Owain answered him, offering a cigarette from his crumpled pack. They each lit their own.

'Shouldn't be a problem.' The other blew out twin streams of smoke from his nostrils and cupped the cigarette in his hand. 'I can give you a lift back to where my van's parked, about two miles down the road, and from there I can take you on into Kerry.'

Damn it, he should have brought Suzannah and Rose with him. They would have made it out of here tonight then. 'I've got a woman and a kid with me, sheltering at a house back down the lane on the left there. The kid's ill, 'flu or something, I guess. I was hoping you'd be able to plough up to the lane and maybe past it. My car's buried up yonder. If we could get that mobile we'd be away.'

The man shook his head slowly and Owain's hopes sank.

'I'm sorry, pal –' He really looked as though he was. 'But I'm afraid no can do. Don't think I wouldn't if I could. This machine's low on fuel, nearly out, maybe not enough to do another hundred yards if I want to get back to the van as well. I'll bring some diesel out with me in the morning but there isn't time to go back for it tonight. We knock off at four. The council aren't paying overtime 'cause they used up the bulk of their snowploughing budget on last winter's snow. Last year we worked the clock round on shifts, ploughing by headlights, but not this year. The foreman'd go crazy if I carried on. There's talk of hiring a couple of snow-blowers from the next county but we won't get 'em before next week. Jeez, you want to see 'em! Blows the bloody lot over the hedges and you can just keep going. This old girl's an antique by comparison.'

Owain sighed. Tomorrow. It was a long time when you were stuck in a place like the Donnington Hotel.

'It'll have to be tomorrow then. I suppose you couldn't plough the lane out for me, could you?'

Again the head shook. 'Afraid not. That's a JCB job. The snow'll have to be lifted, chucked over the hedges. This baby only pushes it to one side, and in a narrow lane there's no place to shove it. See what I mean?'

Owain nodded. The driver was being logical, only obeying orders on which his job depended.

'I reckon I'll have to put up with another night at the place where I'm staying, then.' He grimaced.

'You're not by any chance staying at that Donnington place, are you, mister?'

'You've got it.'

'Holy Jesus! I go there when I'm on the dust-cart. It used to be a head farm, was closed down and then all the nutcases came back to live there. Gives me the bloody creeps and I only go there on Mondays!'

'I'll see if I can get my companions down to the bottom of the lane in the morning. If you can free my car, there shouldn't be any problem.'

'Give us till about eleven then.' He began to close the cab door. 'Half-eleven at the latest. See ya, pal.'

Owain stood and watched the snowplough back up, swing round and head down the smooth surface, its beacon bobbing, becoming fainter as the mist swallowed it. He felt like a ship-wrecked mariner again: the sail on the horizon had passed on. It might return tomorrow, on the other hand it might not. Dejectedly, he headed back once more in the direction of the Donnington Country House Hotel.

'Your daughter does not look at all well, Mrs Mitchell.'

George Clements appeared from out of the kitchen carrying

an empty tray to begin clearing the tables. 'Oh dear, what a pity we can't get hold of Dr Gidman.'

'Perhaps you could find her an aspirin or something?' Suzannah said. 'I'm hoping that Mr Pugh will be back in a bit to inform us that the main road is clear. In which case I'll take Rose to evening surgery.'

'I wouldn't build your hopes on it.' There was a momentary gleam in the eyes sunk deep in the fleshy sockets. 'Last winter they took almost a week to get to us. But you never know . . . Just a moment and I'll see if I can find an aspirin.'

He returned a couple of minutes later bearing a glass of water and a white tablet which he set down in front of Rose. 'There you are, my dear, and what you need most of all is a warm bed. I'll go and change the sheets in your room, put an electric blanket on the bed.'

'Perhaps we ought to wait and see what news Mr Pugh brings.' God, I can't stand the thought of another night here! 'We could be going very shortly.'

'Pardon me for saying so, Mrs Mitchell, but I really don't think your daughter ought to travel. It isn't just the travelling, it's the long walk back down the lane through the snow first. It might be wiser to stay, and if the road has been cleared then I'm sure we can get a message to Dr Gidman somehow. You know how easily pneumonia can set in with the young and the old. Our own daughter died at a very early age.' Meningitis, but I don't need to tell you that.

Cold fingers stroked Suzannah's spine, travelled right the way up to the nape of her neck. 'I'm sorry.'

'My wife has never looked up since.'

'Is she better today?'

'A little, thank you. I will just go and check on her again if you'll excuse me.' He walked back to the kitchen, let the door swing to but open just an inch or so, enough for George Clements to peer through without being seen. With narrowed eyes, he stared with an intensity that rendered him oblivious to everything else except Rose Mitchell as she swallowed the 'aspirin'. A pretty young girl. A few years hence and she would be as beautiful as her mother. Except she wasn't going to live that long because the Master had need of her. Perhaps she would catch pneumonia and die, save him from the necessity of killing her. Death due to natural causes, not murder by persons unknown.

At least the child would sleep; that sleeping tablet of Mother's would put her out for the count. Which was another reason why they would not be able to move her tonight. He turned away; he had better go and see Alison. Surely dearest Elspeth had to be born before another day dawned.

Rose was fighting to keep her eyes open. Her head dropping on her chest, she might even fall off her chair. Suzannah moved her own chair closer, pulled the child towards her and held her. This was no place to keep a sick child but it was better than that awful cold bedroom. Oh, please, Owain, come back and tell us that we can leave and we'll drive straight to the doctor.

The front door banged. Somebody was stamping snow off on the mat just inside the hall. Suzannah's heartbeat speeded up – this had to be Owain surely.

It was. And Suzannah's hopes plunged to the depths of despair as she saw his weary, dejected expression.

In the same instant she felt Rose's body relax against her own and heard the young girl's breathing, deep and regular. Asleep. Flaked out, ill and exhausted.

'The snowplough hasn't made it.' Suzannah saved him the task of having to put the bad news into words himself. She felt pity and admiration for him. Cold, wet and tired, he had done his best and he was still fighting.

'It's not all bad.' He tried to sound optimistic. 'The damned council aren't paying overtime which is why they won't reach us till about eleven in the morning. How's Rose?'

'She's got a temperature.' Suzannah smoothed a hand across her daughter's forehead and felt the warm stickiness of fever sweat. 'She's probably caught a bug. There's 'flu going round at school. My worry is that it might turn to pneumonia. Mr

93

Clements found her an aspirin but she needs something a bit stronger than that.'

'Perhaps I might make it through on foot.' Owain glanced at the window and saw that dusk was already closing in. 'I'm sure they'd get to us in an emergency.'

'No. Please. It isn't desperate yet.' *Don't leave us Owain, I can't face being left alone in this madhouse.* 'If only she had a really warm bed. The bed and the room we slept in last night were a disgrace.'

'I'll go and demand some civilized treatment . . .' He moved towards the door, but she caught his arm.

'Apparently Mr Clements is giving us an electric blanket and that's better than nothing. Maybe . . .'

She broke off as a wretched high-pitched scream echoed from out in the empty hall, a cry of ageing female terror and madness, rising hysteria emanating from the depths of a tortured soul. Again and yet again. Dragging footsteps, the sound of a struggle, incoherent cursing and another scream of fear.

'*Oh, my God!*' Suzannah embraced Rose, instinctively shielding her daughter from whatever horror lay on the other side of the door. Owain was transfixed for a second or two, turned, and in that instant the door flew open, crashed back and stuck on the uneven linoleum.

And framed in the doorway was the gaunt and wasted figure of a man in an ill-fitting rumpled suit that was torn and stained. Wild-eyed, cheeks sunken and deathly white, the mouth appeared to have slipped until it was almost a vertical slit from which babbled meaningless words through a hanging string of spittle. Nostrils flared as though he sought a scent like some hunting beast. His spindly legs were bowed, barely able to support his slight weight, and his arms were swinging from side to side helplessly as he tried to gesticulate, but he had no control over them. He staggered into the dining room, swaying but somehow not falling, seeing them but unable to stay on course for them, and veered off towards the kitchen door on feet that splayed outwards sliding on the smooth floor.

94

The watchers stood in shocked silence, their eyes no longer on the cavorting figure of Harry Clements but instead on the pathetic woman who crawled in his wake, her long grey hair falling over her agonized wrinkled face as she screamed and screamed.

Then she halted, and somehow managed to twist her body round so that she could stare in demented terror at the open doorway, cringing as though she expected some further nightmarish horror to appear at any second.

And for a couple of brief seconds coherent speech returned to the sagging lips of Harry Clements. He fought for words, found them; got them out in a rush before they were lost. A warning cry, it might already be too late, a swinging arm completed a half circle and dropped back down.

'Beware! Satan is here amongst us!'

The effort had exhausted him. Bubbling saliva again, eyelids drooping as his body gave up the struggle, he fell forward, hit the floor and rolled over, sprawled in a still heap.

And Brenda Clements began screaming again.

CHAPTER TEN

The screaming from downstairs jerked Barbara Withernshaw out of her doze and had her sitting upright in the chair by Alison Darke-Smith's bed. Momentary shock set her blood-pressure going, bringing on a feeling of dizziness, but it passed as she recognized the shrieks. It was Mother again, nothing new. Barbara listened, tried to pick out the smash of breaking glass, the tinkling fragments of a broken bottle, but there was none. Maybe the old dear wasn't throwing ammonia this time, just an ordinary tantrum. Bugger her, but at least it hadn't wakened Alison. The poor kid needed all the rest she could get.

Jack Christopher had come in earlier, about an hour ago. Barbara had tensed and somehow managed to restrain herself from giving him a tongue-lashing. He was nervous, ill at ease, and there was no sign of his threatening behaviour now. He shuffled into the room, stood there entwining his fingers, typical of an anxious father awaiting the birth of a first child.

'Nothing yet.' He spoke to himself rather than to Barbara in hushed tones.

'She's peaceful.' A nurse formally reporting on the condition of a patient. 'She needs rest and quiet.'

He appeared not to have heard her and leaned forward, his protruding eyes shining in the last of the daylight.

'What is life but waiting for death?' he murmured. 'But this time He shall not die but shall have everlasting life.'

Barbara sighed. She wasn't going to go into all *that* again. He wanted a damned good kick up the backside for filling the poor girl's head with all that nonsense. The Second Coming, indeed! Jack could well be the father and this a crazy plan for abdicating responsibility. The registrar of births and deaths wouldn't fall for that one!

'I'll let you know as soon as anything happens.' She wouldn't but she hoped he would take the hint and go. Surprisingly he backed towards the door, still watching the sleeping girl.

'It has to be,' he said, still muttering to himself, 'for I was told in a vision and the signs are there.' And then he was gone, fast footfalls down the corridor and back to his own room. Barbara got up off her chair and closed the door. Jack was obviously born in a barn – or was it a manger? She smiled at her own joke but all the same she felt uneasy. Whatever the baby, male or female, the responsibility for the birth was hers for there was no way they could get help from outside.

There was definitely something going on downstairs. Brenda Clements had stopped screaming but there were movements, people going to and fro, muffled conversations. She picked up bad vibes and wondered about going to see. No, they would fetch her if they wanted her. Her job was to stay with Alison.

More footsteps, heavier and more urgent ones this time, coming up the stairs; along the corridor, heading this way. She braced herself: they had come for her after all.

It was George who stood in the doorway, holding on to the open door, supporting himself against it and when it moved he almost fell over. His features were lined and pallid, his grey hair awry and he was breathing heavily.

'. . . Harry . . . you'd better come . . . quickly.'

'What's up with him?' It occurred to her that it might be a crude ruse to get her to leave the room. George was mixed up in this crazy business, too, claiming that the baby was going to be the rebirth of his own daughter. No, he wasn't that good an actor, something really was up with Harry.

'He's had a stroke . . . Mother's fainted.'

'Oh, dear!' Everything was happening at once but that which ought to happen wasn't. Barbara cast a glance at Alison; the girl was sleeping deeply, she would be all right for a few minutes.

'All right, I'll come but I don't see what I can do.'

97

They had somehow got Harry Clements back to his book-filled room and he was stretched out on the bed, his shirt undone. His eyes were closed, he was unconscious, his lopsided face the colour of faded linen.

'Stand back, please.' Barbara Withernshaw pushed her way past Owain Pugh and Fred Ainslow, experiencing a fleeting sense of importance. There was a small shaving mirror on the box that served as a bedside table; she took it and held it to the unconscious man's lips. At first there was nothing, then it misted slightly. 'He's still alive, but I fear not for long.'

She heard George gasp; well, he ought to have known without anybody telling him. Few people came out of a massive stroke like this and those that did were the unlucky ones. A lingering stench had her wrinkling her nostrils; at first she thought it came from the dying man, but no, it wasn't quite right. Too pungent, and not the smell of death . . . yet. It was cold in this room, freezing . . . She shivered and looked at the others.

'Can't we have some heating on, George? Damn it, Harry'll freeze to death before he dies from this seizure!'

'It should be on. I switched the radiators on an hour ago.'

She stretched out a hand and felt the small, old-fashioned radiator half-hidden behind some boxes of books. It was warm enough . . . but for some reason the heat wasn't spreading into the room. As though the cold was too powerful for it!

'Let's cover him up.' She tugged the eiderdown from beneath him, draped it over him and pulled his old macintosh off a coathanger over the bed. It was the best she could do in the circumstances. And she experienced a desire to be away from this room, to flee back up the basement steps. Not because Harry was going to die – she had seen death often enough in her time – but because . . . *there was something in this room, an invisible evil which hid in the shadows, perhaps behind all these boxes, and reached out a cold clammy hand to touch you! And all the time you smelled the vile stench of the beast's lair.*

'Now, somebody will have to stop with him.' She moved

quickly towards the door as though she feared that the others might bar her way, lock her in this place where soon there would be death.

'Barbara, you're the best one . . .' George said, making as if to lumber after her.

'I am needed upstairs.' She was at the door, opening it and squeezing through the narrow gap where a box had toppled over as if the entity within here was trying to prevent her leaving. 'He's *your* brother, George.'

'Mother . . .'

'Mother has looked after herself, and you, for long enough now.' She was at the foot of the steps, starting to climb. Let them sort it out for themselves; she had a job to do, the living needed her more than the dying.

'I got to get the dinner started,' Fred Ainslow pushed away George's outstretched, pleading hand. 'We got to eat, no matter what.'

'I can't leave the little girl.' Owain's concern was genuine but he felt a twinge of embarrassment in case it might be interpreted as a ready-made excuse. 'I'm afraid it'll have to be you, Mr Clements. Unless, of course, you can persuade Jack Christopher to watch over your brother for you.'

They left the proprietor there and tried to ignore his mumbled pleas as they went upstairs. Harry Clements would die before this night was out and there was nothing any of them could do to save him.

'She seems to be sleeping peacefully enough,' Suzannah said as Owain tapped on the door of her room and entered. 'But night is always the worst time when you're ill.' And it's awful here even if you're in good health.

'I'm going to have a bath,' he said, 'presuming, of course, that there is any hot water. These damned taps in the basins are all cold.' He was beginning to shiver, wondered if perhaps his trousers would dry on a radiator whilst he bathed. 'If I'm successful I suggest you take one as well. I'll be back shortly.'

The bathroom was on the first floor. It was small and dirty, cobwebs in the corners, brown paint flaking off the walls and showing bare plaster in places; there was green mould on the cold tap and a crack in the bottom of the bath that had him wondering if it actually held water and when it had last been used. A grubby towel was on the rail, the remnants of a bar of hard soap on the side of the bath. Basic, but it would do if the water was hot.

He let the tap run, watched as it swirled, collected dirt and a dead spider, washed them down the plug hole. He tested it with his finger, almost giving up hope until he felt the temperature change from cold to luke warm. Gradually the water heated until finally there was steam rising. Owain began to undress, and wondered again how he was going to dry his trousers.

Sheer luxury in a pig-sty of a bathroom, lying back, closing his eyes and realizing for the first time just how tired he was; he could easily have gone to sleep. One more night here – it felt like it had been a week already – and then tomorrow the snowplough would set them free. If it wasn't for Rose the prospect might not have been so awful. He felt Suzannah's helplessness, frustration, rub off on himself. They were trapped here and as if to underline the fact Harry Clements was dying, and there was no chance of getting a doctor. That girl was about to give birth and there *could* be complications. Utterly trapped, it was a claustrophobic feeling; it could drive you as mad as those who lived there.

And the place stank. Owain could even smell the stench that had been in Harry Clements's room in here. Perhaps there was a leaking waste pipe somewhere. No, that wasn't quite right: it was a vile but unusual smell, like rotting flesh in a way. He tried to tell himself it was the dustbins out at the back.

The light bulb flickered. He started, seemed to experience a mild electric shock. The light was definitely dimmer; perhaps there was a loose connection in the fitting and the steam had got in. And, damnation, this bathwater was going cold already!

He sat up, leaned over and reached for the hot tap, turned it. Water gushed out but there was no steam. *Ice cold, almost to the point of freezing!*

It couldn't be, there wasn't time. He hadn't been in the bath for more than ten minutes at the most. Well, there wasn't any point in lying in a rapidly cooling bath; he clambered out, began to towel himself.

And that was when he heard the baby crying. There was no mistaking the sound, the insistent screeching of an infant demanding to be fed, yelling. Alison must have given birth and whatever the infant's sex it certainly had powerful lungs. A long way away, up on the next floor, but he could hear it plainly enough.

He dressed, went out on to the landing. There was nobody about; silence, an eerie stillness, and even the baby was quiet now. A sense of loneliness engulfed him, a sensation that everybody had somehow left and he remained in this big house on his own. Like a bad dream, because there wouldn't be any exits, no matter how hard he tried he would not be able to find a way out.

This was too silly for words. Suzannah would be in her room sitting with Rose, George would be in the basement waiting for his brother to die and free him. And Alison Darke-Smith would be holding her newly born baby to her bosom. Total contrasts, the living and the dead. But within these walls death reigned supreme.

Owain quickened his step, found himself glancing round involuntarily. Somebody was watching him, it was unnerving. There was nobody around; there was, but you couldn't see them. Run before they get you. Don't be so bloody stupid! He had to stop himself from running up the stairs.

'Well?' There was relief on Suzannah's face as he entered the room.

'The water was hot.' It sounded silly now that he had proved that everybody had not mysteriously left. 'To begin with, anyway. Then, without warning, it went cold. There's something wrong with the light in the bathroom, too. It dimmed, almost went out. I guess it must have been the steam. Quite obviously nobody here takes a bath. And then, of course, the baby started crying.'

'Oh?'

'Yes.' That sense of uneasiness returned. 'You must have heard it crying here if I could hear it down in the bathroom.'

'I didn't hear anything. In fact, the place has been so silent it was beginning to get on my nerves.'

'Sound can play funny tricks.' He was desperately searching for a logical explanation. 'These thick walls can produce strange acoustics – sounds you don't hear close to but others can hear a long way away.' He was talking rubbish for the sake of it. His skin was goosepimpling. 'How's Rose?'

'Much the same, still sleeping. That's the best thing she can do under the circumstances. Roll on tomorrow morning.' But first we have to face the night.

'I could do with something to eat,' he said. 'Ainslow was going to get dinner on. At the moment I think I could eat even his cooking.'

'I can't leave Rose.' Neither can I go in that dining room again. Suzannah had trembled for an hour after that ghastly death stagger by Harry Clements, and the face of that dreadful woman crawling in his wake would haunt her sleep for weeks. Thank God that aspirin (if it *was* aspirin, and Suzannah was beginning to have her doubts) had knocked Rose out, spared the poor child a horror that could seriously have disturbed her mind. 'I'd better stay with her.'

'Tell you what,' he said, 'we'll eat up here, both of us. I'll go down and bring up a tray of whatever's on the menu tonight.'

'That would be nice.' She smiled. Well, the food wouldn't be but Owain's company certainly would.

'Cheese and spud pie,' Fred Ainslow announced as Owain walked into the kitchen. 'Out of a packet but don't tell the others.' He discreetly dropped the remains of a cigarette on the floor and covered it with his foot. 'Apple tart is to follow, all on individual foil plates. Mr Kipling's but *I* warmed 'em up. Don't expect there'll be many in for dinner tonight anyway, not after what 'appened. Blimey, enjoy yerself while you can, you never knows when it's goin' to be your turn.'

'Has he died yet?'

'If he 'as then the gaffer 'asn't been up to tell us.'

Owain found a tray, began loading it. 'I hear the baby's been born at last.'

'Eh?'

'The baby. Alison's. It's come.'

'It ain't.' The unshaved chin thrust out defiantly. 'Don't you go spreadin' rumours, mister. She ain't 'ad it and I know 'cause our Barb's been down to fetch 'er dinner to take up-stairs, and she should know.'

'Oh!' For a second the kitchen seemed to tilt and spin, piles of unwashed crockery about to cascade on to the floor and disintegrate. Then it steadied and Owain found himself hang-ing on to the edge of the large unscrubbed table. 'I heard a baby yelling whilst I was in the bath.'

'Wax in yer ears, mate.' Ainslow laughed at his own crude joke but it didn't sound funny, not even to himself. 'I get it sometimes. Noises in the 'ead, tin–tin–sommat Dr Gidman calls it. Like you've got somebody talkin' to you all the while. You've got babies cryin' instead, no doubt about that.'

'I must have been mistaken.' Owain picked the tray up and hoped that he was steady enough to balance it all the way upstairs. And once again he had the feeling that somebody was watching him, hidden malevolent eyes boring into him. He had definitely heard a baby crying. It wasn't voices inside his head nor his imagination, no matter what Fred Ainslow said.

George Clements had considered leaving his brother and going back upstairs, anywhere so long as it was well away from this crypt lined with cardboard boxes. It was as though Harry had built his own tomb, a macabre act like something out of one of those books he collected. Well, if Harry wanted to make his crypt he could bloody well lie in it on his own.

But George stayed, because to go upstairs would mean having to sit with Mother and she was really off her rocker now. No bloody wonder! Harry couldn't just have a stroke like any normal person, it had to be melodramatic, staggering into the dining room and collapsing, scaring everybody.

George used the mirror again to check his brother; it clouded but there was only a minute patch of condensation on the glass. Getting weaker all the time.

'And now I haven't got you to keep an eye on our Elspeth when she's born,' he said aloud. 'Mother isn't capable and I can't trust any of the others. So it'll have to be me. And you're stopping me from going up to her, Harry. I'll have to leave you to it soon, so why don't you hurry up and die first?'

And suddenly Harry's lips began to move, a slight quiver at first, growing stronger, like a curled-up earthworm trying to straighten itself out. Wriggling as though trying to reshape the mouth in readiness for words, saliva bubbling to lubricate the dry flesh, the wide nostrils snorting mucus.

No! George wanted to back off, to turn and flee, but his limbs refused to move. Forced to watch as one eye opened, just a whiteness glinting in the dark socket, then the pupil clicked down from somewhere like a sleeping doll's orbs when it was picked up. Focusing slowly, seeing the others, the second eye coming to the help of the first. An expression of bewilderment, changing to hatred. Burning deep into George Clements, a gamma ray of smouldering anger.

Please, Harry, don't blame me. I didn't do this to you!

Life was seeping back into an arm, the muscles twitching, skeletal fingers opening out, flexing. A supreme effort, the limb raised, a human claw spread, reaching out.

George dropped the shaving mirror, heard it smash on the floor, the glass splintering and tinkling. Now I won't know whether you're alive or dead, Harry. Retreating until he backed up against a wall of cartons and was unable to go any further. You can't reach me, Harry, you haven't the strength. For God's sake, *die*!

The extended arm was shaking, the effort was proving too

much for it, life's last gesture. With a sudden jerk George turned his head, gave a throaty cry of terror. The shadow of his brother's arm was cast on the cardboard wall opposite, a magnified caricature, scrawny bony fingers that pulsed with life and clawed for a hold. Growing all the time, the hand of death in search of a victim.

No, Harry! George stumbled, fell to his knees. Now he could see his brother on the bed, the arm falling back down on to the covers, the eyes clicking shut, the mouth shapeless like squeezed putty. Death had come at last, a reprieve for George Clements just when he thought it had singled him out, too.

He stared at the still form of his corpse brother, trembling as he recalled that final expression of hate and fury. He dared not close his own eyes in case he saw it again and breathed deeply, trying to muster up the physical strength necessary for him to flee this room of death.

Kneeling there, sensing rather than hearing a movement behind him, trying to stop his head from turning. Failing. The light bulb was dim. Would that it had extinguished and spared him this new horror. Telling himself that it was a trick of the dusty bulb, that it couldn't possibly be happening. But it was.

A shadow that had not died with Harry Clements; a sinewy hand that crept along those boxes like a giant spider, a thing of hate that dragged itself free of the arm, a stump of a wrist for a tail. Misshapen, bobbing as it found its new strength, easing itself across a gap in the boxes and going on to the next. Purposeful, down on to the floor where it blended with the blackness and became invisible and then emerged into a patch of light by the door.

And then on out through the door where it became lost to George's view. But in his mind he could still see it, that ghastly severed shadow slithering up the stone steps. He dared not follow; he dared not even think where it might be going.

CHAPTER ELEVEN

Vera Brown had remained in her room all day sulking. Her sulks were frequent, particularly when she was refused her own way. As she had been this morning.

She did not like rising early. It was so snug and comfortable lying on in bed and after the first shouting match some weeks ago Auntie Barb had not tried to make her go down for breakfast at nine. Vera basked in the satisfaction of a battle won and was not prepared to compromise. She did not feel like eating at that hour and, anyway, Barbara Withernshaw would not let her have the things she liked; anything fried was taboo, and she had to have either muesli or bran flakes or fresh fruit. So the only way to avoid that was keep out of the dining room.

'You'd stop in bed all day if I'd let you,' Barbara Withernshaw had retorted, already on the retreat, 'and I'm not standing for that. All right, don't come down to breakfast then, I'm sure it will be a lot pleasanter for the rest of us without you creating a scene every morning. But I insist that you come down for lunch.'

'All right.' Vera always stared at the floor during an argument. It was easier than looking her opponent in the eye. 'I'll come down for lunch, p'raps.'

'You'd better or else I shall physically drag you down. And another thing, you must stop . . . doing *that* in company. One of these days somebody might call the police and they'll put you away in a place far worse than this where you'll be made to get up for breakfast. D'you hear?'

'I like doing it.'

'I am fully aware that you do. I . . . but we'll talk about that another time. All right, you may miss breakfast, but I'm warning you — if you don't appear for lunch there will be an almighty row and I shall be *really* cross with you.'

It had ended there, a concession won. But today she damned well wasn't going down for lunch. Or dinner tonight. She'd starve; Auntie Barb couldn't *make* her eat and if she dragged her down to the dining room then she'd refuse any food which was put before her and she'd make sure she embarrassed her self-appointed guardian. Even if Mrs Clements came out of the kitchen swearing and throwing ammonia again.

Now she lay in bed just staring at the bare emulsioned wall. Once she sat up and looked out of the window. It was foggy, a dense greyness outside, so even if she did get up there would be no walks or playing with a ball on the lawn; the lawn was covered with snow anyway. Vera snuggled back down the bed, closed her eyes. But she had slept her full cycle and there was no chance of doing anything more than dozing. Life got so boring and it would be just as boring downstairs. The others would switch the telly on in the lounge and if she started to fidget then Auntie Barb would give her a book. Which was a waste of time because Vera could not read anyway and she had looked at those pictures in *Coral Island* so many times that they were as boring as just staring at the wall, following the patterns on the furling wallpaper with her eyes until she got double vision.

But she was angry with Auntie Barb, and very, *very* hurt. The older woman was the only real companion she had ever had, more like a mother than an adopted aunt. All Vera asked of her was affection, and she had told her countless times how much she loved her. Her worst nightmare was the prospect that one day Auntie Barb would die. And when that happened Vera was going to come up to her room and swallow a full bottle of codeine, the tablets she took when she had one of her migraines. That way, if what Jack Christopher said was true, she would go to join Auntie Barb in another, much better place. So then they would both be very happy even if Auntie Barb might be cross with her at first. But you couldn't always believe what Jack said. She had proved him to be a liar on more than one occasion in the past.

But suddenly Auntie Barb was deserting her. Just because

Alison was going to have a baby she was spending all her time sitting with that fat slob. And it might be worse after the baby was born: suppose Barbara loved the baby like it was her own and Alison gave it to her? Then her guardian would have no time for a girl she had picked up and virtually fostered. Barbara Withernshaw would devote all her time to the baby's constant needs.

Vera trembled with rage at the thought. That Alison was a dirty prostitute, and men had been going into her room at nights. Vera had lain and listened to their voices; muffled conversations on the other side of the wall. She couldn't make out what they were saying but she recognized them. George and Harry Clements, and Jack Christopher. Dirty Jack . . . she giggled aloud at the nickname. He was always showing his thing to other women. He had tried it once on Vera. He had opened the door of her room, hadn't even come inside, just stood there in a 'what do you think of *this*?' pose. She had yelled to him to fuck off and when she had shouted he'd turned and run. He wouldn't get anything from her, no way.

There seemed to be a lot of activity downstairs, people coming and going, and for a time Vera's curiosity was aroused. But as long as Auntie Barb was in the next room with Alison she wasn't going anywhere.

Some time during the late afternoon Vera got the urge; she got it most days and it was irresistible. For the first time that day she moved with a purpose. She threw the bedclothes back, went and fetched the old mirror off the washstand and placed it on the dressing table the way she had done countless times so that she could see the reflection of her own body with her nightdress pulled up above her thighs as she sat back against the pillows.

She took her time, forgot all about Auntie Barb and Alison. A brief, very brief, reminder of Jack; she didn't know why except that she wished he would suddenly open the door, stand there unzipped. No, he wouldn't touch her, he knew that she would not let him. It would be a way of getting her own back on him. He would avert his eyes like he always did in either the dining room or the lounge, embarrassed. Maybe even resort to flight with her laughter echoing after him. You don't like it when it's done to you, do you, Jack? Then she forgot him, forgot everything except her own body and the pleasure it was giving her.

Dusk turned to darkness and the mirror was a blank outline of a screen, a television switched off. Then came the moon, hesitantly creeping in through the undrawn curtains, brighter than usual because of the reflection of the snow, bringing that square of glass to life again. Ethereal, erotic, silvery white flesh that trembled and brought the first moans from Vera's lips. Holding back until it was impossible to delay any longer, crying her pleasure aloud, oblivious of everything except her own sensuousness, the unbelievable feeling which mystified and delighted her.

Her reflection was a blur, her poor eyesight dimmed by her bodily delights. Resting briefly, then beginning again.

She lost all track of time. It did not matter. When she was tired she would sleep, but the night was young yet. She was impervious to the cold; her body heated, her eyes straining to follow that reflected eroticism; a crisscross of moonbeams, silver and shadows, calling out as though the body in the square frame was a partner in pleasure who was too shy to come nearer.

A movement; for one exciting moment she thought that there was actually somebody else in the room. She saw it first in the mirror, a hand with fingers flexing, reaching out for her. It paused, drew back, came on again. Still she saw it in the mirror, but a brief glance showed it stark and black on the rumple of thrown-back sheets, only inches from her quivering thigh. She looked again, first in the mirror then back on the bed. A hand, no arm attached; just a hand.

A trick of the moonlight. She held out her own hands, saw their shadows on the sheets but the third one was still there. Motionless, like a grotesque talon poised to pounce on an unsuspecting prey.

A little gasp escaped her lips and for the first time she

realized just how cold it was, and was aware of how her skin pimpled and a host of tiny shivers spread from her back upwards. Still curious, she reached out for that mysterious shadow, almost touching it, but it moved, evaded her. It had to be her own shadow, which was why it was so elusive. She could see it plainly on the linen but somehow it did not look like her own hand; it was the wrong shape, the fingers scrawny, knobbly knuckles, much older than her own youthful shadow which played alongside it. They were shadow puppets sparring with each other, darting, backing off, but the stranger refused to go away.

It was a kind of game. She was almost enjoying it except that her body was screaming out for the return of her own fingers, the soft sensuous touch that would make her flinch and gasp her delight aloud.

She was tiring of this play, the moonlight was teasing her.

'Go away, leave me alone!'

A flick of her hand, a disdainful gesture of annoyance as her fingers slipped back to her warm moistness and brought about an instant reaction, her thighs opening wide. And that shadowy hand had moved in closer.

'You're cheeky.' Vera's tone, her giggle, was juvenile. 'All right, then. If you really want to, I'll let you feel me.'

She held her breath, a new game, anticipation of a shadowy touch sending little shock waves all over her body. Seduced by a shadow; telling herself, convincing herself, that the shape was a separate entity unrelated to her own shadows. A stranger in her bed, one whom she was going to let have his (it could even have been 'her') way. Eyes closed, head back, the suspense was torturing her. Of course it wouldn't touch her and even if it did she wouldn't feel anything. A game of make-believe, pretend. The only thing that spoiled it was that nasty smell.

The stench came at her, enveloped her, and she found herself trying to hold her breath. It was something rotting, like that time last summer in the heatwave when Mrs Clements had filled the bins with food scraps and the dustmen had missed a week because Monday was a bank holiday.

Her teeth were chattering with the cold. She could hear them clicking like castanets. The room was freezing, the drop in temperature was diminishing her sensuousness, that stink destroying the erotic feeling she had created. She tired of a silly game that had only provided a brief turn-on and when she looked again she knew that the hand would not be there. She had probably imagined it in the first place.

She opened her eyes, looked down. *It was still there.* Definitely it was not her own shadow. The scrawny outstretched fingers moved again even as she looked, edged an inch or so nearer. Vera stared, eyes wide, disbelief now but no fear because shadows did not hurt you.

'Hurry up – ' Her voice trembled with the cold. 'I said you could if you wanted to, but it's cold lying here and I'm going to pull the sheets back in a minute and that'll be the end of you.'

It was stupid, even she realized that. The tail-end of a little game that had gone on too long. But if it had been real she would not have made the offer because she would not allow anybody to touch her, not like Alison Darke-Smith in the next room.

'You stink, too,' she said and reached out for the discarded bedclothes. 'Go on, piss off. You're just a make-believe tease.'

And suddenly the shadowy hand moved, a dart like a snake that has spent too long hypnotising its intended victim and is hungry for the kill. Fingers splayed, closing, grabbing.

Vera experienced a coldness beyond belief on the soft flesh between her thighs, a freezing burning that scalded and froze into the very depths of her maiden womb. Stark physical terror numbed her, had her convulsing, jerking her head so that she saw it all in the mirror opposite.

That hand writhing and twisting, grasping and pulling viciously, a thing demented as it tore at her with its icy grip. A clenched bal. of blackness intent on mutilation, a beast from out of the darkness beyond the moonlight lusting for her flesh.

A combination of pain and terror, she felt herself starting to slide into a yawning abyss, desperately clawing for a hold on consciousness and managing just one piercing yell as she slipped over the edge into a dark nothingness that claimed her and smothered her scream.

Jack Christopher had sensed the sheer overpowering evil in that basement room of death. The coldness, the suffocating odour of putrefaction, the way invisible hands touched you but when you looked there was nothing there. They were there but you couldn't see them. And no way was he going to stay with Harry Clements and wait for death to come and take him.

That was George's job; everybody else ducked the responsibility – even that stranger who had come in last night – and you couldn't blame them. Now, in the safety of his own room, he struggled with his conscience.

He, Jack Christopher, was the chosen one, chosen by his Maker to guard the rebirth of His Son. There was no doubt about that. And now, faced with evil, he had fled. Because his duty was to the one still unborn, he had to be close when the time came . . . But, if there was evil here then it must be destroyed, or at least driven out, before it could harm the holy one.

You must go back and face it, do battle with it, banish it from this hallowed building.

Jack looked at himself in the wardrobe mirror. Pale and insignificant, there was no mistaking the frightened expression in his protruding eyes, the weakness of the mouth which the beard tried in vain to hide. A mere mortal, meek and mild. But was not Christ a gentle man, one who experienced fear? But He overcame it, fought against all odds. And Jack had to do the same; he had to get back down there and face that insidious evil; it would flee when it recognized strength.

It took him some time to pluck up courage. The mother, the holy foetus, they might have need of him. Barbara Withernshaw is looking over them, he told himself. Your duty is to fight that which threatens the promised one. Procrastinate no longer, get below. He moved towards the door, let himself out into the corridor. The light was off, the floor glinting where the brightness of a full moon streamed in through the window at the far end. Its light fell on him, bathed him in its soft coldness. It was not the light, it was the shadows that frightened him, the blackness that seemed to move, to mock him; following him silently to the head of the stairs, driving him on downwards.

Why can't that fellow Pugh go and see? Because *you* are the chosen one. They might seek to harm Alison and the baby she carried, it was a trick to lure him away. The devil's disciples, all of them, might kill the babe before it is born to rule over us. Hurry, there is no time to waste.

At least the light was on in the hall. Both the dining room and the lounge doors were closed and there were no sounds of chattering of the television coming from beyond them. A house of silence; waiting, as if these people knew. It was Alison's fault; she had blurted out her secret, always had been a blabbermouth.

It was all a plot to stop the Second Coming; Clements was attempting to plant the seed of evil in that virgin womb, his own child, the devil's spawn. If he had succeeded then Alison was no virgin and she had lied to himself too. In which case it was already too late and evil had triumphed. But there was still a chance. He had never needed his faith so much before. Nor his courage.

Jack halted outside the door which led off to the Clementses' quarters. He listened. The only sounds were his own breathing and the hammering of his heart. Where was everybody? Had they all gone? – fled the house, left him here alone? Which would have been marvellous, just himself and Alison; he would have to get rid of Barbara though.

No, it was impossible. Nobody could get through the snow-drifts. Those strangers had tried and failed, and they were desperate to get out of here. His brain conjured up a picture of the woman, Suzannah. The thought excited him; he slowed his step. He could go up to her room – he knew which one it was – open the door softly, savour those few seconds whilst he made himself ready for her. Standing by her bedside, perhaps shaking her gently to bring her awake. A thrill that was near-orgasmic coursing through him as those dark eyes flickered open, puzzled, trying to adjust to the soft moonlight and surrounding shadows; widening in horror and disgust as she saw *him*. The headlong flight, the excitement, and afterwards the fear and the remorse. The thought of the way in which he could end it all and destroy the curse of Satan which was surely upon him, the price he had to pay for his brief pleasure.

'Get thee behind me, Satan!' Jack whispered hoarsely, and stared around him into the darkness as though he might catch a glimpse of his tormentor, afraid in case he did. 'You fight me with my own weakness but I shall overcome it, I swear to God.' He clutched at his lower regions in an attempt to halt the threat of an arousement. And then he was afraid again and the feeling went away.

He descended the basement stairs a step at a time, stopping when he came to the end of the shaft of yellow light that filtered down from the hallway above. Beyond was darkness again, more dense than before, a living black mass that seemed to swirl and thicken into a cloud of vibrant wickedness. An impenetrable wall that gave off vile odours, the stench coming at him in an attempt to drive him back.

'Begone, vain phantasm, in the name of the Lord!' His voice shook as did the hand with which he crossed himself as he moved forward. Then he found the light switch and sent those shadows fleeing, laughed nervously after them. But the smell remained and now he was aware of the icy atmosphere, a coldness that ate into him.

He saw the closed door, the entrance to the tomb, the scratched woodwork as if some hungry beast had been trying to claw a way in, scenting the dead human flesh that lay beyond it. Sinister in its shabbiness, but it would not keep him out. He crossed himself a second time and turned the handle.

The room was the same as when he had left it earlier, stark walls of cardboard boxes, a few volumes laid on top of the cartons where space permitted. His eyes roved anywhere but on the bed where that still form lay beneath a grubby sheet. He read the titles on the spines, words that lodged in his brain and had to await comprehension. *Satan and Sorcery, Magic Rituals, The Dictionary of Mythology . . . The Memoirs of Satan* by Gerhardi & Lunn. Stabbing fear amidst the realization as his temporarily numbed mind clicked back into motion, translated. *The works of the devil, volumes of blasphemy!*

The bold titles mocked him. Read and learn! He threw up a hand as if to ward them off, anticipated these books of vileness leaping at him, attacking him. His breathing came fast. It figured; Satan's henchman, this nocturnal recluse who hid in the bowels of this building and spread his evil, prepared himself for the Second Coming, spawning the Antichrist in that maiden's womb . . . Too late. Or was it?

Jack Christopher was driven on by sheer desperation. Clinging to a wavering faith as he approached the bed, he reached out a trembling hand to pull away the bedsheets and reveal . . .

Harry Clements was barely recognizable. The pinched features were sunken, screwed up into a mask of malevolence, the eyes retracted so that the sockets seemed just empty holes. The hooked nose was like some beak with dried mucus clogging the nostrils, the mouth had slipped and twisted, cursing even in death. Dead but still living, Jack sensed the soul that lurked close by, the cold stinking force that was all-powerful, an indestructible beast of the Left Hand Path.

The suffocating mustiness of old books, the cold and the stark, dim light bulb which swung gently in a draught and cast its own moving shadows . . . Shapes that came and went, changed and came again; reaching out for him, snatching back, sneaking round behind him as though to bar his exit.

A soft slithering sound, one that brought a cry of abject terror to his lips. The sheet, the makeshift shroud, was sliding from the bed, dislodged and slipping, landing softly on the floor and spreading itself out. Revealing the near-skeletal corpse for him to view in its entirety.

They hadn't laid it out. *Rigor mortis* had set in in the posture in which Harry Clements had died, death throes which had been preserved: the writhing limbs, bony knees drawn up, an outstretched arm that pointed accusingly at the watcher.

And that was when Jack Christopher began to scream.

For there was no hand, just a deformed stump of a wrist, a ball of stretched flesh which was already dark with gangrene and smelled of putrefaction. A satanic amputation from beyond the grave.

CHAPTER TWELVE

Owain Pugh was jerked out of a deep sleep. A noise, loud and sharp, penetrated the very depths of his exhausted slumber but when he emerged into consciousness he could not recall it, was not even sure if it was real or whether it had been part of a dream. He lay there listening, tensed and waiting for whatever it was to come again. But it didn't.

Instead he heard muffled movements, somebody out on the landing, a door opening and then closing. Voices. He thought one sounded like Suzannah's, and a child's which was most certainly Rose. He was uneasy, he knew he had to go and see. He glanced at the luminous dial of his watch. 11.40 p.m.

He slid out of bed, found his trousers. Still damp, but he couldn't very well go running about a strange household in his briefs. Cautiously he opened the door and stepped out on to the moonlit landing. Now he could hear voices more clearly: Suzannah obviously trying to console Rose, Barbara Withernshaw speaking in a high-pitched tone further along. He moved off down the corridor.

A glance showed him Alison – at least he presumed it was her – sleeping peacefully in bed. Whatever the noise, it had not wakened her. The adjoining door was ajar and through the gap he could see Barbara sitting on the bed trying to console a sobbing girl. Owain tapped, entered.

'Oh, it's *you*!' Barbara glanced up. The girl had her face buried in the older woman's bosom, sobs shaking her young body, her nightdress lifted up, her hands pressed tightly into her crotch.

Oh, Jesus, it's Vera, Owain thought. She's been at it again, got herself all worked up and that's what it's about! He stood there embarrassed, undecided whether to stay or leave.

'It ... *touched me*!' Vera's pallid, frightened features

emerged. She was on the verge of screaming again. '*It touched me!*'

'What touched you?' Owain felt foolish. In all probability Vera had had an erotic dream.

'The shadow. The hand!'

He felt his skin starting to prickle. In this place he could believe almost anything.

'It was some kind of shadowy hand,' Barbara cut in. 'It *assaulted* Vera, did something absolutely obscene to her. Take it easy, my love, it's gone now and it won't be back.'

'It will, I know it will!' Her voice was rising to another scream. 'It was awful, icy cold and it . . .'

'There, there, we know just what it did to you. I think you'd better come and sleep in the other bed with Alison where I can protect you.'

Christ alive! The two of them in the bed. A nutter who can't leave herself alone and a girl who's convinced she's either going to give birth to the holy child or else a reincarnation of the landlord's daughter. I'll finish up going crazy if there's any more of this rubbish. But his flesh was still goose-pimpled.

'I'll go and see if Suzannah and Rose are all right.' He turned back towards the door, glad of any excuse to get out of here.

Somebody was coming along the landing, slow staggering steps as though whoever it was had returned from a late-night drinking session. Owain conjured up a picture of Fred Ainslow drunk and hiccoughing, flicking a trial of cigarette ash in his wake. Owain hesitated and a second later the door was flung back on its hinges, bounced against the stop. Standing there, holding on to a doorpost with one hand to support himself and crossing himself with the other, stood a wild-eyed Jack Christopher. Staring frightened eyes, clothing in disarray, he was breathing heavily, fought to get his strangled words out.

'The hand,' he wheezed, his eyes roving the lighted room, '*the hand is gone!*'

'What hand? Whatever are you talking about?' Owain asked

incredulously. This bloke had really flipped his lid this time, he'd need a place with a padded cell. He wasn't safe to be on the loose.

'Harry Clements's hand.' Jack's head was thrust forward, his eyes bulging like air bubbles that might burst at any second. 'It's rotted off, possessed by his evil spirit, taken on a new form . . .'

'That's right.' They all started as another figure appeared in the doorway, one that they barely recognized as George Clements. He was stooped, a man who looked to have taken a physical and mental battering, his usually ruddy complexion now greyish, eyes rolling, adam's apple bobbing. He seemed to have difficulty in speaking. 'Jack's right . . . the hand is gone . . . *a shadow that crawls and . . .*'

At that moment Vera Brown began to scream hysterically again, clutching at Barbara Withernshaw, trying to hide behind her.

'I told you,' she screeched, 'but you wouldn't believe me. The hand was here, it touched me. Freezing cold and burning too. It attacked me!'

George Clements swayed on his feet, would have slumped to the floor if Owain had not caught him, his head turned, rolling eyes searching the shadows outside on the landing as if he expected to see that shambling crab-like shape manifest itself at any second. He tried to speak but no words came, and he hissed incoherently. Vera was still clinging to Barbara, and Jack had backed up against the furthermost wall. A foursome crazed with fear.

'Now, look –' Owain spoke sharply, somebody had to be logical or else everybody would go mad here and now. 'You've all had a fright, scared yourselves to death. You're imagining things.'

'Go and look for yourself then,' Jack Christopher snarled. 'Go on down to that basement room and see with your own eyes. And may the Good Lord protect you while you're there.' He crossed himself, closed his eyes.

'All right, I will. Just to put an end to this bloody nonsense.

Now, you all wait here until I get back, d'you hear?' He wished those shivers would stop running up and down his spine but this lot were enough to give you the creeps.

Suzannah came out into the corridor at the same time as he did, looking strangely beautiful in the silvery moonlight, a goddess of old in a white slip that served as a nightdress, her long dark hair falling around her shoulders.

'What's the matter, Owain?' she asked, wringing her hands together in anguish.

'That loony bunch.' He jerked a thumb back towards Vera's room. 'They've started seeing spooks now. I'm just going downstairs to try and prove to them what a load of bloody fools they are and then maybe we'll be able to get some sleep for the rest of the night.'

'I . . . I don't want you to go, Owain.'

Oh, for Christ's sake! He took a deep breath. 'I won't be a minute.'

'I'm worried about Rose. She's feverish. She must have had a nightmare which woke her up. She's mithering about something she saw in the moonlight, a shadow on the wall. *A hand.*'

Owain's senses spun and he had to check his retort. This was all going too far. Play it down, that kid's ill.

'Moonlight can cast strange shadows. I shouldn't worry about it, Suzie.' He called her 'Suzie' instinctively; she did not appear to notice. 'Look, I'll be right back. Stay with Rose and . . . and if you've no objection, I think it might be a good idea if I brought my mattress and bedclothes into your room and slept on the floor. Not that I think there's anything to worry about,' he added hastily, 'but this crazy lot could really scare Rose if they don't pack it up. They've got a fit of the frights and it appears to be contagious.'

'I think that's a good idea.' She smiled weakly. 'But, please, don't be long.'

He went on down the stairs. The hall light was still burning and so were the basement ones. He had to admit that he would not have relished this in the dark. Going to inspect a corpse in the early hours of the morning in a snowed-up madhouse was not the ideal way to ensure a good night's sleep. But he had to shut them all up, go back and tell them what a load of silly children they were. He wondered where Fred Ainslow and Mrs Clements were; in all probability fast asleep.

The door of Harry's room was open, swinging in a draught from somewhere, the hinges creaking. The light was on but it was dim because everywhere was piled high with boxes of books that shielded the glare of the bulb from somewhere inside. There was probably a fortune in books and vintage magazines here; perhaps he would make the Clementses an offer before he left. He smiled to himself. You had to be practical to remain sane here. He glanced at the titles of the loose books as he edged his way slowly inside; God, the old boy was certainly into the occult and the collection looked to be a good one, that fraction which was on view. Maybe all this hassle would be worth it eventually. Financially, anyway, if George didn't want too much money.

And then he saw the body, found himself recoiling from it. Some stupid bloody idiot had been messing about with it, pulled off the covers for a ghoulish look and scared himself. George, probably, and then Jack Christopher had come poking his nose in as well and gone back and scared everybody else upstairs. That didn't explain the shadow of that hand, though. He could take George and Jack's version with a pinch of salt, but Rose . . . *That was when his eyes alighted on the outstretched, rigid, pointing arm, saw the grotesque stump at the end of the wrist, the black, rotting flesh.*

He smelled the vile stench that wafted from it, came at him as though it bore him some grudge, filled his nostrils and lungs, had him stepping back, almost throwing up. God almighty, it was true after all!

Dead eyes sought him out, glared hatefully, threateningly, the mouth frozen in an obscene curse. The light bulb seemed to dim still further and the draught blew up a cloud of filthy dust.

Owain turned, stumbled his way back to the door, knocking

against boxes. Some books fell, clattered on the floor, sounded as though something was in pursuit. Thankfully he made it out to the basement area, fled for the steps. Not glancing back as he ran up the stairs, pausing only when he reached the hall, breathless and frightened, knowing that he had to have the answers when he went back up to the second floor, trying to think up a plausible lie for all their sakes. Suzannah and Rose must never know; in the morning they must be on their way and leave this terrible evil behind them; it was none of their business.

A movement startled him: a door opening, a crone-like figure wearing a raincoat with a shawl around her shoulders peered from out of the darkness of an unlit room, a white, wizened ghostly face, anguished and resentful.

'Who's that?' Brenda Clements asked sharply.

'Owain Pugh.'

'Where's George? Have you seen him?'

'He's upstairs with the others.' Owain was shaking but she did not appear to notice.

'The baby . . . has Elspeth been born yet? Tell me, Mr Pugh, is she all right?' A whisper as though she feared the answer to her question.

'No.' He took a deep breath and tried to compose himself. 'The baby hasn't come yet.'

'She's late. Tonight is the night, I know. Tell George to fetch me the moment anything happens.'

'I'll pass your message on, Mrs Clements.' He was already making for the stairs.

'Oh, and have you seen Fred? Fred Ainslow. I think there's something wrong with the boiler. The radiators are turned on but they're cold.'

Owain shivered. It was cold, but maybe not as cold as it was downstairs in that makeshift morgue. 'I'll see if I can get word to him.' He hurried, eager to be away before she could delay him with any more questions. As he reached the first floor landing he heard a door close softly in the hallway. Mrs Clements had retired to her room. To wait.

'Well?' Suzannah had heard him coming and came out on to the second floor landing.

'It's a lot of fuss about nothing.' He didn't think he sounded convincing: Suzannah Mitchell was not an easy person to lie to for some reason. He had better make a better job of it with the others. 'I'll be with you in a minute, I just have to calm these idiots down.'

Vera Brown had stopped sobbing and sat on the bed, head hung low, staring at the floor. George Clements and Jack Christopher were leaning up against the wall as though without its support they would have fallen. Barbara Withernshaw had just come back from checking on Alison. They all stared questioningly at Owain, but nobody spoke. Perhaps they were afraid to ask, would prefer not to hear what he had discovered down in the basement. They all waited for him to say something.

'Your wife was asking where you'd got to,' Owain began, directing his remark at George Clements. 'And she's also looking for Fred Ainslow because she reckons the boiler isn't working properly. The radiators are cold.' And it was damnably cold in this room, his breath clouding as he spoke.

'Did you see . . . Harry?' Clements asked hoarsely. 'Did you see . . . *his hand*?'

'Yes.' It was futile to deny it, just try and find an explanation, but for God's sake *what*? 'I saw it. He had gangrene. That's probably why he died.'

'Gangrene doesn't rot a limb overnight,' Barbara snapped. 'Don't treat us like fools, Mr Pugh. Something took his hand and I'll tell you what it was. *It was his own twisted evil spirit deserting the useless corpse but taking a limb, manifesting itself. And it's loose amongst us!*'

'What rubbish!'

'If it's rubbish then why have these people seen it?'

Vera Brown began to sob again at Barbara's words.

'You know yourself it's true even if you refuse to admit it. The devil himself is abroad in this very place.'

'Aye,' George Clements added, 'Satan's spirit is here just

waiting to be born again into human form. The body he used is dead and useless. He awaits another.'

'Then he's in for a shock.' Jack Christopher pushed himself off the wall, took a couple of paces forward, a boxer who was almost down and out coming back off the ropes. 'For tonight Jesus Christ will be born again and once more Satan will be cast back down to hell.' He crossed himself hurriedly but the pallor remained in his bearded face.

'You can stop all this rot!' Barbara drew Vera to her and turned on the others, a she-lion defending her young against heavy odds. 'There is a girl in the room next door expecting a baby any hour. She's upset. Because of you fools. One tells her she's going to deliver his long-dead daughter, the other Jesus Christ and now you're adding to that nonsense by in-sinuating that it is Lucifer's spawn. How bloody mad can you get? Just think what you're doing to *her*!' She gesticulated wildly. 'All right, have it your own way, believe what you want to, but if any one of you comes near Alison mouthing that rubbish I'll bloody well brain you with the bedside chair. Now get the hell out of here, all of you! There might be evil here but it won't affect Alison's baby.'

George Clements led the way, looking down, not speak-ing, a man terrified by his own beliefs. Jack Christopher fol-lowed him, his lips moving as he mumbled the Lord's Prayer.

'And Vera will be sleeping with Alison,' Barbara Withern-shaw concluded. 'I shall be watching over them. Thank you for your help, Mr Pugh.' She held Vera with one hand, picked up a bundle of soiled bedsheets with the other and walked out through the door.

Owain sighed as he stepped out into the corridor. He didn't have to tell them anything, they had already reached their own conclusions. A macabre fantasy? A lot of it but there was no getting away from that business of the missing hand from the rotting corpse in that basement room. Somewhere, amidst it all, there *might* just be a grain of truth, and that was the most disconcerting factor of all. Boy or girl, god or devil? The old catch-22 situation: nobody would win. And he and Suzannah and Rose were caught up in it all.

He entered Suzannah's room, dragging his mattress and bedclothes, and laid them on the floor. It was damnably cold. There was a thick rime on the windows where the jaded curtains didn't meet. The temperature was surely around minus ten.

'Are you going to tell me what's going on?' Suzannah whispered from the bed. Rose was asleep, her face flushed against the whiteness of the pillow.

'I don't rightly know myself,' he answered, 'except that everybody here is quite mad.'

'Which we discovered about ten minutes after we arrived.' She was determined to know what had happened. 'Rose is asleep, she's cooler now and resting more easily. Go on, Owain, I think I've a right to know. Everybody else seems to.'

Briefly he told her. There was no point in hiding the truth; if he didn't tell her one of the others surely would. She paled, and kept glancing at door and window as though she expected that spectral shadow to manifest itself at any second.

'It's weird but there has to be a logical explanation,' he concluded. 'Christopher is awaiting the Second Coming, Clements is sure that his daughter will be reborn and that she is the devil's daughter, so one way or another there will be fireworks and friction when Alison gives birth. Let's hope that we're well away from here before that happens. We've got about another nine hours until the snowplough breaks through so we'll sit tight, keep together, and then walk out and leave them to it. I just wonder where Fred Ainslow has got to. Everybody else except him is buzzing about like bees round a honey pot.'

'He's probably sleeping off a drunken stupor,' she answered. 'Lucky Fred. Do you think we ought to leave the light on?'

'If you like.' He had already thought about it but did not want to alarm her by suggesting it. 'We'll rest as best we can. Wake me if you hear anything.'

Silence, and that was suddenly the most frightening aspect

of all. No raised voices, no rushing feet, not even the wind howling outside. Just complete stillness and a freezing atmosphere that bit deep into you, seeped through blankets, sheets and clothing.

Owain had slipped into a doze, a kind of semi-conscious state in which his mind refused to relax. Only sheer exhaustion prevented him from getting up and pacing the room in an effort to keep warm. *And pray God that that plough gets through tomorrow. If we have to walk out of here, carry Rose through the drifts, then we'll do it, because the danger is too great to risk another night within these walls.*

His subconscious mind flipped back to recent events; Vera Brown's room, a sea of faces, some familiar, others with strange distorted features, all shouting. Screaming. Crying. Blaming himself. *You lied to us, Owain Pugh.* Jack Christopher in a frenzy, hammering on the wall with closed fists, a heavy tattoo that vibrated and echoed through the whole house.

Thump-thump-thump-thump-thump.

Vera Brown had torn herself free from Barbara Withernshaw and was trying to scratch his eyes out. He threw up an arm to fend her off, felt how cold her touch was. As cold as death.

Trying to push her away but she always came back, grotesquely naked, her body misshapen and still wearing her glasses, the lenses misted up so that she appeared eyeless. Screaming at him now. 'Mr Pugh, you're a liar and a bastard!'

Christopher still pummelled the wall, now using his forehead, making a hollow sound, seemingly impervious to pain. And on the far wall was a macabre shadow-puppet, a hand that looked like a face with its mouth open, laughing at them all. Only Owain saw it. He tried to tell them but his words were lost in the din.

Thump-thump-thump-thump-thump.

'Owain, wake up!'

Suzannah's voice, but he could not make out her face in the mêlée. It was her all right, she was clutching at his shoulder, trying to get to him.

'*Owain!*'

The mist faded, bright light seared his eyes and now he could not see anything at all. Everything came back to him in a rush. Suzannah's room, not Vera Brown's. There was nobody else here except the two of them and Rose. No Jack Christopher insanely banging his head on the wall and yet . . .

Thump-thump-thump.

Louder and more insistent. Real!

'*Owain, there's somebody at the door!*'

A shock wave jerked him up into a sitting position. Stark terror that showed on his face for a second reflected Suzannah's fear. Rose was still sleeping, the hammering had not yet penetrated her deep fever sleep.

'*Mr Pugh. Come quickly!*'

His confused brain took time to comprehend, to put a face to the voice. Angular features with wire-framed glasses which might or might not be misted up. A painfully thin, almost wasted body which might or might not be naked. Dressed or unclothed, lenses condensed or clear, there was no mistaking Vera Brown's shrill panic-stricken voice.

'*Mr Pugh, oh, Mr Pugh, come quickly!*'

Pulses racing, Suzannah holding his arm, he wrenched the door open. Vera stood out there on the landing and why the hell hadn't she put the light on? A white wraith, a pitiful sight as she visibly shivered in a flimsy nightdress, the fear was only too apparent in her expression; the pleading, and any second she would begin to scream hysterically again.

'What's the trouble?' Owain tried to sound matter-of-fact, in control of the situation, for Suzannah's sake as well as to bolster his own courage.

'Auntie Barb says you're to come quickly, Mr Pugh.' Vera was crouched as though ready to run back to her guardian the moment the message was delivered. 'It's happening!'

'*What* is happening?' He was suspicious of a trick or else this unbalanced girl was in the midst of one of her fantasies.

'The baby,' Vera shrieked. 'You'll have to help, Mr Pugh. *The baby's coming!*'

PART TWO

THE SPAWN

CHAPTER THIRTEEN

'No, you must stop here with Rose.' Owain Pugh restrained Suzannah whose instinct was to follow him, a mother who might be able to help if the birth was a difficult one. 'You must. Shut the door and shout for me if you need me. I'll only be a few yards away.'

He turned to follow Vera, but the girl was already running as though desperate to reach the birth, to witness a miracle and satisfy her curiosity. But no, she passed the room where Alison writhed and groaned in childbirth, turned in at her own doorway, stood there framed in the light from within, a crazed nymph, wild-eyed and yelling, 'Go to her, Mr Pugh. *And I hope the baby dies!*'

The door was slammed and for a few seconds Owain stood there alone in the ethereal light of a moonlit corridor. He was stunned by the ferocity of Vera Brown's curse; it sounded as if she meant every word of it. The crazy bitch, he thought, and opened the door of the adjoining room.

'Shut the door!' Barbara was kneeling in between Alison's spread thighs, the girl's body heaving and shuddering; pushing, relaxing, pushing again. Something squelched, the waters had already soaked the bedsheets. 'I need you, Mr Pugh, not to help me with the delivery but to keep those other bastards from interfering. Guard that door with your life!'

He obeyed. It never occurred to him to refuse: there could be trouble with all these people and their crazy notions. Alison was shouting, cursing.

'Push –' Barbara's voice was strained and tired. 'For Christ's sake, push! You're nearly there!'

The girl gave a strangled scream, and then a baby was crying, a sound that brought those prickles back to Owain's spine. All babies cried as they came into the world but not like *that*! The sound was almost animal, howling rather than crying. Vicious.

He glanced round, wishing that he could see past Barbara Withernshaw's bulky form. He saw Alison's head on the pillow, her eyes closed, exhausted by the strain. She might even be unconscious. The older woman was examining the babe, cleaning it off, cutting the cord, but her intake of breath alarmed him. Something was wrong: perhaps Vera Brown's curse had come true and the child was stillborn. Barbara was dipping a bloody cloth in a bowl of water, sponging, squeezing, sponging again.

'Is . . . is everything all right?' he asked at length.

She did not reply immediately but quite obviously everything was not all right. After some seconds she said, 'Come here and take a look at *this*!'

Owain moved slowly, reluctantly. He didn't want to see anything more after what he'd seen in that basement tonight. He approached the bed cautiously, had to peer round the woman's body, noticed how she held the naked baby from her as though its touch was repulsive to her; a tiny wizened human form that squirmed and screeched venomously, a wild creature's cub plucked from its mother's lair during her absence. *The face, oh God, it was monstrous! A hideous infantile mask that seemed to see him and snarl even though its eyes were closed.* The head was abnormally large for the shrunken body, a protruding forehead seemed to hood it, shade the face like it was not meant to be looked upon. A beak-like nose hooked over the distended lips. Owain stepped back from the bed; there was only one word to describe it: *evil*!

No, he told himself. You've seen too much tonight, it's played on your nerves, all babies are ugly at birth. But not as ugly as this one. More than ugly – *grotesque*.

'He's no beauty.' He tried to sound unperturbed.

'*She!*' Barbara corrected him, and added, 'The Clementses will be delighted, Jack will be devastated. Sod the lot of 'em. That's no human face, I'll swear, and I've delivered scores of babies. *But look at the hand, man, just look at it!*'

Owain looked and his brain reeled. Sheer revulsion as he saw the uplifted wriggling arm that stopped at the wrist. *There was no hand!* 'Oh, my Christ!'

'Exactly,' Barbara whispered. 'Look at the hand because there isn't one.'

'A deformed baby.'

'You could put it that way. *Personally I'd say it's Satan's spawn. George Clements in his madness was right all along. This thing I'm holding is their Elspeth, except that she's born of the devil. We had the sign tonight, I feared as much. The hand came to tell us!*'

The baby had stopped struggling and now lay limply in Barbara's arms. Owain could hear its breathing, saw how its chest heaved under the strain and the mucus rattled up its lungs and into its mouth, oozed out in a thick dribble. The mouth opened, a vile cavity gasping for air.

'There's something wrong with it.' That much was obvious, he just had to say something. 'If only it wasn't for the snow we could get it to a hospital.' And get rid of it.

'Well, we can't, much as I'd like to.' She smiled humourlessly. 'Frankly —' Lowering her voice even further in case Alison heard — 'I don't give much for its chances of survival and I can't say I'm sorry.'

Words that elsewhere would have shocked him. But here, in the Donnington Country House Hotel, you understood.

'What are we going to do?' he asked.

'What *can* we do?' A note of despair. 'If Alison will accept it, are we justified in passing on the responsibility? I'd give anything to know who screwed her. My guess is that it has to be Harry Clements after what we've seen tonight. In all probability the poor girl didn't know a thing about it. He might even have hypnotized her. And just bloody well look what he's given her, the vile sod!'

Alison's eyes flickered open, her bucktoothed smile adding to her vacant expression. She struggled up into a sitting position.

'Let me see it, please.'

'You can hold her, Alison. It's a girl.' And may God have mercy on both of you.

The girl took her baby, cradled it, her fingers smoothing over it, the instinctive reactions of every mother after giving birth, checking to see that it was intact, *normal*. Alison's fingers followed that arm down, froze where the wrist ended, sought frantically for the hand and didn't find one. She looked, saw. And began to scream.

'Take it, oh, take it away!' Screeching hysterically, holding the child at arm's length, she would have dropped it on the floor if Barbara had not caught it in time. 'Take it away, *kill it!*'

In his mind Owain heard Vera Brown's last words as she slammed the door on him: 'I hope the baby dies.' It probably would and then both girls would be happy.

'Listen!' Barbara Withernshaw stiffened and turned to face the door. 'I think there's somebody coming. Well, I suppose this solves our problem. Anybody who wants the baby can bloody well have it!'

It was George Clements who threw open the door and stumbled in supporting his wife who still wore the old raincoat which, in all probability, Owain thought, she slept in. And possibly she wore her wellington boots in bed as well. Her face had an expression of fevered excitement, a grandmother arriving at the birth of a new grandchild.

'It is a girl, isn't it?' Fear and hope crowded the bedside.

'Yes.' Barbara laid the baby on the bed and backed off, made as if to leave. 'You needn't worry, you've got your Elspeth. The mother has rejected it, so it would solve an awful lot of problems, in the circumstances, if you would foster it. If only temporarily. I will help you with the feeding, if you need help.'

'Look –' Brenda Clements pointed, first at the screwed-up features then at the handless arm, not a trace of dismay nor horror in her voice. 'It *is* our Elspeth and not the Christ Child after all.'

Owain experienced revulsion, both at the child and the

Clementses' reaction, and something else which had him looking for the doorway — *sheer terror, even greater than that which he had experienced down in the basement this very night!*

Alison struggled up on an elbow, seemed to have to draw a deep breath before she shouted, 'Go on, take it, take the damned thing. Kill it!'

Her words appeared to vibrate, hang in the air. George and Brenda looked at each other and glanced almost guiltily at Barbara. The latter nodded.

'Yes, you'd better take it and care for it. But she *might* just change her mind. She's distraught, she's been through a hellish time.'

'I won't! I never want to see it again.' The effort of shouting had exhausted the mother and she sank back down, turning her face to the bare wall. 'I never want to see it again. It's wicked, I can tell.'

Brenda Clements had the baby in her arms. Owain's fear was that she might drop it, but she hugged it to her breast. The infant was strangely quiet, with an expression on its tiny ugly features of serenity. Owain shuddered. This was awful, bizarre.

George nodded. 'We'll see to it. We've got a bottle and baby milk.' Because we knew that this was exactly what would happen. 'Come on, Mother, we'd best get it somewhere warm.'

Owain turned away. He had seen enough of this and Suzannah needed him.

'Oh, Mr . . . Pugh, isn't it?' George Clements caught him by the sleeve, held him. 'How is your little girl?'

For a second their eyes met and there was something in George Clements's expression that frightened Owain. It was not merely an enquiry after a child's health; there was an intensity about it that was not befitting in an almost total stranger.

'She's not my little girl –' He tugged his arm free. 'She is Mrs Mitchell's. And she's certainly not very well. A fever of some kind.'

'Then you'd be best to stay here for another day or two.' Hooded eyes, words that bordered on a command. 'We won't charge you, Mr Pugh. Free board.'

'Of course –' Brenda stretched her lips in a rare smile. 'We would be delighted to have you as our guests. Even if the snowplough makes it as far as the end of the road, you can't carry a sick child through the deep snow to meet it. She might get pneumonia. But if you have to leave yourself, then don't worry, George and I will be delighted to look after Mrs Mitchell and . . . *Rose*.' The emphasis was on the girl's name as if it was very important to her, had been lodged in her thoughts.

'Thank you.' Owain's mouth was dry. There was something about this pair that disgusted him. 'But I don't think it will be necessary. We shall find a way to leave in the morning.'

'Brenda did not reply but Owain saw burning hatred for him in her eyes. A silent confrontation: the girl will stay behind; only over my dead body. He turned, left the room, hastened along the corridor. And he was relieved to find Suzannah sitting up in bed waiting for him, Rose still sleeping.

'It's a girl.' He spoke in hushed tones as he closed the door, cursed it again for not having a lock or even a bolt on the inside. 'The Clementses have taken it because Alison has rejected it. God, it's an awful thing. Deformed.' He decided not to mention the missing hand. 'But we're definitely leaving in the morning.'

She nodded, not wanting to know any more. Somebody else was shouting now. It seemed to be on the ground floor, or perhaps on the first floor landing. Shrill voices, and among them she thought she recognized Jack Christopher's. She tried to close her ears to the sound even though from here it was impossible to decipher the words. She had to get herself forcibly under control, hysteria was close. Oh God, I feel as if I'm going mad like everybody else.

George and Brenda Clements had reached the first floor landing and were about to descend the flight of uncarpeted stairs to the ground floor when they heard footsteps coming down after them. The light was off. There was moonlight enough anyway and the starkness of electric light would have detracted from their moment of triumph. They had their long-departed daughter back even if there was still a price to pay.

'Somebody's coming,' Brenda said. 'Perhaps it's that young fellow changed his mind and they're going to stay. Or better still, he's leaving tomorrow and the woman and Rose are remaining here.'

A silhouette appeared against the moonlit wall, one which they recognized instantly. There was no mistaking Jack Christopher, 'Crazy Jack' as they called him, even if they could not see his wild bearded face. He was trembling in every limb, shaking as though he had some uncontrollable fever. Then a shaft of moonlight slanted on to his face and they recoiled at the sight. His features were screwed up in maniacal rage and frothy spittle foamed on his lips.

'Is it true what they tell me?' he said, approaching the couple in the manner of a hunter stalking a dangerous wounded beast. 'Tell me they lie, that it isn't true.'

'I've no idea what they've told you, Jack,' George answered, putting himself between his wife and this crazed madman. 'Whatever the others say is none of your business.'

'*Show me the child!*' Christopher shouted and raised an arm threateningly. 'Let me see for myself that it is the Christ Child and, if so, you have no right to it.'

'Keep away, Jack.' George Clements swallowed. He knew that physically he was no match for the younger man. 'It is a girl, *our* girl.'

'Liar!'

'See for yourself, Jack.' Brenda Clements held the baby aloft, bathed its body in the ray of moonlight filtering in through the high landing window. 'See, it is a girl.'

Jack Christopher would have screamed had his vocal powers not suddenly been rendered useless. He mouthed a silent cry that embodied anger and fear and stared in disbelief, trying to will a sex change upon the baby, beauty where there was ugliness, good where there was incarnate evil.

It saw him, met his gaze, burned him with its tiny eyes that flickered open for the first time, a newly-born that saw and hated and breathed malevolence with clouded vapour in the cold atmosphere.

'That is not your child.' Christopher found his speech, a throaty snarl. 'It is the devil's spawn, Satan's own, born of his seed. The girl was bewitched, she tricked us all. The child must die before it is too late!'

It was as though the babe heard and understood. It began to struggle and screech in harsh vibrant tones in which there was no fear, only frustrated rage because it was powerless to attack him. Spitting, wriggling until Brenda almost let it slip through her grasp and lowered it back down for a better hold. And still it fought her, yelling all the time.

'Go away, Jack.' It was a plea rather than a command from the frightened George Clements. 'Your threats are empty and if you carry on like this I shall phone the police . . . as soon as the phone is working again.' A weak threat, for the other could kill them all if he so wished. Clements prayed that he would not launch an assault and wished that there was a weapon of some kind handy with which to defend themselves.

Christopher fell silent. His face was in shadow again, hiding his expression from them. The baby had stopped screaming and there was only the sound of their breathing. And then, without another word, Jack Christopher turned away and began to walk slowly back up the stairs. They stood there listening to his receding footsteps and only when they could no longer hear them did they continue on their way down to the hall.

'Jack's dangerous,' Brenda said as they reached their untidy quarters where an old-fashioned pine crib stood in the corner in readiness for this hour. 'He means to harm Elspeth.'

'We must be on our guard,' George answered, staring with a glazed expression, 'but we still have our part of the bargain to carry out before Elspeth is ours. That girl, the one named Rose, she must not leave this house. Do you understand, Mother? She must be prevented from going in the morning.'

'She is too ill to travel.'

'They will carry her through the snow,' he snapped. 'It is the man, Pugh, who is the real danger. He means to take her away at all costs. The mother we can handle, but Pugh . . .'

'Why does the Master not kill him then? Isn't he here, in the form of Harry's hand? He could kill him if he wanted to.'

'It is not as simple as that.' George said, his tone one which he might use to explain something to a difficult child. 'His spirit took on Harry's body, which was a mistake for Harry was about to die anyway. The spirit left the body and has now entered our own daughter, but the child needs time to grow to womanhood before that possession is truly powerful enough. And in the meantime we are the guardians, the parents, entrusted by the Mighty One to protect this babe, Elspeth. We are *his* chosen servants; he demands a life for a life and we must do his bidding. Don't you understand that, Mother? *The power is only just beginning.* The girl called Rose must be sacrificed and, so, too, must Crazy Jack die. And Pugh, too, if necessary.'

She nodded dumbly. All this was getting beyond her. All she knew was that they had Elspeth back again and this time they weren't going to lose her, no matter what the consequences were.

CHAPTER FOURTEEN

Alison Darke-Smith was confused, totally numbed following the birth of that dreadful creature which was no normal baby. Her dreams of motherhood were shattered in those few seconds following the birth; she did not understand, she never would.

How could she possibly bear the Clementses' daughter when she had not even copulated with George? He revolted her, as had his brother. And Jack. Jack was mad and she had to be mad, too, to believe all that about Christ coming again in her own womb. Of the two possibilities, though, the latter was the more feasible because she was a virgin and only one virgin in the history of Mankind had had a baby. But she hated Jack for his deception. It was some kind of sick trick: they had all conspired to play a trick on her and it was frightening. But not as frightening as that which had happened when she was in the last throes of labour. Now it was all coming back to her. She reached out for the light pull, found it with some difficulty, and flooded the room with electric light.

Oh please, I don't want to be left alone! She almost cried out for Barbara Withernshaw to come back but stopped herself just in time. She didn't want any of them here, they were all responsible. Even *that* ... she tried to push it from her muddled brain but it refused to leave, remained to haunt and frighten her ... It *was* their doing because if she thought it wasn't then she would go out of her mind with terror.

The baby had been starting to come and Barbara kept shouting at her to 'push'. Alison's gaze was beyond the woman kneeling up on the bed with her, focused on a diamond pattern on the wallpaper. The shape shimmered, straightened out, contracted, nearly faded away altogether because her vision was distorted by the pain that only mothers know at the moment of birth.

Alison had closed her eyes, opened them again, saw the pattern through a misty haze. It *was* different now, sort of squiggly, shapeless, wriggling about. She watched it intently. It was taking on a new form, one that was familiar although it did not mean much to her because it was surely all in her agony-crazed mind.

Somewhere, far away, Barbara was cursing, swearing, telling her she could 'push even harder'. I can't, I'm trying. The door opened and that stupid girl, Vera, left. Thank Christ, and don't come back! Push and push again.

It was a *hand* up there on the wall just below the picture rail, a black silhouette with moving fingers, like a caricature of a spider walking along the wall looking for flies. Hunting. It fascinated her, didn't frighten her at this stage. Now it was climbing down in a straight line, hurrying on its way to the floor. Her eyesight blurred again and when she could see once more there was no sign of whatever it was ... except that there was a break in the diamond pattern – *one of the diamonds was missing!*

The baby would come any second now. Alison relaxed, braced herself for the final push that would bring her child into the world. And it was at that moment that she was aware of icy fingers on the inside of her thigh, creeping upwards. An intense coldness ... it had to be Barbara getting ready to take the baby, it couldn't be anybody else. Vera had gone out. There was a man in the room, but he was over by the door. Moving fingers, freezing and purposeful. *Don't touch my baby!*

She sensed the hand before it entered her, filled with a cold burning and she had screamed and tried to push it out, felt the baby go with it. And when she had regained consciousness, for her mind had seemed to slide into a void where there was nothing – neither pain nor fear – she remembered. It was that hand that had made the baby as it was and she never wanted to set eyes on it again.

Alison kept glancing round the lighted room, fearful lest that shadowy shape manifested itself to her again, relieved to see that the wallpaper pattern was complete now; there wasn't a diamond shape missing, there probably never had been. But these mad people had done something to her and she hated them for it.

Footsteps passed along the corridor. She followed them with her ears, heard them go down the stairs. Shouting; she cringed, recognized Jack Christopher's voice. A brief silence then she heard him coming back, his fast walk slowing, stopping. She pulled the sheets up over her as the door handle clicked and the hinges creaked. And she knew that he was in the room.

She kept her eyes tightly shut even though her head was under the sheets. I'm asleep, go away. Her heart was hammering, she thought she might be sick. Sick with fear and revulsion. You dirty bastard, I know what you're doing, you did it once before and made me watch you. You're worse than Vera Brown. I'm scared of you, scared that you'll rape me; I'm a virgin, I don't do that sort of thing.

Alison could hear him breathing, heavy laboured breaths. Oh God, I was right, that was what he came here for. But I'm not going to look. Kill me if you want, put me out of my misery, but don't do anything else to me, *please*!

'Alison?' His voice was scarcely audible. She heard him moving to the foot of the bed, knew that he was holding on to it. 'Alison.'

'I'm asleep. Go away.'

'Stupid girl!' He sounded angry. 'I must talk to you, Alison.'

'I don't want to talk. Leave me alone.'

'Let me see you, girl! *Sit up*!'

She found herself obeying, much as she fought against it, throwing back the bedclothes, oblivious of the fact that she was naked; she had used her nightdress to dry herself. Full breasts with hard pink nipples, a roll of fat hiding her navel. Blood-smeared thighs pressed tightly together, not just to prevent him from seeing *there* but because she was so sore.

She stared at him, amazed because he wasn't doing what she thought he was, frightened because there was a mixture of fear and sorrow in his expression, his eyes red-ringed and glistening as though he had been crying. In a strange sort of way she felt pity for him; apart from Barbara Withernshaw he wasn't like the rest of the guests (inmates). He was cultured, intelligent.

'I want to ask you something, and I want you to answer me truthfully.' He tried to smile.

'Yes.' It sounded silly, the sort of reply she used to give that stupid private tutor whom her parents had engaged in a desperate effort to educate her.

'Alison —' He closed his eyes, spoke softly, almost kindly. 'With whom have you had intercourse?'

She swallowed. She knew that she was blushing, her cheeks burning redly to match her hair. Guilt because he wanted a confession and would not accept anything else.

'I've told you, I'm a virgin. I've never been with a man in my life.'

'Alison —' His tone was firmer now, any hint of a smile was gone. 'Alison, you're lying to me. You've tried to trick me. The Evil One cannot bring about a virgin birth. You are not a virgin, and I want to know with whom you mated. *Answer me!*'

She recoiled as though his words had struck her a physical blow. She knew she was going to cry. The tears were beginning to build up and when they started to come there was no way she would be able to stem the flow. She would sob until she fell asleep.

'All right.' His tone had changed again. 'Perhaps you do not remember, that is possible. Or else . . .' He paled, his expression was one of mounting terror. 'Or else . . . *he* somehow got to the virgin foetus, corrupted it. In its innocence it would have no defence. May God have mercy on us all if that is the case!'

Jack Christopher stood there with bowed head. She saw the way he trembled. And when finally he looked up there was hopelessness in those eyes which seemed to have retracted.

'Had I guessed,' he murmured, as if he was unaware of her

presence in the room, 'then I could have cast the evil spirit from you. It is too late now, the devil's spawn has left you, left you with a soiled and useless carcass, a half-demented girl who has no knowledge of what she has done. Your death would not solve anything, *it is the spawn which must be destroyed*!'

Her earlier plea echoed in her tortured mind. 'Take it . . . *kill it*!' And suddenly somebody was going to take her at her word. Oh, no, you can't murder the baby, no matter how ugly and deformed it is.

'The hand of Lucifer is upon us,' Christopher muttered as he slunk towards the door. 'Satan has returned to earth in vile human form. His exile is over. Even God has not been able to defeat him this time.'

Alison sat up in bed shivering for a long time after Jack Christopher had left the room. A kind of realization, but her brain was unable to grasp it fully. Such was her terror that she was unaware of the cold as she stared fixedly at those diamond patterns on the wallpaper, frightened in case one of them blurred and changed shape again.

Sleep was out of the question, except for Rose. Owain Pugh resigned himself to that after the first half-hour. Scared to sleep, if you were honest with yourself; scared to put out the light. And eventually it became an embarrassment, two people together, not speaking. Maybe if they talked about *normal* things it would help to pass the night hours, hasten the daylight. And they were leaving for sure this morning, two kids at boarding school on the last night of term unable to sleep, lying awake and wishing the hours away.

'At least I've nobody at home worrying about where the hell I am,' he said at length. He waited for her reply, was surprised how tense he was. You're sure to have a husband or a boyfriend, Suzie. Go on, tell me the worst. Because that's how important it is to me even though I have no business feeling this way about you. A passing fancy, comrades in a crisis. It was more than that and he knew it, even if it was one-sided. He held his breath and stared at the wall.

'Nor me,' she said. 'Just Rose, just the two of us.' Her voice dropped to a husky whisper. 'My husband walked out on me. A young girl.'

'I'm sorry.' Liar, you're glad. His pulses raced. Cool it, you're just a friend in her hour of need, after tomorrow our ways will part. 'I suppose I never met the right one.' It sounded silly.

'Do you ever know who is the right one?' He detected a bitterness in her voice. 'I thought I did. As it turned out I was wrong. But at least I got Rose out of it and so it was worth all the heartbreak. You're a second-hand bookdealer, aren't you? I've always been curious about booksellers.' Changing the subject because that one was hurtful.

'A way of making a few bob.' He looked at her now, thought he might just be blushing because Suzannah's cheeks were red. Over the first hurdle and now on to trivialities. 'I picked the trade up as I went along. You deal in the field that interests you. Mine's science fiction and fantasy —' For Christ's sake don't mention 'horror' — 'It's a gradual process. You start a collection, decide to prune it because you've been greedy and there's a lot of stuff you don't want. So you list your surplus, advertise them. Suddenly everybody seems to want your books and as you've made a bit of money you look around for a few bargains to sell at a profit. It gets into your blood and before you know it a hobby has become a part-time business. I was working in an office at the time. I was engaged, needed the security, but when the engagement was broken off I didn't give a damn. So I chucked up my job and went into book dealing full-time. I've got by, I don't make a fortune but I have my freedom. I'm not tied to a desk from nine till five. Instead —' He laughed — 'I work about twelve hours a day and clock the miles up looking for books up and down the country.'

'It sounds fascinating.' She was playing with her hands, looking at them. 'I've always been fond of books. I like reading historical romances. I'd love to see your shop some time.'

'It isn't a shop. Just a couple of rooms stacked with books.

But I'd love to show 'em to you.' It sounded like 'come and look at my etchings'; he hoped it didn't come over that way.

'It's a deal.' She did her best to laugh. 'Out of here in the morning, first stop the doctor's with Rose, and then we'll have a peep at this Aladdin's Cave of yours.'

'Great.' Suddenly Donnington was fading into second place. 'We'll do that.'

Rose stirred, sat up and blinked, looked around as though she was unsure of her surroundings. She showed no surprise at seeing Owain in his makeshift bed on the floor.

'Are you all right, darling?' Suzannah felt her forehead and thought her temperature had dropped a little.

'I'm okay, Mum.' Rose managed a smile. 'For a moment I couldn't work out where I was. I need to go to the loo.'

'It's down on the next floor.' Suzannah glanced at Owain. 'I'd better come with you.'

'No, I'll be all right.' Rose slid out of bed, began padding barefooted towards the door.

'Hey, Rose, just a minute . . .'

'Look, Mum —' Tight-lipped, a young teenager resenting a parental offer to accompany her to the toilet. 'I'm quite capable and, anyway, I'm feeling better now.'

Suzannah checked the words that almost fell from her lips. This isn't an ordinary household. There's a corpse in the basement. The residents are all mad. And . . .

'All right, then. Down the stairs, on to the landing below, and the bathroom's at the far end facing you. Why on earth they don't have one on this floor, I'll never know. Go on, hurry. It's beastly cold and you're far from better yet. First thing tomorrow, when the snowplough's got through, is a visit to Dr Wildman.'

Rose opened the door, closed it behind her, and they listened to her footsteps going towards the stairs.

'Do you want me to keep a discreet eye on her?' Owain asked.

'Yes . . . and no.' Suzannah's smile was far from reassuring. 'She can be a little madam at times. Treat her like a child and she'll throw a tantrum. Treat her like an adult and everything's more or less fine. That's how it is at home, anyway, and I doubt it'll be any different here. We'll give her a minute or two and if she's not back then we'll go and check . . . from a distance.'

Owain was uneasy. He had moved in here to keep an eye on them and now he was letting the child go down to the lower landing on her own. But she had only gone to the loo, she would be back in a minute or two. They found themselves listening but there was only silence. Perhaps this night of madness was over and everybody had retired. Owain hoped so.

Rose hurried down the stairs. She would have been very angry if Mum or that man had followed her. She was fourteen, not eight, in her third year at school, about to take Grade Four piano exam. Which made her nearly an adult.

There was a light on in the toilet at the end of the landing, illuminating the pane of frosted glass above the door. Damn it, she couldn't wait much longer. The sudden denial of the opportunity to relieve herself increased her discomfort. She balanced on one leg, then on the other, wondered if there was another loo downstairs. If there was she had no idea how to find it and, she had to admit, she would feel scared going all the way down there on her own. Here it didn't bother her as her mother was only just upstairs. Then she heard the chain being pulled; twice, three times before the cistern reluctantly flushed in a noisy cascade. A bolt clicked back and the door opened.

Childlike, she didn't even wonder to herself who it might be, didn't give it a thought. In hotels there were always strangers walking about and you ignored them. But as Rose moved towards the opening door recognition of the woman emerging from the toilet had her stopping in amazement. *It was Brenda Clements.*

'Why, if it isn't young Rose.' A smile on that lined face, a genuine greeting, nullifying any harsh thoughts one might have had about a landlady who threw bottles of ammonia in the dining room and cooked in her wellington boots. Mrs Clements wore a faded blue dressing gown and slippers to match, and her usually straggling hair was done up in a bun at the back of her head. Smart by Donnington standards, she put you at your ease and if you were young enough you were prepared to forget. She didn't look bad-tempered, just a homely grandmother type, Rose thought.

'I hear you've been poorly, Rose.' Those eyes scrutinized the young girl as though searching for signs of illness, concerned for the health of a young guest. 'Are you feeling a little better now?'

'Yes, thank you.' Please let me get by you, I'm bursting for a wee.

'Good. Perhaps you'd like another asprin. I think the one I gave you has worked wonders.'

'No, thank you, I'd rather not.'

'Well, all right if you're *sure*.' Mrs Clements made as if to move on, checked, still barring the way to the toilet. 'Oh, I'm sorry, that toilet's not working.'

'I heard the chain . . .'

'Of course you did, but I was just testing. It doesn't flush properly. I think one of the pipes must be partially frozen. It mustn't be flushed again. Mr Ainslow will have a look at it in the morning. I'm sorry, my dear, but if you'll come with me you can use our own private toilet downstairs.'

Rose hesitated. There was a fluttering in her stomach. There hadn't seemed to be anything wrong with this toilet, she had heard it flush all right. Three pulls, admittedly, but it had gone then. Suspicious, tempted to turn and run back upstairs but the discomfort in her bladder was stopping her. Oh, I've got to go, I can't hold on much longer.

And even as she hesitated Brenda Clements sidled forward, took her hand kindly but firmly.

'Come on, my dear, you come with me and make yourself comfortable. Then you can run on back to your daddy and mummy.'

'Mr Pugh isn't my daddy –' She found herself being helped towards the top of the stairs, propelled in a shuffling kind of way, a determined woman who would not take no for an answer. Over-kind, dominant; children don't argue with grown-ups, my dear. 'He's just somebody staying here. He's sleeping in our room because . . . he's looking after us.'

'Oh, he's not your daddy but he's in with your mummy, is he?' The sunken dark eyes were questioning, the brows raised. 'I'm afraid that's against the rules in this hotel. Unless a couple are married we don't allow them to sleep together.'

'He's sleeping on the floor, on a mattress!' Rose was indignant, found herself on the first stair, being helped down on to the next one. 'My Mum wouldn't do anything like *that*!'

'No, I'm sure she wouldn't, but it's still against the rules.' Brenda Clements tightened her grip on the other's hand. 'Come on, let's hurry if you need to go that bad.'

Rose wanted to tug herself free, flee, but somehow she daren't. She didn't want a scene; she would use the loo and then hurry back.

'In there.' The door in the corner of the hall was nudged open and Rose found herself in a kind of large bedsit with clothes and rugs all over the place, a smell of stale cooking hanging heavy in the stuffy atmosphere. A divan bed was in the corner, George Clements sitting up in it wearing a long-sleeved vest, reading a newspaper. He lowered it at their approach, pushed a pair of thick-rimmed glasses up on to his forehead and stared in surprise.

'Why it's the little girl.' His thick lips parted, but his eyes didn't smile with them and that was what frightened Rose most. A hungry look, more as though his wife had returned bearing a plate of steaming food.

'She needs the toilet.' Brenda pushed the door shut. 'It's in there, my love.' She pointed to an adjoining door. 'Go on, you're not afraid of *us*, surely? We're just a harmless old couple. And when you've done you can go back to your mummy, can't she, George?'

'Why, yes!' He laughed, a guttural sound. 'But perhaps

she'd like a quick peep at the baby first. Carry on, my dear, you use our toilet.'

Rose went through into the adjoining room, a cramped bathroom and toilet, just the basics and the walls were in need of redecoration; in places the bare plaster was showing. There was a small window that was dirty, its frame green with mould as though it had not been opened for a very long time. The walls were wet with condensation, the light bulb flickered as though it had a bad connection. There was no lock on the door, something which Rose found disconcerting. She ought not to have come and she wondered why she had. Because the woman's personality was domineering, she had had no option.

Rose finished and made her way nervously back into the Clementses' living accommodation. Mrs Clements was still standing by the door as though to bar the young girl's exit, her husband was sitting on the edge of the bed, a pair of creased trousers held high up above his waist by braces. Elsewhere Rose would have found him a comical sight, a character out of some second-rate TV soap opera, your typical working-class husband of the last generation. But here it was not funny, it was frightening.

'Would you like a peep at the baby?' Mrs Clements indicated a wooden crib next to the bed. It was facing away from Rose so she could not see inside it. Normally she found babies interesting, a kind of curiosity; everybody gathered round to view a newborn one. But for some reason the last thing she wanted to do right now was to look inside that crib.

'Thank you, but I'd better be getting back.' Her voice trembled and she felt heady as though the fever was returning, the room seeming to darken a shade. Her legs were wobbly.

'Oh, come, come, a minute won't make any difference now that you've made yourself comfortable, my dear.' Brenda Clements glided forward, ungainly but silent, and grabbed Rose's hand again. Rose tried to draw back but the woman was too strong for her, dragging her towards the cradle. 'You just take a look at this lovely baby, our Elspeth. Alison doesn't want her so she's given her to us.'

Rose saw that the man was on his feet, too. Child, you're going to look at the baby whether you like it or not!

'Mummy will be worried,' Rose almost shouted. 'She said not to be long . . .'

'She won't be worried, not here.' Brenda's voice was a sinister croon. 'Now, what d'you think of this little darling?'

Rose stiffened, gasped. The tiny face looked up, saw her. Features twisted in evil, a totem mask that moved, pouted its lips, dribbled a thick yellow mucus. It was breathing noisily, wheezing, a kind of sawing sound. Its complexion was a purplish colour; even Rose knew that this gruesome infant wasn't well.

'What d'you think then, girlie?' George Clements whispered, gloated.

Oh my, it's *awful*, Rose thought. She wanted to turn her head away but that would have meant looking at the couple standing at her shoulder. She was frightened, shivering, . . . and then the cot sheet moved and a tiny arm came up from beneath it, pointing threateningly, accusingly at herself. That in itself was bad enough but then she saw that it had no hand, just a deformed stump, and a scream started to rise in Rose's throat. A scream that got stuck halfway, ended in a gasp of terror, had her trying to jerk her eyes away but they wouldn't move, her stare transfixed on that grotesque limb, hypnotised by it.

For Rose time seemed to have stopped. Everything, except the baby, was so remote. She was caught in a timeless void, just herself and that dreadful creature which was threatening her in a sinister infantile way. Pointing with a handless arm, its slobbering mouth moving, cries that became words of hate. *That's the one! Kill her!*

No, please! Rose thought she struggled but she was powerless in a strong grip, her arms twisted behind her back. The Clementses were laughing, a crazy sound. They were mad, they meant to harm her.

We've tricked you, little girl and now we've got you and you're going to die!

Struggling, pulling, kicking out but it was futile, they had her pinioned and helpless and that baby was yelling for them to harm her. Rose felt her senses starting to slip away, sinking into a dark mist as though she was floating. Panicking, but there was nothing she could do to save herself.

Until suddenly somebody shouted, '*What the hell's going on here?*'

At first Rose thought she was in the throes of a nightmare, that she was ill again, but only when they let go of her and she stumbled and fell to the floor did she realize it was real. Somehow she picked herself up. That baby was still yelling. Don't look at it whatever you do. Look away ... and see Owain Pugh standing in the doorway, his face clouded with anger, and now it was he who was pointing angrily at George and Brenda Clements.

The couple were startled, backing away, trying to bluster.

'What are you doing in here?' the woman croaked. 'You've no business to ...'

'And you've no business touching Rose.' Owain strode forward, held the shaking girl to him, turned again on them and had to shout to make himself heard above the baby's screams. 'Damn you, I've a good mind to report you to the police!' Except that the phone isn't working.

'We were showing Rose the baby.' George Clements made a pretence of checking on the infant. 'And then it started crying and for some reason she became frightened. She isn't well, you know, Mr Pugh. She nearly fainted, but we just managed to catch her in time. And you frightened the life out of us, bursting in here like that.'

'And I'll do more than just scare the living daylights out of you if you ever dare touch her again!'

Owain's fist was clenched, it was all he could do to stop himself from driving it into George Clements's fleshy, blood-drained features. Squirm, you bastard, you were up to something, both of you.

'It's nothing to make a fuss about,' Brenda whined, and there was fear in her eyes. 'We *love* children. Aren't we looking after Alison's baby, Mr Pugh? Would we harm Rose when we're caring for a newborn baby?'

'I don't know what your game is but it disgusts me.' Owain began to back away towards the door, taking Rose with him. 'I can only guess at what is going on in this vile place and it scares me to hell. Which is why I'll break your bloody necks if you try anything else. Get it?' He was shaking with anger.

'I hear you're sleeping with the child's mother!' Brenda screamed. 'Adulterer, fornicator! Not under our roof you won't sin. Get back to your own room. Do you think this is a brothel?'

'No, I think it's worse than that.' Owain said. 'It's a house of evil, and the three of us are leaving first thing in the morning if we have to walk through the drifts. And until then, keep out of my way because I'll not be responsible for my actions if you don't!'

He backed out into the hall, kicked the door shut behind him, and lifted Rose into his arms. When he had burst into the room the Clementses had got hold of her, and he had seen the expressions on their faces. There was no mistaking the killing lust: *they were bloody well going to kill the girl!*

That in itself was terrible enough. It did not bear thinking about and he would not dare to tell Suzannah. Pray God that Rose hadn't realized. But worse than that, Owain had caught sight of the baby's face, the deformed thing they called their Elspeth, and that had frozen his blood, rendered him immobile for a few seconds during which time it might have been too late to save Rose from a terrible fate.

For that child from hell had been yelling at them to kill Rose, there was no doubt about that. The creature understood and it had wanted her life in some macabre, inexplicable, form of human sacrifice!

And just as they reached the foot of the stairway in the hall, Owain heard Suzannah starting to scream upstairs.

CHAPTER FIFTEEN

Vera Brown had lain and sulked in her room after she had left Barbara and Owain. And I hope the baby dies! I'll make sure I never have one and if I ever do I'll sneak out at night and drop it in the river so that the fishes will eat it and nobody will ever know. And from now onwards I'm going to eat what I like. I'll have chips and bacon whenever I feel like it.

She huddled under the bedclothes, a frayed housecoat wrapped around her. It was cold, very cold; she amused herself by blowing vapours, wished they didn't disappear and that she could fill the whole room with them. Like a fog. She kept glancing furtively around. That shadow, the moving hand, it had been awful, obscene. And it had touched her right *there*, penetrated her as if it was looking for something and when it hadn't found whatever it was it had crushed her soft, moist flesh in a malicious icy grip. Like it was taking its frustration out on *her*. She wondered where it had gone. Just vanished probably, like the breath she kept blowing now. So long as it did not return, that was all that mattered.

Vera tried to push her terrifying experience from her mind. Now she was shaking with anger as well as from the cold. Auntie Barb didn't love her any more, that much was plain. From now onwards her self-appointed guardian would only have time for Alison's baby. In which case there wasn't any point in stopping here any longer. Vera didn't like it here, anyway. Okay, you were fed (even if you were dictated to over what you ate), most times you were warm and you had a bed to sleep in, all of which cost her nothing because Auntie Barb paid for it all, like she paid for Fred Ainslow to live here. But why?

The girl was puzzled over that one. Barbara Withernshaw didn't get anything out of it, just the reverse. Some kind of do-gooding, picking up waifs and strays and tramps. Walter Gull had been another of her 'finds' that she adopted and a lot of good it had done that silly old sod; he had upped and walked out and got himself run over down on the main road. *He* wanted to leave and at least he had tried to do something about it. Vera attempted to work out how long she had been at the Donnington; too long. She could barely remember the time before she was taken in by Auntie Barb. A terraced house with an aunt who was a real aunt except that she hit you every time you did something she didn't like, and there was no way of knowing what made her angry from one day to the next. Not just a slap, a fistful of knuckles right in your face. Vera rubbed her nose gingerly as distant unpleasant memories filtered back to her; her nose had been broken, never set, the bump was still there on the bridge. And one of her front teeth was slightly loose, but she had learned to avoid chewing with it. At least Auntie Barb didn't hit her and for a long time she had found affection when she needed it most, but now all that was gone. And Vera wasn't playing second fiddle to any baby. No way.

Which was why, in various stages, she arrived at a decision to leave. Now, tonight, without telling anybody. And when they looked for her in the morning she would be gone and it would be too late. She would have left a note if she had been able to write but as she couldn't she wouldn't. So there, find out for your bloody selves and I'll swear all I want to. Auntie Barb does, she effs and blinds and so does Mrs Clements when she's in one of her moods, and those always ended up with her throwing ammonia. So, really, there was nothing to stay here for.

Vera got out of bed, went to the wardrobe and began sorting out some clothes. A pair of dirty jeans, and those leg-warmers which Auntie Barb had bought her for her birthday, those would keep her warm in the snow. Her wellingtons had a slit in one boot but that wouldn't matter much. An old coat, a hand-me-down which fell to her ankles. All very suitable, just the job to keep you warm on a cold, snowy night.

She crossed to the window and tried to see outside. A layer of patterned opaqueness obstructed her vision and she scratched at it, the encrusted ice lodging beneath a fingernail. She sucked her finger and turned away. She wouldn't be sorry to go. A sudden thought crossed her mind – *where* was she going? Her forehead creased. That was a point, but not really an important one. She had her post office savings book with nearly a hundred pounds in the account and that would suffice for the time being. She could always get a job, sweeping up or washing up in some café. She had often helped Mrs Clements. All the same, it would be nice if she had somebody to go with.

Another idea stopped her when she was almost at the door. Fred would like to leave, she was sure of it. Lately he had been cussing about Auntie Barb being domineering, and he was getting fed up with having to do the cooking and not getting a penny for it. Vera trembled with excitement; she would go and ask Fred, persuade him. He could be quite nice sometimes, often more so when he was drunk.

Fred Ainslow wasn't in his room, and quite obviously he had not been in it tonight. An outside observer might have been fooled by the crumpled grimy sheets on the unmade bed, but not Vera. If Fred was around, had just popped out to the loo, then there would, in all probability, have been an open can of Export on the bedside table and a smouldering cigarette end in the overflowing ashtray. And if he wasn't in his bedroom then he would almost certainly be down in the boiler room where it was nice and warm.

She ran lightly down the stairs. Voices came from behind closed bedroom doors but they were no concern of hers. From now onwards the Donnington Country House Hotel was a place of the past for her.

Down the basement steps. God, it was bloody cold down here. Averting her gaze so that she did not have to look towards Harry's room, a pang of fear because a corpse lay in there. Maybe that was one of the reasons why she was going: she never could stand the thought of death. Down a short passage, an ill-fitting door at the end. She had to push with all her frail strength to grate it open. She peered inside. Afraid again. Perhaps there was somebody dead in here too.

She groped along the wall until she found the light switch, flicked it and bathed the room in candleglow of a forty-watt bulb. Coal dust everywhere, a pile of broken black boulders beneath a closed chute in the corner. An old-fashioned boiler in the centre of the floor, its door ajar, affording a view of the glowing fire within. Embers amidst a heap of ashes, throwing out a warmth, and lying on the floor a huddled form beneath the canopy of a dirty navy blue overcoat. A body.

Vera drew back, almost fled. She stared. She couldn't be certain: it was Fred Ainslow all right, there was no mistaking him even under his coat, but was he . . .?

'Fred!' Her whisper grew in magnitude, bounced back off the black walls at her. Waiting, peering to see if he moved, ready to flee if he didn't. '*Fred?*'

'Uh?' The coat stirred, dragged on the brick floor, sent up a cloud of dust as an old man's white features peered from beneath it, toothless mouth screwed up amidst white stubble. Sunken eyes met her own, glared angrily at this intrusion, took some seconds before recognition filtered through. 'Vera, what you doin' 'ere?'

She released her relief in a long expellation of breath, felt faint for a second or two. 'I was looking for you, Fred. You're not in your room.'

'Course I ain't.' He gave a coarse laugh and coughed. 'If I was there I wouldn't be 'ere, now would I? What you want me for?'

There was no point in going into a long rigmarole where Fred was concerned. She said, 'I'm leavin' Fred.'

'You're *what?*' He sat up, pulling his coat tightly round his wiry frame.

'Leaving. Right now.'

'Why?'

'Because I hate it here. I hate Auntie Barb and the rest of them, and she doesn't love me now that she's got a baby to look after.'

''Er'll soon get tired of the babby'. He produced a half-smoked cigarette from his pocket, struck a match on his thumbnail and lit it. When his lungs were full of tobacco smoke and he had finished a spasm of coughing, he said, 'You'll be all right, take it from me.'

'I won't, and I'm going, Fred.'

'Where you going?' He watched her intently. 'There's deep snow out there, you'll die of hypodermia.'

'I won't but I don't care if I do,' she almost shouted. 'I'll find somewhere . . . but it'd be nice if I had somebody to go with. They don't like you either, Fred, so you've got nothing to stay here for.'

''Cept it's warm.' He jerked a thumb at the dying fire. 'God blimey, 'er's nearly out. 'Ang on a tick.' He got up, picked up a shovel and began to scrape at the heap of coal, avalanched it and threw a shovelful into the stove. 'That's better. So you're leavin', eh? Well, I just 'opes you knows what you're up to.'

'I want you to go with me, Fred.' A plea, the whisper vibrant with emotion. '*Please*, Uncle Fred.'

He did not reply immediately. He dropped the shovel on to the floor with a clang and sat down again. 'You know, Vee –' His gaze ran up and down her slight figure – 'you and me . . . well, with your looks and my brains, just think what we could breed between us!' He gave a guttural laugh, joking but serious, trying to cover up what he was thinking.

Vera stiffened, instinctively stepped back. 'No!' A hiss. 'I . . . I wouldn't want to do anything like *that*, Fred. Even if you came with me we wouldn't . . .' Her voice tailed off.

'Please yourself but it's nice to think about it sometimes. After all, you've shown us what you can do.'

'I don't do it any longer,' she said. 'I'm never going to touch myself again after that.'

'After what?'

'It doesn't matter.' She was even whiter than usual, her dark eyes wide with fear behind her thick lenses. 'I'm going, Fred. I just wanted to say goodbye.' She turned and almost ran back through the door, dragging it shut behind her.

'Hey, wait a minute . . .' Fred Ainslow made as if to follow, changed his mind and sank back down to the floor. What was the bleedin' use? Vera would get about as far as the end of the drive before she changed her mind. Tomorrow morning she'd be back in the dining room eating bran flakes and muesli again and Babs would be shouting at her to get her hands from under her skirt.

Suzannah was almost frantic with fear. Rose had been an awful long time; ten minutes seemed an hour. Perhaps she had fainted in the toilet, had been sick. Or else she had taken a wrong turning in this warren-like house and found herself lost. A brief period of relief when Owain went to search for her but if he had scoured the whole house he should have been back by now. Which meant he hadn't found her . . .

She was on the point of going to look for them both when she heard footsteps on the landing. They halted outside the door. Silence for maybe two or three seconds. Her hopes which had soared, began to fall; why didn't he come in? Was it because he had not found Rose and was afraid to confess the truth? Or . . ?

The door was opening.

'Owain, is everything . . ?' She stopped and her consternation turned to shock, a fear that had her wanting to flee except that there was nowhere to go. Wanting to look away but afraid to take her eyes off the newcomer, terror because it was Jack Christopher and he was stark naked.

She wanted to yell at him to get out, threaten him with the police, Owain, anything. All she managed was a kind of whimper, holding on to the dressing table in case she fainted and then he would be able to do to her what he so clearly wanted to do.

'They got to the Christ Child in the womb.' Christopher's eyes were glazed and staring, his lips scarcely seeming to move beneath his beard. 'Satan struck at the weakling babe, the hand of the devil entered the womb and corrupted. It is too late except that I am the Chosen One and there must be

159

another child. It must be conceived at once. Do not fear, I will not hurt you. It is the will of the Lord.'

'Keep away from me.' She backed a couple of steps, came up against the bed and almost fell on to it. 'Don't you dare touch me, you filthy pervert!'

His arms were reaching out for her and in desperation she kicked out, felt her bare foot make contact with his thigh. He grunted, staggered, and in that instant she made a dash for the doorway. A leap springboarded by sheer terror, throwing herself forward, but she had underestimated the speed of his reactions. A sudden grab, his fingers closed over her arm and pulled her back. She smelled his breath, hot and rancid, on her face as he swung her round, read the crazed lust in his protruding eyes. A man gone berserk, one whose fanatical beliefs had been shattered to fragments and who sought to atone for his catastrophic loss.

His free hand caught her long hair, jerked her head so that her lips were only inches from his own.

'Woman, you have been chosen by my Father, the Almighty, to bear His son. Lie with me and be holy!'

Suzannah, acting out of desperation and panic, swung her knee upwards, felt it make contact and saw the expression on that lusting face change to one of sheer agony. The grip on her arm and hair slackened and she tore herself away, fled blindly for the doorway.

Out into the moonlit corridor, running for the stairs, her feet skidding but somehow she kept her balance. She heard him coming after her, his laboured breathing, his profane curses in spite of his claim to be divine. She was almost at the top step when he caught her and now she screamed because in this ethereal silver light his face was that of a wild beast at the rutting stand.

His thigh wedged her against the banisters preventing her from kneeing him again, her wrists were seized and her spine threatened to snap as he bent her back. Below her was the stair well, a deep drop right down to the basement. If she could have squirmed from his hold and jumped, she would have done – flung herself to her death rather than be . . .

She did not know how it happened, only that he seemed to be trying to climb on to her in this precarious place, two toy monkeys flaying about on a horizontal stick; slipping. Suzannah grabbed for a hold, found one, felt her adversary sliding across her, his flesh slippery with sweat. And in that one awful moment he left her, groped blindly and missed.

If he had screamed with her it would not have been so bad. Instead he fell like a rock dislodged in a mountain avalanche, bouncing from wall to wall, splintering the rail of the lower landing as he went, falling faster and faster until, with a dull body-crushing thud, he hit the quarry tiles of the basement floor. The impact seemed to come up at her, an airborne force like the soul of a violent man escaping from the dead body, eager to be free. Going on up past her in the deathly cold atmosphere until there was only a frightening silence left behind.

She fled downstairs because she was afraid to remain on the upper floors. Sheer terror, not just because of what had almost happened to her but because Rose and Owain were missing. And then she saw Owain, bathed in silver light on the stairway below her, Rose cradled in his arms, a saviour knight in her hour of need.

'Suzie,' he called out, 'are you all right?' And thanking God at the same time that she was moving and walking and appeared to be physically unharmed.

'Owain, Rose!' She rushed to them, stared into the child's upturned face and fought against sobs of relief. 'Oh, thank God you're all right.'

'What happened?' Owain had heard the thud from below, but whatever – whoever – it was it didn't really matter if Suzie was alive and unhurt.

'It was Jack Christopher,' she whispered. 'He finally snapped. But I think he's at peace now.'

CHAPTER SIXTEEN

'He's dead,' George Clements announced as he came back into the room, rubbing his hands together with undisguised glee. 'Head smashed in like a broken egg and neck broken as well. Barely recognizable.'

'Who?' Brenda Clements looked up from where she was kneeling by the crib.

'Jesus Christ his bloody self. He must've fallen down the stairwell.'

She returned her attention to the baby. From where he stood George could hear its wheezing breaths, the rattle and gurgle of phlegm in its tiny lungs. 'George –' Brenda's whisper was vibrant with fear. 'I . . . *I think Elspeth's going to die!*'

He stood there stunned, speechless, ashen-faced, his lips moving but no words coming. He swayed and caught hold of a chair to prevent himself from falling. His head craned forward and at last he said, 'No, it can't be . . . she can't die . . . she's immortal, the Master returned to earth. She's not as other mortals. Immortal.'

'Come and see for yourself.' She leaned back. 'We need a doctor, George.'

'No doctor must tend our child, she does not need it. She will be all right.' Fearfully he advanced, forced himself to look down into the cradle.

The baby's face was purple from the labours of drawing breath. Thick mucus ran from its mouth and nose, bubbling as it breathed. The eyes were open, staring, meeting his own. Seeing and seeming to understand. Of course it understood; this was some kind of test for its chosen foster parents, a trial in which they had to prove themselves. Testing their faith in the Master of Darkness. Eyes that smouldered like those coals in the boiler, burning. *Touch me, father!*

No! George found himself shrinking back but those eyes never left him. A command, touch me! Somehow he stretched out a shaking hand, a visitor to the zoo challenged by a keeper to stroke some repulsive reptile. Go on, it won't hurt you, I promise.

His extended fingers made contact with the flesh. He anticipated the warmth of a fevered infant, sweating in the heat of a high temperature. Instead the flesh was cold, icy; *it might already have been that of a corpse.*

George Clements snatched his hand away but it was impossible to remove his gaze from those eyes. They scorched into his brain, mocked him. *I'm dying, father!*

'What can we do, Mother?' A desperate plea.

'I don't know.' She did not look up. 'We can only keep her warm, and hope.'

'This room is freezing.' He dragged himself away, felt at the old-fashioned radiator. It was warm but, as in Harry's room downstairs, the heat did not seem to be emanating from it. He shivered. Elspeth could not die, not after the way that vision had come true. It was impossible; the Master was just testing them, he told himself yet again. All the same, they were expected to do something. But what?

Outside the wind was getting up, howling across the fields at the back. It did not matter, nothing mattered except this child spawned by Satan in the womb of an unsuspecting mother.

'I know –' A sudden idea, something positive to do if nothing else. 'I will fetch the mother.'

'I am its mother,' came a monotone reply.

'Yes, yes.' He spoke hastily as though he might have offended not just his wife but some invisible power which might be listening in. 'I mean, the girl who bore Elspeth for us. She might know what to do. Perhaps some milk from her breasts . . .'

Brenda did not answer, she might not even have heard.

A choking sound came from the baby, as if it was attempting to throw up its lungs. Then its breathing became fainter and

George hastened for the door. They needed help and Alison would help them, he would make her if she did not come willingly. He ran for the stairs, pulling himself up by the rail. In his mind he saw again the huddled, smashed form of Jack Christopher lying in the basement. Another sign that the Master was destroying his enemies; the followers of Christ, sane or mad, would be eradicated from this temple of darkness. In which case Elspeth would not die but he was expected to do something for her.

Alison Darke-Smith was sleeping when he burst into her room. The light was still burning and he could see her face clearly. The birth had left its mark on her.

'Wake up, girl, quickly!' He shook her roughly, pulled back the sheets and saw that she lay naked in a soaking bed that still bore the stains of childbirth. 'Wake up, damn you!' He clenched a fist, would have struck her had not her eyes suddenly opened.

Alison stared, cringed, pressed herself back into the pillow. Terror flickered in her wide blue eyes as the events of the past few hours started to come back to her.

'Get up, we need you.'

'Go *away*.'

'Stupid bitch! The baby is sick, we need your help.'

'No! I won't go near it. I hate it, I hope it dies.'

'If Elspeth dies –' His panic merged with rage and he grabbed a bare shoulder, sunk his fingernails into the soft flesh and made her gasp with pain – 'then you will die, too. That I promise you. Now, come with me.'

Alison was shaking, would have fallen to the floor as he dragged her from the bed had he not been holding her. The effort had him gasping for breath and brought on a pounding in his chest. She groaned and he saw that there was fresh blood on the insides of her thighs. No matter, this girl was unimportant, it was immaterial what happened to her so long as she saved the baby. He managed to get an arm around her, held her upright.

'I'm ill,' she shrieked as they shuffled down the landing. 'I'm going to die, I know it!'

'Not yet,' he panted, 'not yet. Not until the baby is well.'

He found it easier to slide her down the stairs, holding on to her and pushing, her fleshy buttocks slipping from step to step. He dragged her across the first floor landing, then down the last flight, hauled her upright in the hall, pulling her towards the door which was ajar. Mother was still bent over the crib. 'Here, I've got her.' He pushed Alison forward and bent her over the cradle, resisted the urge to kick those fleshy buttocks which were chafed and already showing signs of bruising. 'Now, *feed the child*!'

Alison stared in horror at the grotesque infant face, tried to squirm away from the handless arm which groped for her. But George was behind her, pressing her downwards.

The girl shuddered as those vile, slippery lips pouted and fastened on to a nipple, began to suck. Oh God, its mouth was freezing, it was pinching her as though intent on hurting her, an infantile assault. She sobbed aloud, the dull ache from her tender womb was spreading out to the rest of her body, a festering fire of hatred within her, the scars of a devil-baby.

That arm came up and poked its hideous malformed stump at her. It was not the touch of a loving offspring, rather malevolent goading prods, each touch an icy blow that pimpled her shaking frame. She tried to tear herself free but its mouth was an unbelievably strong suction pad that held her, pulled at her. Screams that could not escape were choking her, bile scorched her throat.

And at her shoulder were the frenzied faces of George and Brenda Clements, expressions of fevered anxiety, their lips moving soundlessly as if they prayed to some awful deity that the babe might live.

Dreadful realization came in stages to Alison Darke-Smith. The baby was no longer trying to suck, its lips merely a token touch against her sore nipple, colder than before. The deformed limb fell from her, lay motionless on the cot sheet. The eyes dulled, were unseeing. And finally the head dropped back on to the pillow, freeing her. The wheezing chest stopped rising and falling. Silence except for the howling of the gale outside, a mournful lament, a wail of grief from the bowels of hell.

Alison forced herself to stand up and the others did not attempt to stop her. They were staring in shocked disbelief at the still form in the crib, their trembling hands vibrating the cot as they clutched at it.

The girl wanted to run but she had not the strength. The pain in her womb was almost unbearable, a penetrating coldness which she had known only once before, a few hours previously when that shadowy hand had become obscenely tangible and had clawed its way inside her. It was as though that terrible manifestation had returned to exact revenge upon her for her failure in this unholy hour.

She watched transfixed as Brenda Clements lifted the infant, saw how it sagged in her grasp. The woman shook it, pleaded with it in incoherent exhortations; held it upright but the head lolled forward so that she was spared the sight of those malevolent features which still retained an expression of sheer evil.

'*Feed it!*' George grabbed Alison and squeezed a breast.

'It wouldn't do any good.' Suddenly the relief began to well up inside her, a sense of freedom which had her wanting to laugh out loud. 'Nothing will be any good now. *The baby's dead!*'

Vera Brown stood for some moments in the porch, just looking at the white wasteland all around her. Surroundings which had been so familiar for years were now virtually unrecognizable. The laurels lining the drive were gone, an uneven wall of frozen snow burying them, ghostly shapes which might suddenly reach out and take her for their own.

But she wasn't going back. The driveway must be where those footprints led and all she had to do was to follow them. She glanced up at the sky; the moon was now a vague watery shape behind fast scudding clouds. The rising wind moaned, a chilling mournful sound. A warning. Go back, Vera Brown, before it is too late. Return to the house of death and evil.

She had to force herself out into the night with a determination which was threatening to wane. She pulled her coat over the lower half of her face like a whore attempting to escape from some eastern harem and, head down, she fought against the elements which were trying to drive her back.

She could feel the soft powdery snow driving at her, stinging her face as the gale whipped it off the landscape, swirled it and piled it up in any sheltered corner. Drifts being demolished to build new drifts, Nature dissatisfied with her original work.

Vera thought she must be in the lane. It was difficult to be sure because those tracks were gone now, the surface an endless smoothness. Once she stopped, turned her back into the wind and waited to get her breath; go back whilst there is still time. But she was not even sure of the way back.

The moon was gone now. She had only the whiteness of the snow to guide her but it was difficult to see as the minute flakes froze her and half-blinded her, soaked through her clothing.

If only Fred had come with her it would have been all right. Her numbed lips called out for him but if they managed to utter his name aloud it was torn away by the gale.

Sinking in the soft snow, falling headlong and dragging herself up again, she was like a battered ship blown off course. She wasn't in the lane now, she was sure, because there were no steep banks to follow. An unending desert and she was lost.

Despair, and then came the feeling that she was not alone. Twice she stopped and tried to see behind her but there was only snow and more snow. Shapes in the darkness came and went and she felt a presence: *somebody was following her*.

She hoped it was Fred. It had to be because nobody else knew where she had gone. He had come after her to bring her back but she wasn't going back. You'll have to come with me now, Uncle Fred, because we're both lost. And when we find somewhere to stay it will be all right.

Where was he? She tried calling again but it was futile. There was no point in stopping, he would catch up with her soon. Those few minutes of panic were gone because she knew she wasn't alone any more.

Her thoughts flipped crazily. From Mrs Clements to Jack Christopher. And on to Alison. That whore had got what she had been asking for, a bun in her big fat oven.

And I still hope the baby dies because that'll serve 'em all right, Jack and George, and Barbara Withernshaw would be weeping. It's no good coming back to me now, Auntie Barb, because it's too late. If you want a baby, you go and get one yourself.

I want the baby to die. The hope became a burning obsession, and made her oblivious of the cold and the snow. If she had stayed behind she would have killed it, done something to it when nobody was looking. Like tipping its cradle over so that it fell on the floor. Or sticking its head down the loo.

She felt a tug on her sleeve, stopped. Turning round wasn't easy but when eventually she managed it there was nobody there. At least, nobody she could *see*. It was Fred, of course. She tried to convince herself that it was but her conviction did not ring true, no matter how hard she tried. Perhaps it was just the wind.

She stared until her eyes watered and she could not see any longer. A sort of stinging, watery blindness that left her in pitch darkness, the shrieking wind tearing at her clothing as if it was trying to strip her naked. Don't touch me, *please*!

Her coat wafted up, icy fingers delved beneath it, and she clutched at herself in an attempt to keep them out. *A hand, an invisible shadow in the wintry blackness, as cold as death, searching her out again.*

Then it was gone. An indefinable shape, barely human, a black swirl in the darkness. You see me, now you don't.

She turned, a hand from behind touched the nape of her neck, which was impossible because she was muffled in thick clothing. Whirling, giddy with terror, she thew up her arms to ward it off. It stroked her face, brought a scream to her lips but it wasn't there when she struck out at it.

Uncle Fred, stop teasing me, I know it's you. Trying to convince herself that it was only Fred Ainslow playing tricks in his drunken state. But she didn't believe it. All the same it was his fault because if he had accompanied her everything would have been all right.

'Auntie Barb,' she shouted. '*Auntie Barb!*'

The wind took her words, killed them. A bizarre game of blind man's buff, shrinking back every time she felt that freezing touch. Exhaustion and fear were slowing her, she was stumbling, trying to run and floundering in the drifts. Sinking. Now the hand pushed her, a hard shove that flung her full length into the softness of the snow, buried her face. She gasped for breath. It was holding her down, trying to suffocate her, kill her!

Again it drew back, allowed her to struggle up to her knees, waiting. And still waiting.

She was crying, had given up hope, wanted to end it all. I'm sorry, I really am. I didn't want the baby to die. I hope it lives and makes Auntie Barb very happy, really I do.

The wind seemed to drop for a moment, one final swirl and then stillness. Vera glanced fearfully about her; she could not see anything in the blackness but she felt the emptiness, knew that whatever it was had gone. Gone, and left her to die in peace.

CHAPTER SEVENTEEN

Alison had left the Clementses' living quarters in a numbed daze, staggered out into the hallway and instinctively made for the stairs. The pain inside her was just a dull ache and she shook herself like an animal, trying to clear her head. Her brain had reached the terror-barrier, burst through it, and now it was like a kind of anaesthetic; she did not really believe what had happened. Except that the baby was dead and that was a good thing. All the same, she did not want to return to her room.

She walked slowly upstairs, pausing for frequent rests, and tried to determine what she was going to do. Where could she go? As far away as possible from George and Brenda Clements but that didn't leave her a lot of choice. She could not remain on the ground floor since one of them might emerge from that filthy pigsty of a room and make more bizarre demands upon her.

There were two corpses down in the basement so she wasn't going there. A sudden idea – one that had her bare feet moving up the steps more purposefully: when in trouble go to Barbara Withernshaw. Barbara always had some advice to offer. If you didn't like it you didn't have to take it, but at least she might be able to suggest *something*. Christ, she couldn't stop in this place, not with that vile hand likely to appear at any second and . . . she caught her breath . . . she might go and have another baby! There was no way of knowing, and I swear to God that I'm a virgin. At least, I *think* so. Her mind was confused, but she would not have let any man go the whole way. Sure, she had let one or two fondle her during those late night chats with nocturnal callers to her room; George and Harry, and once Jack, but she couldn't be *sure*. She had only allowed them to touch her because she was afraid what they might do if she refused. She had to be a virgin because she had been telling herself – and everybody else – that ever since she had come here and nothing had happened before then. So she had to be right.

She tapped lightly on the door of Barbara Withernshaw's room, waited. No answer. She knocked again, less timidly this time. Knock and wait was Barbara's rule; Alison had once been severely scolded for entering unannounced. Anybody would think that Barbara had something to hide.

But she wasn't answering. Alison glanced up and down the landing then turned the knob and pushed the door open.

The light was on but the bed was undisturbed and there was nobody in the room. An array of suitcases lay by the wall, some closed, others open and spilling out a variety of contents from books to unfolded clothes. It was always like that: Barbara seemed to live out of her luggage rather than unpack everything and put it away in the cupboards. Like she was always thinking of moving on but never had. Certainly the older woman wasn't here; perhaps she had just popped out and would be back in a minute. Yet Alison got the feeling that the other had been gone some time.

She remained in the doorway, afraid to enter in case she was reprimanded for trespassing. Shivering, only now aware of her nakedness, she glanced down at herself, embarrassed, saw the streaks of dried blood on her legs and that started the soreness again. She ought to be resting. But how could she if Barbara wasn't here and she was afraid to return to her own room?

And then she remembered the new people who had come in out of the snow two nights before; the man and that woman and her child. They might help her. He had seemed nice enough during their brief meeting when the baby was born. She thought about going and putting some clothes on but changed her mind. No, she could not return *there*. Anyway, the man would understand. After all he had seen her without anything on when she was giving birth.

She tried to work out which room he was in. It was on the

second floor and had to be either the end one or the one next to it because there weren't any other vacant ones. She padded softly back down the corridor, paused to listen at the door of the furthest room. There was only silence, she sensed the emptiness and her hopes fell. Then, just as she was about to turn away, she caught the sound of low voices coming from the adjoining room. The man's voice, she was sure it was his.

Alison tapped on the door and the talking stopped. A moment or two of silence and then a voice asked, 'Who is it?'

'Me,' she whispered and became aware of how her heart was thudding.

'Who's me?' The tone was impatient, almost a 'go away'.

'Alison.'

Somebody was walking across the room. She almost fled, and then the door opened and she recognized Owain Pugh, hair tousled, dressed but looking as though he had slept in his clothes. They stared at each other and then he said, 'I think you'd better come inside.'

She stood there, hands clasped in front of her, trying to hide her nakedness, staring down at the floor. The dark-haired woman was sitting up in bed and the child was asleep at her side. Suzannah Mitchell looked distraught, and eyed Alison suspiciously.

'You need to see a doctor,' Owain Pugh said, his voice kind, 'but as that it is out of the question at this moment, the next best thing to do is to lie down and rest.' He indicated the makeshift bed on the floor. 'That's the best I can offer you, Alison.'

Gratefully she lowered her body on to the mattress and pulled the sheets up to cover her. That was better; she closed her eyes for a second or two.

'A man has died tonight.' Owain spoke in a low voice, presumably so that he did not wake the sleeping child.

'Jack Christopher,' Alison answered, 'and nobody is going to cry for him.'

'I think you had better tell us your story, the whole story.' He seated himself on a chair and glanced at Suzannah; this girl's nutty so don't get scared, his look said. Take it all with a pinch of salt. 'I think it's high time we got to know exactly what is going on in this place.'

Alison told her story, falteringly, glancing around the room in case that shadow should suddenly appear, white-faced when she came to the episode of the baby and what the Clementses had forced her to do.

'Jesus God!' Owain looked at Suzannah again; she was scared all right and so was he. They had to stop trying to cover everything up with pseudo-logical explanations. Those they would keep for Rose's sake, she must not know. It could do irreparable damage to the young girl. Thank God she was still sleeping. 'I half guessed as much but it was just too incredible. Now that we know what we're up against at least we know what to expect.' And that was small consolation.

'What can we expect?' Suzannah asked.

His voice dropped to a whisper. 'I'm still guessing a lot, making the jigsaw pieces fit, if you like, because I've run out of logic. Alison had a baby; she had no knowledge of having intercourse so two theories were put to her. A Second Coming or the Antichrist in the form of the Clementses' long-dead child. When Harry Clements died his hand shrivelled up, gangrene I thought, but then this shadow appeared and, according to Alison, entered her womb. Whatever the baby was destined to be, it now became a malformed child which the Clementses took away. They realized it was dying and got Alison to try and save it, but it died. The way I see it, the evil left Harry Clements, possessed the baby in Alison's womb and now . . . *there's a restless satanic spirit on the prowl which would well account for what Christopher tried to do to you tonight, Suzie!*'

Suzannah, her face pale, leaned back against the headboard, a protective arm around the sleeping Rose.

'Don't you think you're being a bit fanciful, Owain?' she asked at length. 'I mean, we have to take into account that everybody here is as mad as a hatter.' An almost apologetic glance at Alison; I'm sorry to be so blunt, my dear, but you are quite clearly ninepence for a shilling like everybody else.

'I sensed the evil soon after I arrived here,' Owain continued, 'although I didn't really recognize it as such. A cold damp atmosphere, the smell, the whole bloody environment. And what better place for the devil, speaking metaphorically of course, to breed his spawn? Madness and evil. Too much has happened tonight for us to discount the theory entirely.'

'What are we going to do then?' Suzannah glanced at her watch. 2.30 a.m. Five or six hours of darkness still to go. It was a terrifying thought.

'We can't do much, I'm afraid, except sit it out here.' He listened to the wind outside, conjured up a vision of deep snow being blown off the fields, piling up in the lane, drifting across the main road. It was no different from a blizzard out of the sky; snow was snow when it was blocking every escape route.

'You think . . . we'll be able to get out at daylight?' She had to ask the question even though she was frightened of what his answer might be.

'We're going to have a damned good go,' he replied with as much conviction as he could muster.

In his own mind Owain was piecing together the events of the last few hours; the birth, Jack Christopher's madness and death, the Clementses' attempt to lure Rose into their room. That was the most sinister of all: they needed her for something, and with their deformed baby now dead there was no way of knowing what their next move might be. He wished that he had a weapon of some sort.

George and Brenda Clements sat staring at the dead baby in grief and terror. Grief because within a few hours of having their dead child returned to them from the grave they were bereaved again. Terror because they had failed the Master and they feared retribution, vengeance and punishment.

The tiny corpse was laid on the floor, staring up at the ceiling with dead, sightless eyes, its mouth and nostrils clogged with thick yellow mucus. The watchers waited in vain for a sign of life, a bubbling of the vile matter, perhaps those lungs starting to wheeze again. A sign, any sign. But there was none. The child was dead, just as if it was human and had succumbed to the ravages of pneumonia.

George Clements spoke at last. 'We have to return Elspeth whence she came.' He shifted his position, creaked the chair.

His wife stared at him. She had some difficulty in forming her words, almost as if she had suffered a stroke. Her mouth was slanting and she dribbled. 'We can't put her back in the womb, George,' she lisped.

'Stupid fool!' he rasped. 'I did not mean that. I mean she must be returned to the Master. Perhaps then he will give her life again and send her back to us. I can think of nothing else.'

'How do we return her?' Brenda stirred, seeming to come out of her trance.

'There is only one way,' her husband answered and he was shaking, terribly afraid of the idea which had been born in him; perhaps it was the commanding voice of the Master who had spoken to him. 'She must be given back to the flames, consumed by fire and her spirit returned to hell whence perhaps it will be given a new body.'

'You mean . . . *burn her?*' Surprise but not shock, as if she should have thought of it already.

'Exactly.' He stooped and lifted the corpse up in his arms, cradling it tenderly to his body. 'Ashes to ashes, a cremation of the useless human shell with due reverence. The spirit has gone. Cannot you sense the emptiness in this frail form? A spirit that will wander until it is at peace. Just as it left Harry's body and went in search of our beloved one. A tormented soul in search of another body. First it searched out Vera but found her womb to be empty of a foetus, so it found what it was seeking in Alison. A holy child, if what Jack said was right, so it had to drive out the existing spirit and take it for its own. See, the hand is a scar of battle, the last curse of the Christ Child. But the struggle had taken its toll, sapped the strength of the newborn, and physical life has to begin all over again. Let us beseech the Master to give us back Elspeth as he once promised.'

'You're right.' She stood up, her back bent as though arthritis had crippled her spine. 'Where, George, *where?*'

'The furnace in the boiler room,' he said unhesitatingly. '*Let fire consume this flesh so that Elspeth may yet live again.*'

Barbara Withernshaw had gone in search of Fred Ainslow. The old fool was doubtless kipping in the boiler room; she should have left him in that shack on the railway line at Lampeter since he was quite obviously ungrateful for a comfortable bedroom with everything provided for. She had wasted her money, cast pearls before swine. She needed him to look after Vera whilst she kept an eye on Alison. The girls were in danger, there was no doubt about that. Too long had Barbara tried to bury her head in the sand, turned a blind eye to everything. She ought to have recognized those possessed by evil spirits. Harry was a classic case and she had dismissed him as an eccentric. She had heard Jack Christopher talking to himself in his room, as though he was carrying on a conversation with somebody. Sure, there might actually have been somebody in there with him but she doubted it. There was but a narrow barrier between madness and possession but she had chosen to ignore it. And now it might be too late.

Vera was sulking alone and Alison was sleeping and needed medical attention. She felt sorry for those strangers who had sought shelter here in the height of the blizzard. Pray God they didn't get caught up in all this, especially that child; she was a beautiful girl.

First, she had to talk to Fred. He would undoubtedly be drunk but she had controlled him in that state before. Sometimes he was more reliable drunk than sober.

And it was time he fixed this bloody door! She had to put her full weight against it to scrape it open.

The boiler room was in darkness, just the glow of the fire through the open stove door, enough for her to make out the slumbering form of Fred on the floor, his old coat spread over him. You fucking pig, she thought, and kicked him sharply.

He grunted, stirred, mumbled something unintelligible and clutched his coat even tighter around him.

'Fred, wake up!' Barbara pushed him again with the toe of her moon-boot.

'Whassup? Who the 'ell . . . oh, it's *you*, Babs!'

'It's *Barbara*,' she replied curtly, 'and I want to talk to you, Fred, so get up. God, you stink like a bloody brewery!'

'Just a tot to 'elp me sleep.' He grinned in the half-light. 'Christ, I thought you was Vera come back, 'aving found it bloody colder than she thought out there.'

'Out *where*?' There was a sinking feeling in Barbara's stomach, a sudden fluttering that brought on a feeling of instant nausea.

'Out in the bloody snow, of course. Silly bitch, she'll get lost, freeze to death. I bloody told 'er . . .'

'Oh, my God!' Barbara felt herself starting to panic, 'Whatever are you thinking of, letting her go out there? You stupid bloody fool, she could be dead by now!'

He gaped at her, the smile dying on his lips as stark realization penetrated his drunken daze.

'I'm sorry, Babs, I didn't think she'd go. Are you sure she 'as? She might still be in 'er room.'

'She *might*.' Barbara clutched at a faint hope but knew in her heart that Vera, in one of her sulks, was likely to do just anything. 'I'll go and check straight away. If she isn't there then I'll have to go out into this God-awful night and try and find her.'

'D'you want me to come with you?' he asked fervently hoping that she didn't but he had to offer otherwise she would never forgive him. She probably wouldn't anyway.

'The last thing I want is the added responsibility of looking after *you* in the snow, Fred. Just go back to bloody sleep.' She stalked out, moving as fast as her bulk would allow, striding for the stairs, knowing that Vera Brown would not be in her room. A search was a foregone conclusion; she thought about asking Owain Pugh to come with her but dismissed the idea. The woman and the young girl needed him. It would not be safe to leave them on their own.

177

Fred closed the door after her. In a way it was like shutting himself off from Barbara and Vera. He didn't want to think about them. He groped in the corner, located a battered tomato crate and his trembling hand found the last remaining can inside it. There was only one answer to his current problem; he popped the ring, took a long swig of the fizzy liquid, spilling some of it down his shirt, and belched. That was better.

Christ, she was coming back! He couldn't remember how long Barbara Withernshaw had been gone. It might have been ten minutes or half an hour. His conception of time was hazy during the night hours. Footsteps, and somebody was struggling with the door. A moment of panic as he set the can of beer down, knocking it over, cursing and trying to retrieve it, sending it rolling into a dark corner. Fuck it!

'Well, 'er was in 'er room after all, then?' Barbara must have found Vera otherwise she would not have returned. Unless she had decided that she did want him to accompany her on a search for the missing wench after all.

He squinted. It wasn't Barbara outlined against the basement light. Oh Christ, it was George and bloody Mother! What the bleedin' 'ell did *they* want? And what the bloody 'ell was that George was 'olding? It looked like . . .

'We have to serve the Master.' George Clements spoke in rhetorical tones, a nasal intonation that sent a chill through Fred's sparse body in spite of the heat from the fire. 'Elspeth must be returned to her father and you must help us.'

'Hey, that's a *babby*!' Fred recoiled, almost fell over. 'What's the bleedin' game? It's *dead*!'

'Merely sleeping before it lives again.' Clements held the infant corpse out so that the firelight glinted on its still, almost gargoyle features. 'Poke the fire, make it blaze and let us begin without delay.'

'What . . . what are you goin' to do?' Fred whispered.

'Fool!' George's eyes blazed angrily in the firelight. 'Do you not understand, imbecile? We have to conduct a funeral befitting one who is the Master's own child and who was entrusted to us. *This sacred corpse must be burned, consumed by fire*!'

CHAPTER EIGHTEEN

Barbara Withernshaw sensed an overwhelming futility, the sheer hopelessness of trying to find Vera Brown as she set off into the stinging, driven snow. It came in gusts, vengeful particles from off the fields and hedges, a vicious driving force that had her sheltering in the hood of her duffle coat, turning her head away to draw breath. Her small torch was virtually useless, a dim yellow beam that showed only snow.

The stupid bitch, she cursed to herself, and I must be as crazy as her to come out in this looking for her. Where the hell did she think she was going? Vera, in all probability, had not given it a thought. Of course, simple as she was, it wasn't the girl's doing: *they* had driven her out, a very convenient way of getting rid of her. Suddenly the dark powers which had lurked in the Donnington shadows these past few months were concentrating all their evil energy on the place. A Christ Child that wasn't, and now a devil-baby which would surely not survive unless *they* protected their own in some miraculous way which defied all the logic of freak and deformed babies. It wouldn't live; Barbara could not make up her mind which was the lesser of the two evils, for it to live or to die. Whichever, it boded ill for the rest of them.

She paused to get her breath at the bottom of the drive where it joined the lane – at least she thought it had to be the lane. If Vera had got this far then she must have turned left because the other way was a dead-end about a hundred yards further on. Barbara tried to shout but it was a waste of time, the gale took her words, was aiding the dark forces in their work.

She tried not to blame herself; she could not have left Alison to the perils of childbirth, cast her on the mercy of either Jack Christopher or the Clementses. If Vera wanted to sulk then that was up to her; just as it was her decision to do a Titus Oates on this vile night. I'm going outside, I may be some time. Vera had threatened suicide on more than one occasion, which was why the older woman had taken charge of the sleeping tablets prescribed by Doctor Gidman and administered them when the girl asked for them. But there were numerous other ways of doing away with yourself if you really wanted to. Barbara just restricted the possibilities.

The poor lass. Tears welled up in Barbara's smarting eyes. She had done her best for her, done everything to protect her from the rest of the world. Simple rather than mad, she was a girl who craved affection and men would only have taken advantage of her insatiable sexual desires. Those sensations were probably her only pleasure in life and one could hardly deny her the compulsion of masturbation although recently it had got out of control. But at Donnington it didn't matter. Jack was as bad when the mood took him, a religious fanatic who thought he was Jesus Christ one minute and the next he'd be showing somebody what he'd got.

Barbara permitted herself a wry smile as she recalled that day he had exposed himself to Brenda. God, it had shocked the old dear out of her mind. She'd grabbed a kitchen knife and chased Jack all the way up the stairs to the second floor. He'd shut himself in his room and shoved a chair under the handle. Brenda had hammered on the door for the best part of half an hour and told him in no uncertain terms, and in very colourful language, what she was going to do to him when he came out. Jack hadn't come out, he'd stopped up there for most of the following day until hunger finally drove him down to the dining room. By which time Mother had completely forgotten the episode.

Barbara struggled with a drift, found a way round it. Christ, it was all a waste of time. They'd find Vera when the thaw came. Her favourites were letting her down. Walter Gull had run off just like this, but that had been George and Brenda's fault. There were ways of administering injections other than holding the poor bugger down and treating his arse like a pincushion. Sure, he had to be confined to his room but it need not have been a prison cell. Treated right, shown a little compassion, he would have gone naturally. She should have been firmer, got those needles off them and given the injections herself.

There was only old Fred left now and she feared he would not last long. He was drinking and smoking himself to death and what was left of his body would pack up soon. At least he'd had more sense than to go off into this blizzard with Vera, but that didn't excuse him for not coming and warning Barbara. She was cross with him about that.

All in all, they were a bunch of failures and society had a lot to answer for. An awful lot. She half suspected that it was a deliberate plot by the government, giving everybody a massive intake of harmful food additives, keeping the masses down. Dull their brains, stop them from thinking too much, reduce the population and cut the dole queue. A subversive Nazi régime ready to take over when the time was right, when there were too few left to revolt. They let you harden your arteries with fatty foods, damage your heart, smoke and drink all you want. They could do with the revenue, and fags are a lot easier than machine guns and gas chambers. Which was why nobody would publish Barbara's book. One publisher even claimed to have lost the typescript, another lied and insisted he had never received it. Which was why she had taken a number of photo-copies. They couldn't eradicate it; there was a copy in safe custody in her bank and another with her lawyer. All she needed was an understanding publisher, one with guts. He'd make a fortune out of a bestseller and she wasn't bothered about royalties. All she wanted was to let society know what was going on before it was too late. Maybe it was already too late, and the people weren't bothered because they were all victims of this diabolical plot anyway.

She had to admit to herself that she wasn't going to find Vera. She was probably dead by now. Guiltily, she turned her back on the wind and began to retrace her covered footsteps. Then a nagging worry struck her, relegating Vera Brown to second in her list of priorities. Alison should never have been left, they might be up to their tricks with her!

She tried to hurry, blundered through the drifts, fell several times, but her latest sense of urgency kept her going. Alison needed her because the girl had nobody else. She also needed a doctor but that was out of the question tonight. George and Brenda, or Jack Christopher, might already be interfering with her . . . she tried not to think what those lunatics might be getting up to.

Her frustration built up as she battled with the elements; her torch was a mere dim pinpoint of light, a psychological aid. Without it she would have been at the mercy of the darkness with its eerie white glow. By sheer good fortune, she found the entrance to the Donnington Hotel for a deep snow-drift had built up in the lane beyond, forcing her to turn to her right and she found herself in the mouth of the driveway.

The weighted laurels seemed to scowl at her, would have reached out to impede her progress had not their boughs been weighted down by snow. Run, woman, before we get you! She stumbled round the bend, saw the lights in upstairs windows and prayed that everything was still all right – at least, no worse than it had been when she left and that had to be a good two hours ago.

Vera was dead, she had no illusions about that. The poor kid was frozen stiff by now, the drifts hiding her corpse. The dead were beyond help and Barbara must concentrate on the living. She forced the hall door shut behind her and stood listening. Not a sound, just a faint smell of . . .

Somebody was cooking something, probably that crazy old woman preparing a nocturnal feast. It smelled rancid. Barbara wrinkled her nose. It was vaguely familiar and yet not quite. Like pork in a way, a joint that had been left forgotten in the oven and was burning. Well, that was Brenda's problem. If she chose to serve fatty flesh foods loaded with cholesterol then that was up to her and the fools that ate it.

Barbara pondered a moment or two. Should she check the basement first? No, there wasn't any point. Fred was probably in a drunken stupor and she could not rely on any help from him. Alison was her priority.

The evil was strong and growing stronger by the second. She sensed it as she began to mount the stairs, the penetrating coldness, the atmosphere that was *alive* with invisible demons; watching her, stretching out their icy cold fingers to stroke at her.

She knew that she would find Alison's room empty even before she opened the door. She sensed the loneliness, the despair of a vacated bed seeming to come at her in a cold wave that prickled her skin. She surveyed the lighted interior, the untidy bed with its saturated bloodstained sheets, hollow in the middle where the old mattress had sunk, mocking her. You're too late, I've gone!

She did not go inside, there was no point. Instead, she turned away and began checking on the other rooms, a vain hope but even at the height of despair she had to be systematic. Her own room, Jack Christopher's, Vera's, all empty as though the occupants had left and weren't coming back. An air of finality, a burgled house with its contents gone. You stood there, closed your eyes and tried to convince yourself that when you opened them again everything would be all right. But you knew it wouldn't be.

Where the hell was everybody? Out in the blizzard, dead like Vera Brown? There were precious few places left to check; she wasn't going near George and Brenda – they were the last people she wanted to see now. Maybe Fred Ainslow was missing, too, from his cellar hovel. Just those other two rooms, the newcomers' . . .

She stood outside the door of the last room but one. She saw light coming from inside, heard a low murmur of voices. Barbara took a deep breath, raised a clenched hand and rapped soundly on the woodwork. Mr Pugh had come before when she had sent for him; there was no reason to suppose that he would not help her again.

The voices stopped suddenly, there was a tense silence from inside and then a man's voice called out, inquiring who it was.

'Barbara Withernshaw.' Barbara thought her voice sounded distant, unrecognizable, as though it no longer belonged to her. The door was opened and she saw Owain Pugh framed in the light from within.

'You'd better come inside and join the party,' he said, trying to be light-hearted and making a hash of his façade. He was obviously exhausted.

'Thank you.' She squelched over the threshold in her soaking moon-boots. 'I'm looking for . . . *Alison*!'

Alison Darke-Smith turned a pallid freckled face upwards and pulled the sheets up to her chin. I don't want even you to touch me, Auntie Barbara.

'Oh, the poor girl! What a trauma for her, Mr Pugh. And Vera is missing out in the snow and . . .'

'I think there are one or two things you should know, Mrs Withernshaw,' Owain said, and he told her how Rose was nearly abducted by the Clementses, how Jack Christopher died, what the Clementses had forced Alison to do and that the devil-baby was dead.

'And we are just waiting for daylight,' Owain concluded, 'when we can make a break for it. Rose needs to see a doctor, so does Alison. And I've no doubt that the police will be very interested to hear what's going on here.'

'I doubt the police will be able to do much,' Barbara said. She sat down on a chair, thought about removing her boots and decided against it. 'The evil here is not tangible, you can't lock it in a prison cell. George and Brenda are merely pawns, the madness has spawned something beyond our ken. We should be drawing a pentagon on the floor and all sitting inside it to protect ourselves, but as none of us knows anything about black magic we'd probably make a hash of it and our defences would be useless. So in that case we'll save our energy and just sit here, and hope and pray.'

'Sh!' Owain saw Rose stirring restlessly, raised a finger and sighed his relief aloud when she settled down again and did not waken. 'We've got to spare Rose the truth, for her sanity's sake.'

'All this has been brewing for a long time.' Barbara stared at the floor as she spoke. 'I've felt it, told myself that I was imagining things, that everybody here was mad and that was explanation enough. And now that escalating madness has become a powerful, evil force and we are in deadly peril. I think Jack was killed because, deep down, he was a Christian. *They* had to remove him to be sure. But what they wanted Rose for I daren't imagine.' *Because she's a child virgin? And virgins are powerful sacrifices! Like Vera has been sacrificed to the elements.*

'Four o'clock,' Owain looked at his watch. 'At least three hours of darkness left, four if it's a dark morning.'

'We'll never get out of here on foot,' Barbara whispered. 'I've been out there and I *know*. The snow is blowing off the fields, filling the lane. At this rate the drifts will be ten or twelve feet deep by morning.'

'We're going somehow,' Owain answered. 'If necessary I'll get through alone and bring back help, a helicopter if need be. They're used to helicopter rescues in this part of the world when the snow cuts the outlying villages off and somebody has an emergency.'

'There used to be a small village on down the lane,' the older woman went on, 'but it died. Folks left because there wasn't any work, and the younger generation want the city lights. Houses were put up for sale but there were no buyers. Almost as though the devil himself had chosen this place for his return to earth.'

'Stop being so bloody cheerful.' Owain found himself glancing at the door. He realized how puny that chair was which he had wedged beneath the handle. It might keep the likes of George and Brenda Clements at bay but they were mere frail human puppets in a diabolical plot which defied human logic. 'Have you ever known anything bordering on black magic rites to be practised here?'

'No, I doubt if they know anything about rituals.' She smiled wryly. 'Just evil, playing it by ear, so to speak. I've sensed it, though. This place has given me the creeps for a long time. I've kept my bags packed as I didn't want to be permanent, although I've been here for years. I've had an urge to leave for a long time and I would have done if it hadn't been for Vera and Fred. I couldn't just walk out on them, could I?'

'No, I suppose not.' Deep down, Owain admired this eccentric woman; she was nuts, but in a lovely way. 'I'd feel easier if there were locks on the insides of these doors so that . . .'

He stopped, cut off in mid-sentence by the sharp metallic click that came from the outside of the door, a sound that seemed to echo in the room. They all heard it, knew what it was, stared with frightened eyes at that door with its scratched paintwork. Suzannah opened her mouth to speak, closed it again and left the job to somebody else. Come on, somebody, tell us the awful truth.

'I suppose that's it.' Owain dropped his gaze. He didn't want to look at the others. 'We won't be going anywhere now, not even at daybreak. Because somebody has shot the bolt on the outside and locked us in. *We're prisoners!*'

CHAPTER NINETEEN

'Stoke it,' George Clements ordered, his features a slobbering mask in the glow from the fire. 'Stoke that stove until it burns with a white heat!'

Fred Ainslow backed away, could not take his eyes off that thing which Brenda Clements was clutching to her breast like a stiff plastic doll. A baby, a corpse; this had to be some awful nightmare, it could not possibly be true. They were going to burn the poor little bugger, cremate it! Wake up, for God's sake, wake up! He tried to force himself out of a macabre dream but when George shook him roughly, mouthing something incomprehensible, Fred knew it was real.

'You can't . . .'

'Stoke the fire, I say. And if you don't, God help you!'

The old man moved to obey. He fumbled with the shovel, scraped at the mound of coal, created another avalanche, lumps sliding and rolling. He scooped up a shovelful but most of it fell off and bounced on the floor.

'*Hurry!*'

He was trembling so violently that he could scarcely hold the tool, and, though he managed to get some in through the open stove door, the rest missed. He worked with a zest of fear because he knew only too well that they would do something terrible to him if he failed. Blackening the embers, piling up the fuel, pulling out the damper and sending a thick column of smoke up the ancient flue.

'We'll 'ave to wait for it to burn up.'

'How *long*?' There was a desperate urgency in George's tone.

'Five minutes, p'raps ten. This boiler's old, you shouldn't stoke it right up. It might blow.'

The warning went unheeded. They waited, the old woman

crooning to the dead child, her husband clicking his tongue with impatience, glancing round the boiler room the whole time as if he expected to see some awful monstrosity hiding in the shadows. The fire hissed, there was a glow of deep red, a tiny tongue of flame poked up through the heaped fuel and licked hungrily at it.

Fred leaned on his shovel and thought that he might faint. He would be better sitting down but that might make George Clements angry. He tried not to look at the baby and wished that Barbara might show up; she'd sort 'em out, she always did. She'd stop this bloody nonsense. But there was no sign of Barbara Withernshaw. She had gone out into the snow to try and find Vera. Maybe they were both lost, freezing to death. Fred couldn't stand this much longer. He felt in his pockets, his gnarled fingers locating a nubbed-out cigarette. He needed a smoke badly.

He cupped his shaking hands round the crumpled cigarette, struck a match and drew the tobacco smoke deep down into his lungs, starting off a fit of coughing.

'You can stop that!' It was an hysterical scream from Brenda which penetrated his spasm. 'I won't have smoking in this house. Throw that cigarette on the fire at once!'

He was obeying even before the meaning of her words had sunk into his confused brain, an instinctive response because she had caught him having a sly smoke on more than one occasion. The cigarette hit the smouldering coal in a shower of sparks, dropped out of sight. He glanced up fearfully but the other was bent over, kissing those tiny dead lips. She had already forgotten the episode.

The fire was starting to burn up now, black coals turning to red. Fred stared at them and thought again about this antiquated heating system. If you stoked it too much the pipes clanked and the stove itself glowed red. It could easily explode, like a bomb. He found himself moving away a yard or so, saw how George Clements was studying the fire intently, mentally urging it to burn to a white heat. A funeral pyre awaiting an infant corpse.

The heat was intense, scorching out at them through the

open door, a furnace roaring for more food, its greed insatiable, its square mouth seeming to open still further. *Give me the child, let me eat human flesh.*

'It's ready.' George straightened up and turned back to Brenda. 'Let us make our sacrifice to our Master and beseech him to return Elspeth to us once more. The Christ Child has been destroyed, that may appease him.'

Brenda Clements hugged the still, rigid form to her bosom and hesitated. Her lips moved. The words were not audible but her expression was that of reluctance, a mother refusing to part with her dead baby.

'No ... George, we can't ... not Elspeth ... let us bury her as we did before in the churchyard.' A hoarse plea, a hand raised as though to fend off her husband.

'Are you mad?' His face was contorted with rage as he shambled towards her, arms outstretched. 'The Master will strike you down for such blasphemy. Do you not realize that the child is his as well as ours, that we must return its body to him? And after that we must make yet another sacrifice to appease him.'

She did not reply, merely clung to the baby, wrapping her arms around it.

He grabbed her, forced her hold apart, tore the baby from her arms and held it by an ankle so that its head scraped on the floor. Even as he turned away she flung herself at him with a screech, her broken, dirty nails gouging his fleshy neck, bringing a cry of pain from his lips. He staggered, almost fell, struck out at her but could not dislodge her. Now she had a hold on one of those frail infant arms and was preventing him from throwing the dead body on to the flames. Struggling, cursing each other, both of them incensed by a desperation to do what they believed must be done. George's foot slipped on a piece of coal and he lurched and fell, taking his wife with him, their unholy burden slipping from their grasp.

Fred Ainslow stared aghast at the writhing, grunting, cursing heap of demented humanity on the floor, hypnotized by the bizarre scene; he had forgotten all about flight.

George was in a frenzy. The baby hit the floor with a resounding crack that was surely its skull shattering. He had no need to continue this attack upon Mother, but his fingers encircled her throat and reduced her yells to choking cries of terror. The firelight glinted on her staring eyes, the orbs were surely being squeezed out of their sockets like blackheads being popped. Her booted feet kicked, her clenched fists hammered at him, but he appeared not to notice. Trying to throttle the life out of her, banging her head on the floor as he squeezed. Fred's frightened gaze met her bulging eyes: help me, Fred, he's going to kill me! A moment of conscience, Fred glanced about him. If only Barbara was here, she'd bloody well stop this nonsense. *Help me!* I can't, I daren't, I'm only an old man minding my own business.

Brenda sagged, went limp, and with a curse George released her. He groped for the dead child and dragged it towards him. He lifted it, turned and saw Fred, and a bestial grin touched his lips.

'Either you're with us or against us, Fred,' he said, breathing heavily. 'Which is it, man? Speak up, for the Master is listening.'

Ainslow swallowed, gulped. 'I'm ... with you, Mr Clements.' Because you'll kill me, too, if I say I'm not.

'Good, that's what I like to hear.' The very tone of the other's voice spread an icy chill over Fred's body and, too late he thought of flight again. George held the baby up, thrust it outwards as though it was some kind of offering, or perhaps a raffle prize being handed to the winner. Take it because we're in a hurry and there are more prizes to be drawn.

Fred recoiled, felt the beer in his stomach starting to rise would have turned his head away to throw up if he had been able to drag his eyes from George's. Trembling, he raised his arms to take the corpse, aware of its coldness, its stiffness. So very dead.

'*Commit it to the flames in the name of Satan, the Master.*' George Clements's voice was suddenly calm. He no longer struggled for breath. A vicar conducting a funeral service ashes to ashes, dust to dust. 'And pray that we might be saved when the Master himself returns to earth in human form.'

Fred found himself obeying, an automaton controlled by some invisible force, his very soul rebelling but it mattered not. He turned, was aware of the other close behind him, saw that square of fire, the stove beginning to glow redly. The heat was intense, he felt the sweat beginning to pour from him, smelled his own stale odours. He moved a step, then another, stooped, saw how the coals were stacked up at the rear of the fire-box; the baby would stand almost upright inside it, cremated on its feet.

The fire shifted as if to make a space, ravenous for this offering. He held the child at arm's length, tossed it forward. It hit the fire, tottered, and for one terrible second he thought it was going to overbalance and fall forward. Then it leaned back as though it had found a comfortable position, almost relaxed, arms and legs rigid, standing to attention as it revered the Master in its own way.

Fred tasted something sour in his mouth, spat it out, almost spewed. That baby was watching him, its face a scorching mask of hatred and . . . *pain*, the lips curling as it cursed him for what he had done to it. *Fool, don't you know that I am the Christ Child, corrupted in the womb and now burned to satisfy Man's wickedness?*

Flames licked at it, the flesh began to melt, a giant candle with tallow running and dripping from it, giving off ghastly odours of human cremation. Charring, the white skin turning darker by the second, a multi-racial offering to the gods of old. The mouth chanted its own prayers, the eyes closing. Fred wanted to slam the cast-iron door shut on it, pretend that it had never happened, that such a babe had never been conceived. But he knew he would have to watch until it was all done.

The corpse was disintegrating, shrinking in the intense heat, burned, nearly unrecognizable, stinking, smouldering mass. The stench was overpowering, the rancid roasting odour filling the room, seeping out through the door. Fred coughed, could not control the spasm any longer; bent double, retching, his smarting eyes mercifully sparing him the final collapse of that infant body as a fall of red-hot coals buried it from human view. George was muttering, meaningless incantations that pleaded for mercy and the return of Elspeth.

Fred started. Something was moving on the floor close by. He gave a strangled cry, expected to see a fire-burned infant form wriggling and writhing towards him, begging to be put out of its agony. Instead the shape was much larger, gigantic by comparison, white-haired with wrinkled features, rubber-booted.

'*Mother!*' George Clements whirled and spat at the crawling shape. 'So you still live, you who turned traitor in our darkest hour; you almost brought the wrath and scorn of our Lord and Master upon us. For you there can be no mercy!'

Fred Ainslow cowered. He knew when the other lifted up the bent shovel what he was going to do with it. A ragged blade, as sharp as an axe, raised, held poised.

Fred screamed mutely. His cry would have been futile even had he managed to utter it. The woman's head was uplifted, a victim on the executioner's block, scrawny neck outstretched. Whimpering, but it was too late.

The firelight glinted on the shovel as it descended, a flash of deadly lightning seeking a conductor and finding one. Cutting deep, slicing through aged flesh and shattering brittle bone. The lips parted in a final cry of agony but the vocal chords were already severed. The head jerked, then snapped back, would have gone spinning except for an elasticated sinew that pulled it back. The body shuddered, pitched forward, lay twitching as blood began to fountain.

A cry from George Clements, one that embodied lust and vengeance, hate and sorrow, and then the weapon was swung again. Chopping motions like a workman using a pick on stubborn concrete, chipping and cutting until that last sinew was severed and the head rolled away on the uneven, sloping floor. Somewhere in the shadows it hit that discarded beer can, clinked and lay still.

A silence that might have been the beginning of eternity for Fred, a numbed daze through which he saw George leaning on the shovel, pensive at first, then nodding and smiling. Whatever had happened tonight was meant to be and there could be no recriminations. Those who are not with us are against us. Even Mother.

Finally George cast the shovel aside and turned to Fred, held him by the sleeve of his old coat and thrust his sweating face close.

'I need you now, Fred.' His tone was both commanding and beseeching. 'Our enemies are all around us. Some are dead, others live, but there is much work to be done before the day dawns.'

Fred Ainslow's resistance, if he had ever had any, was long gone. He would do as he was ordered – this man would accept nothing less than total obedience. The penalty for less was death in its most terrible form.

'Good!' George was rubbing his hands together as if he was washing them, lathering them with soap in an effort to remove the coaldust and blood from them. 'Elspeth has been returned to her father in the darkness beyond in the hope that she may be reborn. But the Master desires yet another sacrifice before he is appeased. You remember that young girl that came in out of the snow with her mother . . .'

Fred's stomach again threatened to throw up the remainder of the beer still swilling inside it.

'She is the one,' Clements went on, 'pure and innocent, her blood will be vintage wine to the Master. But it will not be easy because her mother and that man, Pugh, are with her. All in one room –' He smiled – 'which helps. They plan to leave at daybreak but we cannot allow that. They must be kept here at all costs and that is where you can help, Fred.'

'What d'you want me to do?' Fred asked and knew that he would do it, whatever it was.

'Quite simple, even you can do it.' George was already steering the other towards the door. 'Creep silently up on to the second floor landing. They will be in the room which is the second one on the left. There is a bolt on the outside of the door, remaining from the days when this place used to be a nursing home. Shoot that bolt home, and they will not be leaving then!'

Fred Ainslow nodded.

'Just one thing worries me . . .' It was as though George Clements was talking to himself, voicing his innermost fears. 'The shadow, the hand. *Where is it?* It left poor Harry, entered Elspeth who died, and was forced to wander again in search of a body to possess. It is here somewhere, I can feel its presence, but *where?* Has it found that which it seeks? I had hoped, feared, that I might be the chosen one but it has not touched me. It passed me by that time because it wanted the baby, the foetus. If it has already found somebody then there is a disciple of Satan under this very roof more powerful than I. I am just a willing tool and I will serve the Master, but I fear the one who has the shadow!'

Fred nodded again. He did not understand. Another coughing bout as he stepped out in the basement, almost tripping over Jack Christopher's mangled body. Then he made for the stairs and slunk silently up them as he had been bidden to do.

'Oh, my God, what are we going to do now?' Suzannah tried to keep the hysteria out of her voice as she asked what everybody else was thinking.

'I daresay we can break the door down.' Owain Pugh noticed that Rose was stirring and that was bad; if only the poor girl could have slept through all of this. 'But let's not do anything rash right now. Why have we been locked in here? Because we might see or interfere with anything that is going on downstairs. Let's face it, the opposition doesn't amount to much, the Clementses and old Fred.'

'Under normal circumstances we wouldn't have much to worry about,' Barbara Withernshaw said. 'But these aren't normal circumstances. Harry, Jack, Vera, all dead and . . .'

'Mummy, what's happening?' Rose awoke and clung to Suzannah's hand as memories of the past few hours came back to her.

'It's all right, darling, you're quite safe,' Suzannah assured her daughter with more confidence than she felt. 'We're all together, nobody can hurt you.'

'If we can get out of here I'm going to make a sledge,' Owain went on. 'There's bound to be some pieces of timber in those outbuildings at the back, and failing that I'll smash up some furniture – the dining room tables for a start. That way we can get Rose and Alison over the drifts and to a doctor.'

'Jolly good idea,' Barbara said. 'D'you know, when I was in the Girl Guides . . .'

Whatever anecdote she was to relate was cut short by the room being plunged into darkness. The light bulb flickered once, went out. Gasps all round, everybody hoping that it might come back on at any second in the way that the power supply was often restored during strong gales by the authorities responsible immediately switching the current on to another transmitter.

Waiting in silence, their eyesight becoming accustomed to the semi-darkness, the ghostly white gloom of reflected snow from outside the window. Silhouettes became dim features, everybody looked to everybody else. Glad you're here, please don't go away because I need you.

Still waiting but there was not so much as the promise of a flicker from the light. It was dead and it would not be coming back on.

Afraid to speak, fearful of having your worst fears confirmed. Concentrate on trivialities: the crisscross pattern of the window frame on the wall, the shadow of the bedside lamp like the caricature of a static clown whose head was too big for his body; fidgeting with bedsheets, clothing, rustling.

Suddenly Alison Darke-Smith screamed and pointed upwards with a shaking hand, tracing something that shimmered on the ceiling, a shape that did its best to hide in the darkness. 'Look . . . *the hand*!'

They all looked, saw something; something that moved quickly like a bounding rabbit on the edge of a cornfield that knew it had been spotted and sought cover. A glimpse, no more, and then it was lost in the other shadows and might never have been. Except that you knew it had; you sensed a cold and evil presence.

'It was the hand, I know it was.' Alison was sitting upright and the others saw how she shook, felt the hysteria that threatened to swamp her.

'It could have been anything.' Owain tried to sound calm, unconcerned. 'The gale blowing a branch outside the window, casting a brief shadow.' I'm lying, lying for Rose's sake most of all, the poor kid can't take any more tonight. We'll have to smash our way out of here, we can't wait for daybreak.

Another scream, deafeningly loud. Everybody started, cowered, clutched at the person nearest to them. You recognized it but for a split second could not think who it was.

Until Barbara Withernshaw fell backwards from her chair, convulsing, writhing, grappling with an invisible attacker, her choking cries dying to a wheeze. And then there was only shocked silence again.

CHAPTER TWENTY

The building was shaking, shuddering as though below its foundations the tremors of a mighty earthquake were beginning. Floors vibrated, window frames rattled and threatened to shatter their glass panes. A living force within a frail body of bricks and mortar, a house of cards that might come tumbling down at any second.

'What did I tell yer?' There was terror on Fred Ainslow's face. 'The central heating can't take it and neither can the old boiler. The whole bloody place'll go up!'

'If it does then it is the wish of the Master.' George Clements seemed undeterred by the vibrations. They were back in the dowdy living quarters which he had shared for years with Mother, bless her. It wasn't her fault what had happened, the enemy had got to her and once that happened there was only one solution. Fortunately he had had the courage to do what was necessary.

The clock on the mantelshelf said 4.40, give or take ten minutes either way. It usually wasn't far out. But the night was slipping away and there was another vital task to be done if total disaster was not to befall them.

'You did well, Fred, very well,' he said.

The other grinned feebly, responded to the compliment in spite of its sinister implications.

'I did me best, bolted the buggers in, good and proper. They won't get out o' there. These doors are old but they're strong. They don't make doors like that today. I'll tell you because that new door I 'ad to put on the linen room, the one you ordered last summer, it's what they call an interior door, bloody 'ollow in the middle. Not them upstairs, they . . .'

'Quite, quite.' George was becoming impatient again. 'But I've another job for you, Fred.'

'Oh?' The old man had that sinking feeling in his stomach once more. 'Well, you'll 'ave to find me a torch 'cause all the lights 'ave gone out. Bloody queer, just after I'd bolted the door and was on me way back downstairs . . .'

'I turned off the master switch – ' A declaration rather than a confession. 'They're better in the dark. Demoralizes 'em if they're thinking of any escaping antics. And besides –' A leer, his face thrust close to Fred's – 'darkness is our friend, Fred. We are the servants of darkness.'

'What 'ave I got to do?'

'It's quite simple, really. You enjoy a smoke, don't you?'

'I got the 'abit,' Fred Ainslow was wary. Mother had always gone barmy if she even smelled nicotine on his breath and her husband backed her up. Was this some kind of trick question?

'Well you can have a smoke with my blessing, and I'm sure that on this occasion Mother, wherever she is, will give you hers.' Glib, watching the other from beneath half-closed eyes. 'But first there's work to be done. In the hall cupboard you'll find a stack of old newspapers, those you use to light the boiler in the mornings. Take a good pile up to the second floor landing and crumple them up into a heap. Then pile up any furniture you can find, chairs, bedclothes from out of the empty rooms. You get me?'

'You mean . . . *build a bloody bonfire on the landing*?'

'You've got the idea, Fred. Then, when that's done, you can have a smoke, and maybe you're getting a little careless so that you throw your lightened match away . . .'

'Hey!' Fred started to shake again and the lighted candle standing in the middle of the table became a blur. 'You . . . you're askin' me to commit *murder*!'

'Not murder, *sacrifice*, Fred. You don't understand, let me explain. Elspeth was committed to the flames so that she might be returned to her father, the Master. Now the Master demands another sacrifice, preferably a young virgin. We have the girl here but securing her is a problem. You have done excellent work in imprisoning her and her guardians in one room, but there is no way we can segregate our sacrificial victim so . . .' He drew himself up to his full height. *'We can still sacrifice her by fire and, as an added bonus, the others with her. Do you understand?'*

Fred Ainslow understood, only too well. He was trembling in every limb but he managed to nod, knew he would do as the other asked because for some terrible, inexplicable reason he was powerless to refuse. He could have left this room, gone straight out through the front door, like Vera and Barbara had done, but even then he could not escape. Because it was as though invisible beings monitored his every moment; he felt them, shadows that followed him, herded him, would do unspeakable things — far worse than death — to him if he tried to run out on George. They had got him just where they wanted him, whoever they were, and now this mythical Master was no longer a figment of George's imagination. Some terrible power had killed Harry and Jack, sent Vera and Babs out to their deaths. There was strong evil here and he was caught up in it. He would do their bidding, whatever.

'I get you,' he mumbled, turning away.

'You will be well rewarded,' George whispered after him, 'if not in this life then in the everlasting one when you will meet Satan face to face. But beware, the shadow is still not accounted for. It is on our side but it is dangerous . . . it may have plans of its own!'

Fred picked up the rubber torch off the chair by the door, and tested its beam in the darkened hallway. George was talking in riddles but he gave you the creeps more than if you understood. It was perhaps best not to understand.

Owain was stooped over Barbara Withernshaw, a sense of inadequacy and helplessness as he shone his waning torch on her, saw the whiteness of her face, the way her body sprawled limply on the floor. Alison was on his right cowering, would perhaps have fled if there had been anywhere to run to; as it was, she was trapped in the corner, trying to tug the bedclothes over her.

Suzannah was attempting to comfort Rose, murmuring

something to the shaking girl. Oh God, Owain thought, this is all I need! The older woman might be dead, or at the very best in a coma, a heart attack or a stroke brought on by the shock of that shadow that nobody had really seen, a flitting shape that might have been anything. What the hell do I do? I'm doctor and undertaker all rolled into one. He tried to think; massage her heart? Give her the kiss of life?

'She's dead!' Alison wailed, a near-hysterical shriek.

'Shut up,' he muttered. 'Keep quiet and let me have a look at her.'

The girl lapsed into silence. He could hear Rose sobbing softly, poor kid. His fingers struggled with the toggles of the sodden duffle coat, managed to undo the top three, and then he was faced with a thick hand-knitted, roll-neck sweater. He couldn't get it up over her head so he would have to pull it up from the bottom. Jesus, a thick woollen vest was underneath; he felt the softness of her huge breasts as they lolled in an oversize bra, smoothing up rolls of surplus fat like gentle waves rippling the shore line. Ebb and flow, they ran beneath his fingers, and somewhere under all this lot was a damned unhealthy heart, no matter how much she preached against the evils of cholesterol.

He was almost sure she was dead, was on the point of asking Suzannah for her handbag mirror, when Barbara groaned, a sound that seemed to come from the depths of her huge body and vibrated his fingers as they still searched for where her heart was supposed to be. Shock, relief, he started, snatching his hand away, a guilty adulterous lover surprised by a jealous husband. An expellation of breath, and he directed the torch on to Barbara's face, saw the eyes open slowly, bewilderment and then fear flickering in them.

At least she was alive. He watched her intently. A slow return to consciousness, trying to say something, resting, trying again.

'It's all right.' It was all he could think of, even if everything wasn't all right. 'You just fainted.' A shrewd guess as she seemed unharmed, and he was certain now that it wasn't anything serious.

'*The hand* . . .' Her eyes rolled and, she turned her head as if searching the shadows in the room, expecting to see that macabre shape crouched in a corner like a huge bloated spider. 'It . . . touched me. So . . . *cold*.'

'Our nerves are getting the better of all of us,' he said, and that was certainly true. 'If it was this damned hand then it isn't here any more.' He swung the ailing torchbeam in a full circle and brought it back to focus on Barbara. 'See? There's nothing there.'

With an effort she sat up and pushed his restraining hand away. 'It's all right, Owain, you don't have to mollycoddle me. I'm not going to be a passenger in all this. That hand touched me . . . here.' She felt at her neck, winced at the memory. 'Just a touch, nothing more. Let's hope that I wasn't the one it was looking for.'

'Obviously not.' We all have to be optimistic, he thought. 'But you need to rest for a while.'

'Only for a minute.' She smiled weakly. 'We don't have time to hang about. Now, do you think you can break that door down, Owain?'

He stood up and went around the room in search of something which would serve as a battering ram. There was just the dressing table, an oak, high-backed piece of furniture on castors, the upright mirror like a sail on an ungainly ship. He studied it, stroking his chin; it was short and chunky, too high really, but the castors would help him to get a run at the door. Primitive, makeshift, but it would have to do.

'I'm going to give it a go with this.' He handed the torch to Barbara. 'Just shine the light so that I can see what I'm doing.'

Owain struggled to manoeuvre the piece of furniture away from the wall, manhandled it across to the opposite side of the room, crouched behind it and tested its mobility. Unwieldy, like one of those large trolley baskets one used at supermarkets to wheel one's purchases out to the car park; you had difficulty in keeping it on course, were afraid of scratching somebody else's car on the way to your own. It did not move easily, it would need all his strength behind it.

'Right,' he addressed nobody in particular. 'I'm going to have a go. Stand by – whatever happens there's going to be a God almighty crash.'

He took the strain and, using the wall behind him as a springboard, he pushed himself off. There was a rumbling sound as the wheels rolled, and gathered momentum. He was using every ounce of strength he could muster, going forward and bracing himself for the impact. Any second now! It seemed an eternity, like he was pushing this thing twenty yards instead of four, gathering force like a Viking assault on the gates of a besieged castle. Then came the shuddering contact, a splintering and tearing of woodwork, and he fell back as though he had been struck a blow which banged every bone in his body. A rendering noise, glass breaking and tinkling on the floor. He tried to see the effects of his attack upon the door.

A small circle of yellowing torchlight told him all he needed to know. The dressing table was at right angles, one of its uprights snapped in two, drawers open and smelling strongly of mothballs. A jagged silvery scar where the mirror had been, shards of grass glinting in the light, mocking him. He stared, felt his hopes falling, let them go. Oh Christ, the door was intact, little the worse for wear, but the dressing table sagged where a castor had snapped off, rendering it useless for a second attempt. It had splintered, broken woodwork and a smashed mirror: a Mini trying to ram a juggernaut and the driver was lucky to escape with just bruising.

He walked forward and surveyed the damage. 'Well, I guess that's that.' He scraped some of the glass towards the skirting board with the side of his shoe. 'If anybody has got any other ideas, please speak up.' Or else bloody well shut up. 'The most we've got out of that is seven years' bad luck.' It was meant to sound funny, but it didn't.

'Listen! What's that?' Barbara Withernshaw was on her feet, an arm raised for silence.

Owain tried to listen; all he could hear at first was a roaring in his ears, his chest pounding after the exertion. The floor seemed to quiver, an unpleasant sensation which began with the soles of your feet and travelled right the way up your body. Juddering you, like standing on a pavement close to a workman who was using a pneumatic drill. A rumbling and clanking, it might have been vibrations echoing and re-echoing inside his brain.

'Can't you hear it?' Barbara shouted at him. 'It's like the . . . the start of an earthquake!'

'Don't be bloody silly!' He had to play this down, for in the reflected glow of the torch he saw the white, terrified features of the other three. 'It might even be the missing snowplough come right up to the front door.'

And that was a bloody silly thing to say, too.

'I know what it is!' Barbara had recognized the noise and the way the old radiator was shuddering and clanking, had heard it once before in this very house, some years ago. 'The boiler's been overloaded. It happened a few years back and we all thought the whole place was going to blow up. I'll bet my bottom dollar that's what's happening now. That silly bloody fool Fred is to blame. We have to get out of here, Mr Pugh, and fast. This house is like a bomb!'

'Okay, *you* work something out.' Owain leaned back against the wall and, folded his arms. 'Maybe if you didn't spend so much time yakking you'd have a few ideas.'

'You're bloody rude!' She turned on him, brandishing the torch like a club. 'You're the most self-centred man I've ever met. You're conceited, too. And just because you've let us all down it's no good trying to push the blame on to me.'

'I think you're being very unfair, Mrs Withernshaw.' Suzannah spoke angrily as she held her daughter to her. 'Mr Pugh has been absolutely marvellous. The door was stronger than the dressing table and that isn't his fault. And he's right, you talk too much.'

'Very well, I shan't have anything else to say.' She sat down on the bed and held the torch out to Owain.

And that was when they heard the noise immediately outside the room, a rustling and scraping, somebody moving about.

Owain smelled cigarette smoke, heard whoever it was outside dragging something heavy down the landing, pausing. A fit of coughing. It died away and the dragging noise commenced again, finished up against the outside of the bedroom door with a soft thud. More rustling. He identified the sound: newspapers being crumpled, unfurling themselves. The cigarette smoke was really strong now.

'It's Fred,' Barbara forgot her vow, whispered in a puzzled and frightened tone. 'Whatever can he be up to?'

'Well, ask him,' Owain replied. 'I thought he was a buddy of yours. Perhaps he'll tell you.'

She stood up and went to the door.

'Fred?' She raised her voice to a hoarse shout. 'Fred, is that you?'

There was no reply, the shuffling to and fro, the movement of heavy items across the floor, the rustlings of paper ceased. Silence; whoever it was might have gone except for the smoke from his cigarettes seeping under the door.

'Fred, I know you're there. Come on, what are you up to?'

The coughing began again, a paroxysm that reached a retching peak and then died slowly away to laboured breathing, as though the other was an asthma sufferer.

'Fred, will you stop being a silly bugger and tell me what the bloody hell is going on out there? Be fair, Fred, haven't I paid your keep all this time when, but for me, you might still be sleeping rough in that shack up at Lampeter? Think what I've done for you. You might even be *dead* by now. Come on, I demand to know what you're doing!'

'Please don't ask me that, Babs.' A cringing whine. Owain imagined the old man's face, tortured by anguish, afraid of the woman who had dominated his life these past few years, and bullied him for his own good.

'I *am* asking you, Fred. Enough of this nonsese, just you tell me or I'm going to be very angry with you. I'll take every penny of your pension off you and I'll see to it that you don't have a drink or a smoke from now onwards.'

'It ain't my fault Babs. I couldn't 'elp it. Mr Clements

made me do it. 'E made me burn the baby and then 'e chopped Mother's 'ead off!'

Good God almighty! Barbara clutched at Owain for support. Not for one second did she doubt the truth of what Fred Ainslow was saying. He was a bloody old liar at times but he didn't have to lie now. She sensed also that she was able to dominate him again even though there was a bolted door between them.

'They could put you away for a very long time for that, Fred,' she said. Take a firm but sympathetic line with him; it always worked. 'But I won't tell the police if you will cooperate with me. Now, for the very last time, just what *are* you doing? Come on, I want an answer or else I'll see to it that you'll be in *very* big trouble.'

'I'm makin' a bonfire, Babs, like George said. Paper and furniture, and then I'm going to set fire to it.'

Owain caught his breath, felt the others in the room shrink back in horror. Except Barbara. Suddenly she was in command again and that moment of sheer terror was virtually forgotten. This was a real and terrible danger, not some partly visible shadow that they thought they might have seen.

'That's a very silly thing to do, Fred. If George told you to put your finger in the stove I suppose you'd do it.'

'I'd 'ave to, the way 'e is now Babs. 'E's a devil and 'e's been in touch with the devil, too. That's why I 'ad to burn the baby and Mother got 'er 'ead cut off 'cause 'er tried to stop 'im. You see what I mean Babs?'

'Vaguely.' She was trembling violently, now more with rage than fear. 'But that doesn't explain why you have to burn all of us too, Fred.'

'Because . . .' He hesitated, his shaky voice now so low that those inside the room could barely hear it, as though he was having to search his memory in an effort to remember why he had to burn them. 'Because of the little girl, that's why. 'E says that we 'ave to make another sacrifice if the babby is to come again, and it 'as to be the girl. And 'e reckons that it'll be a bonus if you lot are fried as well.'

'Charming!' Barbara Withernshaw was tight-lipped. She sensed the urgency for getting out of this room but it had to be played right. She had cast her bait, the old man was hooked, but he still had to be landed. 'And do you realize that you've overloaded the boiler and it might explode at any minute, taking us all up with it, you included?'

They could hear the water boiling in the central heating pipes, expanding the old lead, taking the strain – but only just. Something clanked and rattled, set off another tremor of vibrations.

''E made me stoke it up, Barb, said it 'ad to glow white.'

'He's mad –' Like everybody else in this goddamned place. 'There's only once chance for you, Fred. *Open this door and let us out!*'

A few seconds of silence. Rose was crying softly and Alison Darke-Smith was hidden under the bedclothes on the floor.

'Fred, this is your last chance, open this door. Or else I'm going to report you to the police and I'll see to it that you don't have another fag or another can of beer. Ever. Come on, open up!'

Shuffling footsteps that crinkled rumpled newspapers, a frail hand scratching on the woodwork of the door. An intake of breath and a grunt as Fred wrestled with the stiff bolt. Then it shot back and in that same instant Barbara had grabbed the handle and pulled the door open before their senile gaoler could undergo a change of mind.

'Thank God!' Owain staggered out into the gloom of the darkened corridor, tried not to see the scattering of papers, the pile of chairs and the broken coffee table which normally resided beneath the window at the other end. All he saw was an old man in a frayed overcoat, an effigy that had come in off the fields for warmth, a mindless being that stared in blank amazement around him.

'Well, at least we're out.' He hung back, waiting for Suzannah who appeared in the doorway, her arm around Rose, Alison, a blanket over her shoulders, trailing behind her. 'Now, let's get outside as fast as we can.'

The entire house seemed to be shaking under the strain of the old boiler, the floorboards quivering under their feet.

'Hold on –,' Barbara Withernshaw caught at his arm. 'We'd better check on George first.'

'Damn George, we . . .'

'He's evil and dangerous.' Her voice was a whisper, her lips pressed close to his ear. 'He may have some other fiendish trick up his sleeve. Fred could be all part of a decoy plan.'

'You're crazy. You check on George if you want to but I'm getting these girls out of here this very minute.'

For a moment fury clouded her shadowy face and then she nodded. 'All right, have it your own way and . . .'

Suddenly Fred Ainslow seemed to stiffen, an arching of his stooped back, stretching up on his heels and falling back against the wall, holding his balance for perhaps a second, then slowly crumpling, folding, slumping down to the floor. The coat fell open, revealed the thin figure clad only in a holed vest and ragged long pants, the upturned face a white mask with mottled stubble and blackheads, lips struggling to move.

Barbara dropped to her knees, slid an arm under him and glanced up at Owain and said, 'This has all been too much for him, poor bugger.'

'You don't understand –' Cracked undertones, but for all Fred Ainslow's ramblings Owain recognized a flash of lucidity. More than that, a warning which the old man was fighting against time to get out. *'The 'and, it's gotta be around . . . George says that it's . . . the 'and of Satan and . . . and the evil will carry on . . .'*

Fred Ainslow's words trailed off. His eyes glazed over, and his head fell slowly forward. Barbara remained on her knees beside him.

But Owain was not waiting. He took Suzannah's and Rose's hands, checked that Alison was following, and began to descend the stairs. If Barbara Withernshaw chose to stay then that was entirely up to her.

CHAPTER TWENTY-ONE

The hallway was deserted when they reached the ground floor, an elongated tomb where their footsteps echoed, the walls a spectral white from the reflection of the snow through the skylight over the front door. A door that seemed to beckon them, taunt them: come on, death by fire within, death from the snowdrifts outside. Take your choice, either way you die.

The boiler was louder now, like some demon in the vaults immediately beneath their feet, a monster that pulsed with demoniac fury, trying to lift up the floor to get to them; heaving and pushing, creating its own background symphony with a rattling of crocks and cutlery in the filthy kitchen behind them.

They felt the evil stronger than ever now, a living force coming at them, a macabre game of cat and mouse. Run for the door but you won't make it. An invisible barrier, relenting then closing in again. And outside they could hear the wind shrieking at them, knew that it was piling up drift after drift as it sought to aid the dark forces in the Donnington Country House Hotel.

Owain experienced a helplessness again, almost a surrender. Forcibly he dispelled it because of Suzannah and Rose. And Alison. He had to battle for their sakes.

It seemed to take him an eternity to reach the front door, aware that the other three were at his heels; he experienced an urge to turn and tell them to go back because he did not want them to see what was out there. He grasped the old doorknob, closed his eyes for a second . . . I don't want to see, either. Christ, my nerves are shot!

The wind was pushing at the outside, gathering like an invisible battering ram. He sensed its power, braced himself, and it was all that he could do to stop the door slamming back against the wall. Hanging on to it, feeling the light feathery snow gusting in, a white hurricane that spilled its contents en route. A wail of triumph from the elements because it had burst through the door at last, wedging snow against the jamb to stop it from being slammed. Shrieking inside, fluttering a lace cloth off the hallstand, floating it towards the stairs.

'Oh, God!' Suzannah saw and clutched Rose to her, turned away because she did not want to see any more. Alison stared in shocked silence, perhaps did not fully understand.

Owain struggled to force the door shut, kicked at some of the fallen snow with his foot, managed to close it but the latch would not click. He pushed the bolt across, brute force, but it went and held, leaving a gap below through which more snow found an entrance and took a diagonal line across the floor. He closed his eyes again, was afraid to face Suzannah because he had run out of hope. They wouldn't be going anywhere, not even out into the snow. His temples were pounding in time with the thumping of the nearest radiator. They had no choice but to stay here and be blown up in a fiery explosion.

She did not ask what they were going to do now because she knew only too well that there was nothing they could do. He thanked her silently for not putting the responsibility on to himself. I love you, Suzie, and I wish I had the guts to tell you before we all die.

Finally he turned to face her, saw that she smiled weakly. She said, 'I suppose that's it, isn't it? No more escape plans.'

He nodded, saw Barbara Withernshaw disappearing down the basement steps. What she hoped to find down there he had no idea, didn't care. She seemed in an awful hurry, her obese figure moving amazingly swiftly.

He said, 'Let's go through into the kitchen. Perhaps we can make a cup of tea. At least we're assured of hot water!'

There was a candle well burned down in the centre of the large pine table, its flame flickering in the draught as the door opened, an odour of burned tallow greeting them. Perhaps George Clements had been sheltering in here. He hoped he would not return.

'Well, let's see . . .' He looked around and saw the kettle steaming on the hob. 'Kettle's boiling, we'll have a cuppa in about a minute flat.'

'What about the boiler?' Suzannah asked.

'It'll probably cool off.' The least he could do was to show optimism. 'These old boilers are pretty resilient. Over the years they've been overloaded scores of times.' Until finally they can't take the strain. He poured water on to some teabags in the pot and tried to shut out the howling of the wind and the clanking of the hot water pipes.

'What's that, Mummy?' Rose whispered, gripping Suzannah's arm.

'What, darling?'

They all found themselves listening. A noise: it sounded like a human voice, a shout of anger or fear – it was difficult to tell which – from somewhere below. Owain moved, picked up the heavy poker and held it tightly.

'Perhaps it's Barbara,' Owain said. It couldn't be anybody except her or George Clements because there was nobody else left alive. Or Vera, missing and presumed dead. Perhaps she had found her way back out of the snow. No, nobody would return alive out of a blizzard like that.

He poured some tea into mugs, listening all the time. An extra cup for Barbara if she joined them. Damn her, if she chose to do her own thing at a time like this then that was up to her.

Alison had sunk down on to a chair and appeared to be asleep, exhaustion and pain having taken its toll on her. She ought to be lying down, Owain thought. Perhaps he could find a couch somewhere and bring it in here. At all costs they had to stay together. What little safety remained, if any, was to be found in numbers.

'Somebody's coming.' Rose shrank against her mother, eyes wide with fear and fixed on the doorway.

The others heard the footsteps, soft, padding ones, and knew that it was Barbara even before the door opened. She closed the door behind her and leaned up against it as if she was barring it against a pursuer.

'It's George,' she said at last.

That icy chill prickled Owain Pugh once again, mingled with fear and revulsion.

'Dead?'

'No.' She looked at him steadily. 'But Fred was right: Brenda is. George cut her head off down in the boiler room. He . . .'

'All right, don't give us the gory details.' Owain said. 'There's a mug of tea there for you.'

'And can I use it!' Barbara stepped forward, lifted the mug and slurped the hot tea noisily. 'It's a damned good job for all of us that I went to look for George. That hand, you know, the shadow that touched me upstairs? Well, it found what it was looking for, all right . . . *George Clements!* *He's* the possessed one now and no mistake. I found him down there with . . well, you know what I found him with and the bugger nearly had me. Fortunately I was too quick for him. Too strong as well.' A pause. There was no mistaking the note of personal pride in her voice. 'I wrested the shovel off him and got the better of him. I couldn't leave him walking about the place, now could I?'

'What . . . what have you done with him?' Owain asked, and wished for Rose's sake that he hadn't.

'I've locked him in Harry's room.' She smiled. 'It was the best thing to do. There's a good strong bolt on the outside of the door because they often used to lock poor old Harry in, sometimes for days at a time. He had epileptic fits, you know. Well, George is in there now, keeping his brother's corpse company. At least he can't go anywhere and as long as he doesn't die we're all right, because if he dies that bloody spirit will go in the search for somebody else.'

'I see.' Owain took a gulp of tea. He didn't really understand but suffice it that George Clements was locked up where he couldn't harm anybody else.

'I've also pulled the damper down on the boiler,' Barbara continued. 'With luck it'll quieten down before long. Christ, they'd stoked it to capacity.'

'So you reckon we're safe?' Owain said at length.

'For the moment,' she replied. 'Anybody who could hav[e] harmed us is out of the way and if the boiler doesn't explode and I don't think it will, then we've just got the snow t[o] contend with.'

'Which doesn't alter our priorities: a doctor for Rose an[d] Alison. One way or another we've got to get out of her[e] Barbara. Once it's daylight we'll see what can be done.'

'You'd never get through those drifts,' she said. 'They'r[e] horrendous. They'd find you when the thaw comes, alon[g] with Vera. And it was only by the grace of God I didn't peris[h] out there as well.'

He sensed an easing of the tension; it had been a traumati[c] night but hopefully all those dangerous nutters were accounte[d] for. His eyes roved the room, spotted chairs and a workin[g] surface top that was loose, a toolbox on the shelf above it.

'I still reckon we could make it on a sledge,' he mused. A[t] least it would give him something to do, ease his frustratio[n] whilst he built it. Basic woodwork, nothing fancy, a few piece[s] of wood and some nails.

'You're crazy,' she said, 'but carry on if it makes you happy[.] But this kitchen isn't exactly comfortable, it it?'

'Meaning?' Owain's eyes narrowed.

'George and Brenda's room is much more comfortable, it['s] just as warm as in here, and there's a bed.'

'*No!*' Rose shrieked. 'Mummy, I don't want to go in *ther[e]* again!'

'Nor you shan't,' said Suzannah protectively. She flashe[d] an indignant glance at Barbara. 'Use your brains. Rose isn['t] going in there after . . .'

'All right, all right, forget I suggested it.' The other turne[d] away. 'In which case I'll leave you to it. You can make you[r] sledges and go to sleep on upright chairs, do just what yo[u] bloody well please!' She walked through into the hall an[d] slammed the door shut behind her.

'Well, it doesn't take much to offend Barbara.' Owain trie[d] to laugh. 'It's almost as though she's changed her mind an[d] ants to stay here now.' Which, on reflection, was a disturbing thought. Possibly she was unwilling to leave because Vera was lying out there somewhere, felt guilty about abandoning her even if she was dead. And Fred Ainslow, too. But it was the living who needed help, Rose and Alison most of all.

The making of the sledge was not as simple as Owain had at first supposed. Working by candlelight, all he had at his disposal in the way of tools was a hammer, a pair of pliers and an assortment of nails, most of them rusty and second-hand. The chairs were pre-war, utility but made of hard strong wood, and the nails did not penetrate easily.

After some searching he found an old hacksaw and began the laborious process of cutting a length off the loose piece of hardtop. It wasn't easy: the handle jammed in the sawn slit and he had to keep prising it apart. Any minute the blade could break and that would be that.

Miraculously the blade did not snap and sometime later he held up a rather unevenly cut square of wood, topped with formica, and began to nail runners made from chair backs on to it. Surely there was a piece of rope lying around somewhere, but he would search for that later.

'One appreciates how prisoners of war got their kicks out of improvisation.' He paused for some more tea and was aware for the first time that he was sweating.

'How are you going to pull it?' Suzannah was not happy at the idea of her daughter being dragged over the snowdrifts on that.

'I'll wade through the snow,' he replied, 'She'll be quite safe on it. Somehow or other I'll get through.'

'Wouldn't it be easier just to go for help?' There was a hint of sarcasm in her voice which she instantly regretted.

'Maybe and maybe not. That sledge will take both Alison and Rose, they can help to hold each other on. They'll be at the doctor's hours before any rescue attempt gets through here.'

'I'm coming with you,' she said. 'Christ you don't think I'm stopping here on my own, do you?'

'All right. Now, I'm going to take this out to the back door and see if I can find a length of rope somewhere. I won't be many minutes.'

He carried the unwieldy homemade sledge out through the door into the hallway and down the passage towards the rear door, his torch giving him as much light as he needed. At least the wind wasn't battering the back door, and that was a small bonus.

Owain noticed a small cupboard on his left, stopped and opened the door. A dark recess that contained all kinds of jumble, broken vegetable boxes for use as kindling wood, flattened cardboard cartons, empty jars and ... his fingers closed over a piece of nylon rope, pulled and it began to unravel.

'*Eureka!*' he spoke his triumph aloud. 'Just what the doctor ordered, all four feet of it!'

He tied the rope on to the front of the sledge and propped it up against the door. A sense of purpose had rekindled his flagging enthusiasm. At least there was hope again.

He went back to the kitchen. From down in the basement he thought he heard a faint pounding noise, like feeble fists banging on a stout door, accompanied by muffled curses. He tried to push it out of his mind.

'Well, I even found some rope and we're all set to go,' he announced.

Rose was asleep against Suzannah's shoulder and Alison appeared to be sleeping too. Just the two of them awake, himself and Suzannah. Oh, Christ, in some ways I wish we didn't have to go.

'We must fix up a date for you to come and look at my books,' he said, unable to look at her.

'I'd like that.' She sounded as though she genuinely would. 'I must admit life gets a bit boring these days. Apart from the last couple of days, that is.' She smiled wanly. 'I've been in a sort of vacuum ever since my husband left, like being dead in a way. If it hadn't been for Rose I don't think I could have kept going, Owain.'

'Maybe things will change for you from now on.' He looked up and their eyes met suddenly and he noticed a sparkle which had been absent up until now. 'You know, things go from bad to worse and then when you hit the bottom there's only one way to go and that's up.'

'I hope so.' She seemed to blush slightly and then they lapsed into silence again.

Silence. Even the wind seemed to have dropped and Owain could no longer hear that hammering down below; the pipes were still, their crisis, too, it appeared, over. He found himself dozing, let himself drift. One big effort lay before them, then they would be back in civilization and they could try and forget this nightmare. Sinking slowly into a blissful sleep, he sagged in the uncomfortable chair.

'Owain . . . Owain –' Somebody was shaking him gently. He started, surfaced from a deep sleep and saw Suzannah's silhouette against the window. The candle had burned out and there was a white glow filling the room, light seeping through the snow that plastered the glass pane. 'Owain . . . it's daylight!'

'Oh . . . great!' He was stiff. His limbs creaked as he stood up uncertainly. Rose was awake and Alison, too, the latter holding the blanket around her and standing rather awkwardly as though she was in pain but was fighting it. 'Well, we'd better have a cup of tea and . . .'

'All ready,' Suzannah said briskly. 'Tea and toast.'

They ate and drank quickly. They were eager to be away but knew that they had to fortify their bodies against the elements outside.

'Still no sign of Barbara,' Owain said. 'She's probably back upstairs in her room, fast asleep.'

'And none of us are going up to look for her,' Suzannah replied, 'and we're not even going to shout up to her.' Because you don't know what you might disturb in a place like this. Blow her, frankly.'

Which set her thinking about why they were here in the first place. Because of Mrs Blower and her damned rehearsal.

If Rose had not been so insistent about going then the
wouldn't have ended up at the Donnington Country Hous
Hotel. Which – she glanced slyly at Owain Pugh – would hav
been a pity in spite of everything that had happened. And sh
could not wait to look at those books.

'Right, let's go.' Owain stood up and looked at the others
'Alison and Rose on the sledge and we'll do our best to pull it
Come on.'

It was 8.45 by his watch. The morning light was beginnin
to fill the hall, cold and grey, as sinister as the darkness of th
previous night. They glanced about them, seeing the step
going down to that awful basement and knowing that Jac
Christopher's mangled remains sprawled at the bottom, an
in the boiler room the old woman known as Mother lay decapi
tated. And in that dreadful basement room was the corpse witl
the shrivelled, rotted handless arm, kept company by its de
mented brother.

They saw the stairs and remembered the old man who ha
died in the second floor corridor, who had meant to incinerat
them because he had been instructed to sacrifice Rose to th
dark gods. And somewhere was the strange, dominant woman
maybe grieving because she had been unable to find tha
halfwit girl out in the snow. They were best left here, the dea
and the living, and those who still had their sanity must escap
whilst there was still time.

They sensed the evil again, those clammy invisible hand
reaching out to claw them back. Run, before it is too late!

Owain turned into the passage. It was darker here becaus
there were no windows. The cupboard door still swung oper
creaked faintly in a draught, hung wide as if to hinder their pro
gress.

He pushed it closed, stepped past it, his eyes peering int
the gloom, a hand outstretched for where the sledge was lean
ing up against the door.

Something was wrong. He sensed it even before his finger
located the heap of rough wood. No longer were the piece
nailed firmly together. They seemed to have disintegrated int

216

a pile of rough firewood, sharp edges and protruding nails scratching the palms of his hands, sending icy shockwaves through his body.

Disbelief, trying to shield the wreckage from the others, lifting it up and hearing it clattering on the flagged floor, splintered wood, some of it still held crazily together.

'What is it?' Suzannah was trying to push past him. 'What's the matter?'

He took a deep breath, did not trust himself to speak but he knew there was no way he could hide the truth. It was there for them all to see, a pile of matchwood, chair backs that were split and torn, a length of useless rope coiled like a dead snake. They might as well carry it all back to the kitchen and stoke the stove with it for all the good it was to them.

'The sledge . . .' he closed his eyes, opened them again and knew he had to tell them. *'It's broken . . . smashed! Somebody's wrecked it to stop us getting away!'*

CHAPTER TWENTY-TWO

'Who . . . who on earth could have done this?' Suzannah stared at the pile of broken wood strewn across the floor and knew she had to believe that it had really happened.

'Well, there's only one person left who could have done it, isn't there?' Owain said. 'Everybody else is either dead or locked up. Barbara did this, though for what reason I can't even guess. But she obviously doesn't want us to leave here, that's plain enough. We'd better return to the kitchen. There isn't anywhere else to go.'

He led the dejected party back, looking at the stairs as they passed as though he might see Barbara Withernshaw suddenly appear, but there was no sign of her. Back into the kitchen, the kettle still simmering on the hob, a faint aroma of toast still lingering in the atmosphere. They sat down and looked at one another, but there was nothing to say. The shock was still seeping into their systems.

'I'll have to go it alone, I've no choice,' Owain said at length. 'You three must stay here, keep together and don't go outside this room for any reason. Keep this poker handy and if Barbara shows up, use it. I can only conclude that she's as mad as the rest of them were.'

Madness or evil . . . was there a difference? he wondered. Could all this have come about simply because they were in a house of maniacs? Was the evil just a cover-up they had used? Or vice versa? There was no way of knowing but there was certainly danger all around them.

'I'm going now before anything else happens.' He rose to his feet and at that instant the radiator pipes began to vibrate and shudder again. 'Oh, Christ almighty! The pipes are starting to boil again.'

'They can't be,' Suzannah said. 'It's impossible.'

'Not if the old boiler has been stoked right up,' Owain muttered, 'and there's only one person who could possibly have done that. Her bloody ladyship! She's bust the sledge and now she's trying to blow us all up. Damn it, I'm going down to that basement to see what the bloody hell *is* going on!' As he spoke he snatched up the poker. 'You lot stay here, I'll be right back.'

His flesh crawled as he began the descent of the basement steps, seeing the body of Jack Christopher in the dim light, stepping over it and forcing the door of the boiler room . . . *Great Jesus, Mother's severed head was set up on its neck, staring balefully at him with its dead eyes, the mouth wide in what might have been either a curse or a warning.*

Beyond it lay the splayed body, a useless shell cast off, the light from the roaring fire inside the open cast-iron door illuminating the dirty room, throwing the shadows back. One frightened glance told him that there was nobody else here, nobody *living* anyway.

It was the emptiness of the place that was most terrifying of all; *the living vacuum.* You couldn't see the evil but you smelled it in a variety of different odours. The stench of death and burned human flesh, the thick cloying atmosphere. He almost panicked, caught his foot and stumbled, just managed to save himself from falling. He was mad to come here at all, there was no reason. Except Barbara Withernshaw, and she most certainly was not here.

He staggered out through the door, forced his eyes away from the gruesome carnage that lay out there. Poor Jack, he was just another of their victims, a pawn for whom they had no further use. Like the others who had died.

'Help me!'

The feeble cry froze him, had him throwing up an arm to shield himself from some attack, clasping his hands over his ears to try and shut out the cry if it came again. He recognized it, pathetic as it was, would hear George Clements's plea for help in his nightmares for years to come, along with all the other horrors of this awful house.

No, I don't want to hear you.

'Please help me.'

Cold fingers gripped his stomach and compressed it into a tight ball, almost forcing him to throw up. He leaned back against the wall, staring at that bolted door. Harry was in there, too, what was left of him.

Fingernails scraped the woodwork, a dying caged beast making a final futile attempt to escape from its prison. A sagging bump as though George had slipped to his knees, still scratching at the woodwork.

'I can't help you, George.' It's true, I dare not free you because of what I know. He forced his fear to turn to anger, remembering how he had rescued Rose from their devilish clutches. 'Remember the girl, George? When the police get here they'll put you away for life.'

'You must . . . listen to me, Mr Pugh.' The words were barely audible. Perhaps George had had a heart attack or a stroke like Harry? Oh, God, please don't let him die, not till we're away from here. Don't let that awful thing be loosed again.

'Listen to me . . . Mr Pugh, not just your lives, your souls are in danger!'

Reluctantly Owain crept towards the door. Compelling, fearful words, he knew now why the wedding guests were forced to listen to the Ancient Mariner. A kind of hypnotism. But I'm not going to open the door, I won't free you. They'll find you in there when they get through the snow.

'Can you hear me . . . Mr Pugh?' It sounded as though Clements was retching, a fit of coughing turned to a gurgling.

'I can hear you, but you'd better make it quick because I don't have time to waste. I know all about you, George Clements, what you are and what you planned to do to us. But you're helpless now. And if this bloody boiler blows up you'll roast in your own hell down here.'

'It isn't true. I am only a frail mortal and the Master is punishing me for my failure, just as he has punished the others. The shadow . . . the hand . . . *it has gone and found a new host, the most dangerous of all!*'

'You're lying, it's you who is possessed, George.'

'No, I swear it, please believe me and don't set me free if you don't want to. Just hear me. Satan is amongst you in human form at this very minute and you will all die!'

The boiler hissed and shuddered, the pipes leading from it rattled. A time bomb, but how long to go? And *who* had stoked it again?

'What are you trying to say, George?' I don't want to hear it, I don't want to know. But I have to, for all our sakes.

'It's her.' His voice was low, a terrified whisper, fearful in case he was overheard. '*It's Barbara Withernshaw!*'

Owain recoiled, his brain numbed, refusing to accept what his ears heard. Barbara? No! But it all fitted, the shadow in the room, her scream and collapse and yet . . . It could only have been her who had stoked up the boiler again and smashed the sledge. To keep them here. But why, for Jesus Christ's sake, *why*?

'She's going to sacrifice the young girl.' George Clements was talking quickly, as though time was running out for him. 'All of you. Unless you leave now, you'll die. She told me, mocked me through the door. She could have killed me but she wants me to suffer like the rest of you, to writhe in a hellfire. There's no hope for me, but go and try to save the others.'

Owain turned away, staggered blindly for the steps, aware of his own helplessness now. The bitch, she had toyed with them all and even the elements were on her side. Oh, please, let the others be safe up there!

It was like a slow-motion film in which he was the principal actor. He dragged himself back up the stairs and into the hallway, filled with fear that he might already be too late but somehow unable to hurry. Or perhaps he was hurrying. Groping for the door, crashing through it, pulling up and scanning the dining room with frightened eyes. The room was empty: he had half-expected to find Barbara in here. Moving on to the door that led through to the kitchen, pausing outside it; listening.

Somebody was sobbing. It sounded like Suzannah – low constricted sobs that racked her body. Globules of sweat turned icy on his forehead.

He kicked the door. It flew back, and he stared in awful horror at the sight which greeted him, his worst fears confirmed. Barbara Withernshaw was there. At any other time she would have looked comical in a thick fur coat draped over a layer of sweaters, her grey hair awry and straggling. But her eyes were terrible to behold, orbs that rolled and showed their whites, glazed, then cleared, saw him and gloated. Saliva dripped from her stretched lips, the snarl of a ravenous wild beast that has cornered its prey, a mask of madness and evil that defied logic.

He stared, saw the meat cleaver in her raised hand, poised directly above Rose's head, the serrated blade of a bread knife held against the child's throat. Rose was deathly white, eyes closed, might even have already fainted and was propped up against the woman's bosom.

Suzannah was seated on the chair opposite, hands wrung together, lips mutely pleading; Alison was beside, her, seeming devoid of comprehension. One move, the knife or the cleaver, and Rose would be dead.

'You've kept us waiting, Mr Pugh.' Barbara's voice was unrecognizable, deep-throated and manic, slobbering as she spoke. 'Your puny efforts to escape have all come to nothing and now the time is nigh. The child must go to her Master, as must you all. Listen, can you not hear the fires of hell roaring in readiness to receive their latest offering?'

The boiler would explode this time, Owain had no doubt about that. The first stoking had weakened it and it could not stand the pressure of a second. Suzannah's head moved slightly, her eyes met his. Owain, can't you do *something*?'

'I'm sorry, Suzie.' He experienced an urge to cry, to release his pent-up terror and frustration. 'I should have stayed with you.'

'It would have made no difference,' Barbara cackled. 'You kept us waiting, that was all. The sacrifice is ready.'

'I've been talking to George,' he said. He had to say something, just talk and keep talking, delay this awful blood sacrifice and pray for a reprieve, though God alone knew how. Perhaps God would intervene.

'You could have saved yourself the trouble and talked to me.' She bared her teeth, displayed a number of dark fillings together with some gold crowns. 'Yes, *I* am the chosen one and I shall not fail our lord as these other wretches have done. One after another, bungling fools who could not even commit a virgin sacrifice. Now it is left to me.'

'You're mad,' Owain said. Useless but true, his words seemed to linger in the atmosphere against the background banging of the central heating system, a menacing tom-tom tattoo.

'We're all mad.' She let out a chilling peal of rippling laughter. 'Even you, Mr Pugh. Everybody at Donnington is mad because it is the Master's way. You, these people here, even his child now. Her mind is gone, I can feel the void inside her skull' – she brushed the back of her hand, still holding the cleaver, across Rose's forehead. 'Our Master is merciful at times, he has spared this child the final terror of what must be.'

Suzannah screamed and slumped back in her chair. Owain wondered if he might jump Barbara in time. He tensed and then relaxed again. No chance, the blade was firm against Rose's throat and whilst there was still life there was the faintest of hopes, even if they were diminishing by the second. The floor rippled with a tremor, an empty saucepan on the draining board toppled, crashed and rolled.

Barbara Withernshaw's body tautened and the others saw it with horror; a brief closing of her eyes, the knuckles of the flabby hand holding the knife handle whitening. *The moment of sacrifice had arrived.*

'Wait!' Owain grunted.

Barbara's eyes shifted on to him, mocked him. Do not attempt to delay me! And then her expression changed as a faint sound came through the shuddering of the house, a

stealthy movement out in the hallway and the thumping of th
front door as though the wind had finally torn it free of tha
ancient bolt and was banging it back against the wall . . . Yo
can't keep me out, I'm coming to get you.

'What's that?' Barbara's voice was tinged with fear, th
whites of her eyes rolled again until the pupils virtually disap
peared.

'It's just the wind thrown open the front door,' Owai
almost replied, but he checked himself. This was no time t
give simple explanations. The woman was scared, it woul
waste another few seconds. If only that knife would com
away from Rose's throat.

There was definitely somebody out there in the hall. Owai
and Suzannah turned their heads towards the door goin
through to the dining room while Alison continued to star
blankly ahead of her. Rose's eyes flickered briefly but did nc
open.

'Who . . . is . . . it?' Barbara asked hoarsely, but nobody re
plied.

It has to be George Clements, Owain decided. The bugge
had broken out of his prison. It didn't really matter. It was
diversion and was unlikely to make any difference to Rose'
fate because George would have done exactly the same to he
a few hours previously but for Owain's intervention.

The door from the hall into the dining room opened, the
heard it, felt the icy draught from outside pushing against th
kitchen door like some bizarre usher announcing the comin
of whoever it was. It *had* to be George. Come on in and joi
the party, George; the more the merrier because we're a
going to die.

The newcomer was standing inside the dining room, strug
gling for breath, a rasping of phlegm-filled lungs. Maybe who
ever it was wouldn't make it after all, would collapse on th
floor and die. And then Rose would be sacrificed and th
whole house would explode. And they would never know wh
it was out there. *For God's sake, we want to know!*

'*Who are you?*' It was a bizarre scream of anger and fea

224

om Barbara, but the knife never once shifted its position, as clasped firmly against the tender flesh of the young girl's throat. Owain feared the worst, a moment of panic and it could all be over.

They heard a rustling of material, something thudding softly on to the floor out there, the other gasping for breath as if with the strain of the exertion. And then the footsteps came again, the door handle clicked faintly, was depressed and held down, the mysterious stranger suddenly afraid to enter.

'Come on, let me see you!' Veins corded on Barbara's forehead, twin spots of crimson began to flood her sallow cheeks. 'Enter, for I am a disciple of the Lord of Darkness and I command you to show yourself!'

The door swung open and they all saw. Owain grunted, there was a strangled cry from Suzannah, even an intake of breath from Alison. They heard the cry collecting inside Barbara's lungs, a shriek that gathered force and left her snarling lips in a rush; a scream that embodied terror and surprise, and a kind of macabre delight.

Vera Brown stood in the doorway, a pathetic wasted naked figure with her sodden clothing trailing across the floor behind her. Her glasses were gone, her eyes blinking as though dazzled by the daylight, an expression of total confusion upon her angular features.

'Auntie Barb –' Vera looked, from one to the other of the occupants of the kitchen as though her poor eyesight was incapable of recognition. 'You called me, Auntie Barb, and I came as quick as I could. But the snow's so deep it took me a long time. I heard you calling me. I promise you I'm a virgin, I really am. That's what you wanted, isn't it? I promise I am. You do believe me, don't you. Auntie Barb?'

CHAPTER TWENTY-THREE

'You!' Barbara Withernshaw whispered. 'It can't be . . . *you're
dead*!' Her eyes protruded, the flush on her cheeks paled, and
the hand holding the knife so close to Rose's neck shook
dangerously. She seemed to have difficulty clasping the hilt,
her fingers were shrunk and twisted, as if with arthritis.

'It's me, Auntie Barb.' Vera's voice was high-pitched, child-
ishly excited as she stepped forward swaying slightly. 'I'm all
right, honest I am. It was awful out there and I got soaked
through so I took my clothes off. You don't mind, do you?'

'You shouldn't have come.' The older woman's words
seemed to grate out through clenched teeth, harsh and frag-
mented. 'I didn't want you to come, Vera. Better that you had
died.'

'But you kept calling me, Auntie Barb, I wouldn't have made
it if you hadn't. I thought I was going to die but you called me
on when I would sooner have lain there. You kept asking me if I
was a virgin because you needed a virgin. You do, don't you?'

'Yes, I do.' The blade had inched away from the child's
neck, the knife handle shaking in the deformed fingers that
held it as if it might fall from their grasp at any second. 'I
want you, Vera, but I wish you had not come. Oh, how cruel
our Master can be at times!'

'I don't understand.' Vera stopped a couple of feet away
from her self-appointed guardian, her face screwed up in bewilderment. 'You want me but you don't? That's silly. You do
love me, though, don't you, Auntie Barb?'

'Yes, I love you, Vera.' Barbara's eyes closed for a second
and the knife arm dropped to her side. The other wavered, the
cleaver descending slowly, resting on Rose's shoulder. 'I love
you so much, Vera, that I can hardly bear to do what I have to
do.'

'What's that, Auntie Barb?' Vera Brown moved forward nd, flinging her arms around her, began to sob uncontrol-bly.

In that instant Owain moved, a leap that carried him across 1e distance between himself and Barbara, an outstretched and grabbing Rose by the arm, pulling her roughly, toppling er against himself. He caught her, swung her behind him.

There was a shriek of rage from Barbara Withernshaw as he realized what had happened, a roar like a cow which has ad her calf taken away. Brandishing bread knife and meat leaver, she would have charged insanely except that Owain icked out and sent a chair spinning into her path. It hit her nees, brought a yell of pain from her, bounced and caught 'era a glancing blow. The latter squealed, clutched at her ompanion and further impeded her attack.

'Follow me,' Owain shouted at Suzannah. 'I've got Rose. un! You, too, Alison.'

In spite of her terror, Suzannah caught Alison's hand, ulled the girl up out of her chair. Run with us and if you on't it's your own damned fault.

Owain crashed the door of the dining room open, paused or a split second in the hallway. The front door was wide pen and there seemed to be a six-foot drift spilling in through ; but if Vera had entered that way then surely they could use : as an exit? There was no time to be lost, Barbara would be fter them with her kitchen weaponry and he dared not chance topping to try and overpower her; the crazed were said to ave double the strength of sane people and armed as she was e could not take the risk. His priority was to get the girls to afety.

Suzannah was hard behind him, Alison stumbled in their vake. Poor kid, in her condition and with only a tatty blanket or protection he didn't give much for her chances outside in hat Arctic hell. But to remain was certain death.

'*Help me!*'

The plaintive cry drifted up from the bowels of this house f madness and evil, was drowned by a chugging noise like that of a steam engine about to move off from the platform George Clements's final plea for help but they had to ignor it. Owain reminded himself again of that scene in their livin quarters only a matter of hours ago. Your turn to die now George.

The boiler was clanking furiously, shaking every pipe an radiator on all the floors as it built up heat and pressure lik some monster stirring in its underground lair, bent on reveng against those who had imprisoned it for so long. A stench scorching paintwork, a suffocating heat.

Owain saw where Vera must have squeezed past the dri which blocked the porch, found a gap against the nearsid wall. He widened it as he forced his way out, glanced behin and saw that Suzannah was close behind him, Alison at he heels. You could see the pain on her freckled face and ther was blood running down her legs. And when she falls do w . . .?

No, you leave her because you can't risk the other two.

Outside it had stopped snowing. There was not even sno blowing off the fields and hedges. The wind had dropped an it was uncannily still. As though some terrible power ha commanded a lull, a total cessation of movement. Stop an watch the actors in this awful finale, see them run down an slaughtered by . . .

There was no sign of Barbara Withernshaw. Owain halte halfway down the drive. Suzannah took Rose's hand. Aliso was still up with them, her trail marked by bright scarl droplets of blood in the white snow.

He looked for Vera's footprints: follow them and surely h would be able to avoid the worst of the drifts. A chill ran ove his body which wasn't entirely due to having emerged fror the hot and stifling atmosphere of the Donnington Countr House Hotel into the freezing wilderness left by the blizzar *There were no footprints, not a single track to be seen anywhere.*

Probably the wind had blown the snow over them, he trie to convince himself. And, anyway, there was no way of know ing how long it was since Vera had come in out of the snow she could have been skulking somewhere indoors for the past couple of hours. Unless you told yourself that you would go crazy with terror.

'Alison'll never make it,' Suzannah panted. 'God, look at her, Owain, she'll collapse any minute!'

Owain turned, saw how the auburn-haired girl was bent double, clutching at a wall of snow, trying to use it to hold herself upright but it powdered in her hands. The blanket slipped from her shoulders. Oh, Jesus, I can't just leave her. But I can't carry her, either. And I'd feel easier if I knew just where Barbara was.

Seconds later he was left in no doubt concerning the whereabouts of Barbara Withernshaw. A movement against the face of the tall red-bricked house caught his eye, had him looking up. The large glass doors opening on to the first floor balcony moved outwards, and through them came a naked girl with long fair hair. Behind her, towering over her, an arm encircling her waist like a heavyweight wrestler attempting to throw a lightweight opponent, came Barbara Withernshaw. She still had that bread knife; the weak rays of the morning sun attempting to infiltrate the hazy clouds glinted on its jagged edge.

Like royalty emerging on to the balcony to wave to the watching crowds below, Barbara and Vera moved to the low, snow-covered parapet. The latter was leaning over it, bent forward, a princess bowing to her subjects. And even from that distance the watchers could hear the thumping of the angry boiler as it expanded every tentacle of piping, condensation clouding the insides of the windows and melting the plastered snow.

'Come back!' Barbara's insane futile shriek hung in the still atmosphere. 'Come back, you have no right to leave, the Master needs you.'

She bent forward and stared past Vera, almost as if she actually expected them to turn back.

'Crazy as they come,' Owain muttered but he could not drag his gaze away, half-anticipated the next move of the woman up on the balcony.

'*Oh, my God!*' Suzannah pulled Rose to her, buried the young girl's face against her so that she should not see.

Vera was bent right over the snowy stone ballustrade, seemingly willingly, for those below thought they detected a smile on her face. And now that serrated blade which had threatened Rose's tender jugular vein was pressed up against Vera's; Barbara was smiling banefully, her lips moving as if she uttered some blasphemous prayer to the one whom she called 'Master'.

They did not want to watch but there was no way they could drag their eyes away, a terrrible hypnotism compelling them to gaze upon the blood sacrifice which Satan had been demanding throughout the night hours. The blade was drawn back and forth, sawing steadily, blood beginning to ooze from the horizontal neck wound, dripping steadily in scarlet splashes that went right down the wall on to the snowy roof of the porch below.

Still cutting steadily, the victim offering not the feeblest resistance, and then, without warning, the jugular opened and the blood spouted way beyond the wide front steps, a gush of claret so vivid against the whiteness below.

Vera fell forward but her executioner held her, stopped her from toppling over, laughing crazily until the flow began to slow, became a sluggish trickle which formed a thick pool and dripped off the balcony. Only then did she release her hold on her victim and step back, leaving the still-twitching girl slumped across the low wall, head downwards, a slaughtered animal hung up to drain its blood in an abattoir.

Suzannah thought she was going to faint, but for the mercy of God and the help of Owain Pugh that limp and bleeding form up there might have been Rose hung over a chair in that filthy kitchen. Suzannah held on to Owain and between them they supported Rose, making sure she did not see. They glanced sideways at Alison; she was staring upwards but there was no revulsion, no fear on her face, just a blank expression. Her mind was gone and she had been spared this ultimate in human degradation.

'We'd better move on and . . .'

The ground beneath their feet shook, trembled with the force of an underground explosion. The bones in their bodies vibrated, their teeth rattled. And even as they watched they saw the panes of glass in the house windows cracking, zigzag patterns weaving in every direction, pushing outwards. Glass was showering downwards, huge shards and cascades of tiny splinters scintillating in the sunlight, crashing through the deep snow below.

And behind those yawning window frames they saw an orange glow that became a glare, shooting tongues of flame that licked upwards at ceilings and began to devour woodworm-infested timber. A gathering, gushing roar, a wall of fire leaping upwards, securing hold after hold as it climbed. A fiery mass, an inferno that was born in that hellish basement and knew no boundaries.

Against that background of fire, Barbara Withernshaw stood unmoved. Her head was bowed so that they could no longer see her face. Her arms hung by her side. Alone with her thoughts – whatever they might have been – her thick clothing already beginning to scorch and steam. A devil-woman of fire. Smoke rose from her but still she remained upright in that immobile posture, now flames appearing on her fur coat, running up and kissing her grey hair, blackening it. Her head was on fire, the hair shrivelling, hissing, balding, until she resembled some drunken artist's caricature of a giant wizened monkey.

Finally she lurched forward, and that was because the timbers of the balcony were bowing, cracking the concrete flooring as they succumbed to the mounting furnace. A final collapse in a cascade of sparks, shooting Barbara and her blood-drained victim downwards, cremating them in the inferno beneath.

Owain thought he heard one last cry amidst the crackling of flames and snapping of timbers but he could not be sure. If so, then the voice was male, that of a very frightened man who still pleaded to be released from his basement prison.

Or it could have been the echoes of his own mind.

CHAPTER TWENTY-FOUR

Suzannah, Owain told himself, was the most beautiful woman in the world. Everything about her was perfection: her looks, her poise, so natural in everything she did from drinking a cup of coffee to pretending to be interested in his untidy shelves of books. The flat was a jumble; he ought to have done something about it before her visit. He tried to hide his nervousness, found himself talking for the sake of it, talking nonsense really when there were so many important things he wanted to say but could not bring himself to put them into words. Like 'I love you, Suzie'. A fear that this might be their only meeting and that when she drove away from here to fetch Rose from the rehearsal he might never see her again. Perhaps a brief encounter at the inquest on the bodies the firemen had dug out of the ashes of the Donnington Country House Hotel, and then a parting of the ways.

'Fiction is rubbish really,' he found himself saying. 'Just lies, even if some of it does have literary merit. Stories for the sake of stories, which you don't need after . . .'

'We have to try and put all that behind us even if we'll never be able to forget it.' Her hand touched his arm, remained there. Perhaps she could feel that he was trembling. 'At least all's well that ends well. For us, anyway.'

In the end the flight through the snow away from that blazing house had presented few difficulties. The lane had drifted badly but they had managed to find a way round the worst of the snow, and somehow even Alison had kept going. And when they were within a hundred yards of the main road they had heard the whine of snowploughs, seen the welcoming flashing of yellow lights. The council had brought in the snow-blowers, and conceded to pay overtime on a twenty-four-hour shift in order to clear all the arterial roads in the county.

A giant fountain of powdered snow marked its progress and even the worst blockages were cleared at a speed faster than walking pace.

They had been transported back in a council Bedford van which ran smoothly over the cleared tracks, and Rose and Alison were receiving medical care within the hour. The latter was suffering from exposure, hypothermia, and had been rushed to hospital. Rose had been allowed to go home with her mother. And then Owain had spent the rest of the day at the police station making lengthy statements to incredulous officers.

That had been a week ago. And now the thaw had come as suddenly as that early winter blizzard, a mild front that brought with it two days of torrential rain, turning the snow to slush and then washing it all away. A kind of clearing-up operation organized by a repentant Nature.

'You were marvellous, Owain.' Suzannah's face was close to his own now, her perfume making him heady. 'Without you both Rose and I would be dead.'

Her upturned lips were an invitation he could not refuse and the moment his own touched them the barrier that had existed between them disintegrated. He kissed her, held her to him, felt the softness of her breasts against him, the way she trembled too. Neither of them was interested in those books. They had served their purpose, the excuse for this meeting. Holding on to each other and laughing away their nervousness, they went back into the lounge.

'I'd go through it all again just for this,' she murmured when they finally disengaged.

'Pray God we'll never have to.' He was suddenly serious. 'The madness bred the evil. Each one of those residents at the hotel was consciously or subconsciously bent on destruction. And as they died the evil was passed from one to the other, like some kind of contagious disease. At least, that's my version of it and I doubt if they'll be able to come up with anything better at the inquest. They'll pass it off as some kind of mania, make it sound as logical as possible. I'll bet the papers will have a field day, though.'

And they both laughed. Suzannah looked at her watch.

'I'll have to be going to pick up Rose from her rehearsal. At least there won't be any snowdrifts, and I swear I won't even glance towards that dreadful lane when I drive past it!'

Owain kissed her at the door.

'Perhaps we could have dinner tonight? Suppose I call for you around eight?'

'That'd be fine.' She smiled. 'I can get Mrs Ward next door to sit in with Rose, no bother.'

'See you then, and drive carefully.'

He watched her go, stood listening to the car being started up, driven off. Then he turned back into the small hallway and a nagging thought returned, one that he had pushed to the back of his mind this last couple of hours. Standing beneath the light he held out his left hand, flexed the fingers. The joints were stiff. He almost had to force them and experienced a deep-seated ache that seemed to go right down to the bone.

He had difficulty in extending the fingers and gasped aloud at the pain. They did not seem to be able to stretch properly, wanted to curl up as though they were deformed, withering, the knuckles standing out starkly. A moment of near-panic but he controlled it, looked away.

Arthritis, probably, he told himself with forced conviction, the damp and cold of that couple of days last week had got to him. It couldn't be anything else. No, Christ, it *wasn't* anything else. And right now he didn't want to think of anything except that dinner date with Suzie tonight.

He went on through to the bedroom to get changed.